EARL'S CHOICE

(REGENCY ROYALS BOOK 2)

JESS MICHAELS

For Michael, who always helps me figure out what path to take and loves me no matter which one it is. And who reminds me that I'm more than just my stories.

AUTHOR'S NOTE

There are a lot of conversations about the concept of Content Warnings in books and for other media. Having suffered from panic attacks that were triggered by trauma, I would NEVER wish that on my worst enemy. I want you to enjoy what you're reading, never be pulled away because you were surprised by triggering material. So, I will do my best to include Content Warnings in an author note in each book from now on. Also, look to my website for them, so that you don't accidentally buy a book that might give you pause.

Content Warning: assault (on page), parental death (described not on page)

PROLOGUE

The Island of Athawick, 1800

Sasha Killick's fingers flexed in the much larger gloved hand of Dashiell Talbot, and she glanced up at him as moments seemed to stretch to hours. She was only six, but she knew what the last few days meant. Mama and Papa were dead, lost when their ship sank on the way back to Athawick from London. Dashiell had told her that meant they wouldn't ever come back. Her heart hurt at the thought.

"Chin up, poppin," Dashiell said, smiling down at her.

He had a serious face, but it was gentle when he smiled. She liked him. He had worked for her father and had always been kind to her. She'd wanted maybe for him to take care of her now that she was all alone, but she'd overheard some talk amongst the servants that she had to be presented to the king and queen first.

"Are they nice?" she whispered.

He blinked. "Nice?"

"Will they send me away?" she asked, wishing she weren't about to cry. All the grownups kept telling her not to cry, to be good, and it was so hard.

Dashiell crouched down and took both her hands, his blue eyes holding steady with her own. "No one is going to send you away," he said softly. "My duty is to see you safely taken care of since you have no other family, and I swear to you, Sasha, that is what I'll do. Your mama and papa were important people in Athawick, and we are a very small country, aren't we? The king and queen wish to pay their respects to you, and perhaps they will even offer some help. But I promise you, on my honor, that you will *never* be sent away."

She nodded. She believed this man, this grownup who held her hands so tightly in his own. He would take care of her.

The door to the chamber opened, and Dashiell got to his feet and turned them both to face the two people who entered. Sasha had seen the king and queen before, but never so close up. He was tall with blue eyes, and she was...beautiful. Sasha almost couldn't breathe from it as she stared up at her.

"Your Majesties," Dashiell said, and executed a bow. He squeezed her hand gently and Sasha managed a wobbly curtsey that she had been hastily taught just that morning.

"This is the child?" King Alastair asked, and sniffed at her. Sasha edged a little closer to Dashiell. The king seemed exactly like the kind of person who would send someone away, no matter what Dashiell said.

"Yes. Her name is Sasha. She was Magnus Killick's daughter," Dashiell said. "Her mother was also Sasha."

"Yes, I recall them," King Alastair said. "They were doing some diplomatic work in England, were they not? Involved in the sinking of the *Greystone* a few days ago. Terrible business, that. We lost a great deal of goods."

Dashiell got a bit stiffer at her side but said nothing. He didn't have a chance, for Queen Giabella moved closer. "How old are you, Sasha?"

Sasha swallowed. Her voice was like music and it soothed her a little. "I-I'm six," she whispered.

"Speak up, girl," the king said, and it was like he pulled her voice entirely from her body when he did it.

Queen Giabella sent him a look. "Alastair," she said softly, and then dropped down closer to Sasha. "Don't be afraid, sweet," she said. "How old are you?"

"S-six," she repeated, a little louder to please the beautiful lady.

"Younger than Ilaria," the queen breathed. "And she looks so like her."

The king shrugged. "I suppose a bit. We're sorry for your loss, girl. I'm sure the matter of her future will be attended to. Best of luck."

He pivoted, and Dashiell moved forward a step. "Your Majesty," he began, but the queen shook her head ever so slightly, and he stopped.

"I'll stay a moment," Queen Giabella said to her husband, without taking her eyes off of Dashiell and Sasha. "You go ahead about your business."

The king harrumphed and then strode off without so much as a backward glance. Sasha felt like she could breathe again after he was gone, but she still backed a little farther into Dashiell's legs.

"Now then, Sasha, whatever shall we do with you?" Queen Giabella said softly, and reached out to touch her cheek gently. Sasha found herself turning into the touch. Mama had always done that too.

The queen stood up straight. "She has no other family on the island?"

"None, madam," Dashiell said. "There are some distant relatives on the continent, but she's never met them and I have not received any word from them yet, obviously, since I wrote to inform them of the tragedy."

The queen pursed her lips. "She is a child of Athawick—I would not feel right sending her to some other place, some unknown people to whom she has no connection."

Dashiell nodded. "I tend to agree, but I am open to any suggestion. I have no legal right to offer to be her guardian, and even if I did, I am looking for new employment as well as lodging at present, so I have no stable environment for her."

"Of course, because you were...you were man of affairs for Mr. Killick, yes?"

"I was, madam, since I arrived here from England five years ago," he said.

The queen looked down at Sasha again, and her smile was so gentle and kind. So warm and comforting. Sasha wanted to go to her, but she held back. "Her parents died in the service of the king," the queen mused, almost more to herself. "Does the king not have an obligation to what they left behind?"

"What do you mean?" Dashiell asked.

"I propose that the royal family take her in. Adopt her as one of our own."

Dashiell took a long step back. "I...I beg your pardon?"

The queen nodded, and she looked very certain. "It is the right thing to do, is it not? And I admit it is hard to look at her and not wish to take care of her. To love her."

Sasha swallowed. "You would...you would be my mama?"

The queen's face softened even further. "I would be, if you would wish for that."

Dashiell took Sasha's hand again, and she held tightly to him as he said, "What would that entail, Your Majesty? I would not wish for her to be taken in without understanding what her future would be. How would she be treated? Accepted?"

The queen met his eyes. "You are truly concerned for her welfare. That is a fine quality, Mr. Talbot. I assure you that she would be treated, at least by me, as a full member of this family. She would not be allowed title, of course, but in any other way she would be my daughter."

"And what of...what of the king?" Dashiell pressed.

"The way he just treated the child is nothing worse than he treats his own, I assure you." The queen had stiffened as she spoke. "And he owes me a boon, so he will not argue. *I* will take responsibility for the girl and her treatment."

Dashiell considered it a moment, and then he drew Sasha to a settee behind them. He placed her there and sat beside her. "Do you understand what Her Majesty is offering, poppin? For you to live here in the palace and be raised as if you were the daughter of the queen?"

Sasha worried her lip. She liked the queen very much, and the idea of living with her felt better than just not knowing what would happen. But she still hesitated.

"But...but what about you?" Sasha asked. "I want to still see you."

"Well, perhaps that could be arranged as well," the queen said. "You mentioned you were seeking a new appointment, did you not? I know that there is a vacancy on my husband's staff, Mr. Talbot. And I think you would fit the bill. You would be living here and would be able to regularly see Sasha."

Dashiell's eyes were wide as he stared from Sasha to the queen and back. "Sounds like we would both have a wonderful opportunity."

"Together," Sasha said.

He looked down at her and held her gaze. "We would say yes together or not at all. So what do you think?"

Sasha nodded slowly. The queen smiled and opened her arms. Dashiell placed a hand on the small of Sasha's back and nodded as he urged her from the settee and toward the queen. She edged forward, uncertain and wary, but also happy. Queen Giabella's arms came around her and she held tight.

"I will always keep you safe," she said into Sasha's hair. "I promise you that."

Sasha buried her face into the queen's shoulder and all the fear and uncertainty that had come with her parents' death faded a little.

She still felt the pain, oh yes, that was true. It was like an ache that throbbed so deep she feared it would never get better. But her future, it seemed, was no longer a blank page.

And that was enough for now.

CHAPTER 1

Spring 1817
Seventeen years later

Despite having grown up on an island, forever surrounded by and transported by ships, Sasha Killick had never cared for the rolling waves of the sea. She didn't get sick from them, thank heavens, but she found no peace in the rocking. Though perhaps some of her discomfort at present had to do with her current destination and all that lay ahead.

King Alistair of Athawick had died a year before, after an illness that had stolen his strength but never the sharp cruelty of his tongue. Sasha knew she should have felt the loss. After all, the man had been...in theory, at least...her father figure for nearly two decades. But she didn't.

As for Athawick? Well, Sasha, like many others, privately believed their island was far better off with the new king, Grantham. Watching her adopted brother take over in the recent months had been wonderful.

And now they were all on their way to London for a celebration tour. Mourning was shed, and Grantham could be hailed by those with power as the new leader of their small but important nation.

All should have been well, but it wasn't. Sasha had felt a strangeness in the air since the family's departure from Athawick a few days ago. A tension she couldn't place. Something was about to happen, and she worried over what it could be and if she would find her place in it. After all, she was a part of this family, wasn't she? Raised as their daughter, their sister, with only a lack of title separating them.

Though in more recent years, even that had changed. Once she had come of age, King Alistair had demanded she take on a role more suited to a servant than a family member. She was Ilaria's companion—and sometimes her body double when they needed someone to wave from a balcony or smile from a carriage.

Sasha might have pondered that fate a little longer, even allowed herself maudlin thoughts, but before she could, the chamber door flew open and Princess Ilaria burst into the room. Her cheeks were flushed with high color and she slammed the door behind her, leaning against it with both hands as she struggled for breath.

Sasha moved forward. "Ilaria?"

Her adopted sister didn't respond, but continued to lean on the door.

"Ilaria?" Sasha repeated, and then, "Your Highness?"

That seemed to yank Ilaria from her thoughts. She pivoted toward Sasha and then rushed forward to grasp her hands. "They are going to marry me off to some titled twit."

Sasha's mouth dropped open and all the anxious energy she had felt all around her during their voyage now clicked into place. "What?" she gasped as she urged Ilaria to sit before the fire.

Ilaria did so and Sasha took her place on the settee, grasping Ilaria's hands tightly for support.

"Mama and Grantham have told me they are bartering me for connection to England, to protect Athawick's position!" Ilaria gasped. "They expect me to marry some titled nitwit in an arrangement for power and money and position."

She went on, but it was all theatrics. Not that Sasha fully blamed her. Ilaria had always been one for flourish, and in this case, she might have earned it. Still, she blocked a great deal of it out and stared into the fire. As Ilaria's companion, she would likely be expected to go wherever the princess went. That included if she stayed in England with a new husband. Once that happened, there would be no more pretending that she would be seen as an equal to Ilaria or Grantham or their middle sibling, Remington. She would truly be only a servant at that point. Would she ever see Queen Giabella again and be treated as her child? And Dashiell Talbot, the queen's personal secretary, who she adored as a father...would she be permanently separated from him, as well?

She realized Ilaria had stopped talking and seemed to be waiting for an answer. "I suppose we might have guessed this would happen," Sasha said slowly. "After all, royal marriages are very rarely for love or by choice of the particular parties. Look at your mother and father. *They* were a union to shore up alliances between Athawick and the Kingdom of Everlay."

"And two more miserable people you never could have met," Ilaria sighed. "And *this* is what they wish for me. In these modern times."

Sasha pursed her lips. "I think you're being a little silly, if you thought you would ever be truly in control of your future. You know that is not what your family is about."

Ilaria bent her head, and Sasha could feel her fear and pain and disappointment as if it were her own. It certainly merged with her own emotions, and everything felt very...sharp at present.

There was a light knock on the door, and Ilaria shook her head. "Probably my mother come to scold me."

Sasha squeezed her hand as comfort and then went to the door, heart pounding. She did wish to speak to Giabella, to try to determine what her thoughts were, if any, about Sasha's position. But when she opened it, it was not the queen but Prince Remington who leaned in her doorway.

"Sasha," he said with a wink that loosened some of the tightness around her chest. Remi was always the one she could depend on for levity.

"Your Highness," she returned as she closed the door behind him.

"Ugh, please don't do that," he said. "We're practically brother and sister, and I hate it."

"*That's* why I do it," Sasha teased, and then she frowned. "And also because Blairford would blister my ears if he heard me being overly familiar."

She knew she would find allies in her hatred of Grantham's lead courtier in this room. No one in the family had liked him when he served Alastair, and the feeling had not changed in the past year. For a moment Remi and Ilaria complained about their own dislike for the man and then Ilaria's predicament.

Remi grabbed for Ilaria's hand at last, and for a moment he actually looked serious, which was stunning enough for Sasha. He never looked serious. "I am...sorry, Ilaria."

"I know." Ilaria rested her head on his shoulder. "I wish I could be like you and thwart them at every turn."

He chuckled. "If you started doing that, they'd have me shot for being a bad influence. Are you trying to get me shot?"

"If it would distract from this plan of theirs, perhaps?" She twisted her lips and batted her eyelashes at him. "Just in the leg maybe? Or the arm?"

He snorted out a laugh and pushed back to his feet. "Look, I'll try to talk to Grantham for you, but he doesn't listen to me anymore, not since he took the title. But I'll make the effort."

"Thank you," Ilaria said softly.

He gave the most ridiculous bow of all time and then saluted Sasha. "Ladies," he said as he swept from the chamber.

Once he was gone, Sasha turned back to speak to Ilaria again, but found the princess with a thoughtful expression. "What if I did that?"

"Shot him in the leg?" Sasha asked in the hopes it would lighten the mood. "He might deserve it."

Ilaria smiled slightly. "No, not shoot him. Thwart *them*. What if I thwarted their plans just like Remi always does?"

"By drinking too much and seducing young women and generally having a good time?"

"I've never seduced a young woman," Ilaria mused. "I don't know that I'd hate it. But I think playing a little fast and loose with a young man or two might be the better way to frustrate their plans. Our island might not be so prudish about that sort of thing, but I know *theirs* is."

Sasha didn't like the sound of that idea. After all, where Ilaria went, she was bound to follow, and that included knee-deep into trouble she wanted no part of. "Ilaria, think this through. There would be consequences for any actions you take against the Crown. Your mother and the king are not to be trifled with."

She could see Ilaria understood her meaning, but she still shook her head. "But are there not consequences for falling in line, as well? Namely a loveless, empty union to some man who will marry me only for money and power?"

Sasha bent her head. She didn't want those things for Ilaria. Her friend was too much of a romantic to simply accept something so empty. She would be miserable and it would change her.

"You aren't wrong. I just want to see you come out of this as undamaged as possible," Sasha said gently. "Perhaps don't make any hasty decisions until you meet the men your family will parade before you. See if you could *like* one of them. If you could, then everyone would win."

Ilaria sighed. "You are correct, as always. It's almost unforgiveable of you."

"And yet you always forgive me." Sasha laughed and Ilaria

couldn't help but join in. For a while they changed the subject and talked about other things, including the packed schedule for the upcoming tour. Sasha winced at the implications. They would none of them have a day's rest for the next few months. Worse if the family was truly hell-bent on marrying Ilaria off to some titled gentleman.

"Let me go speak to Dashiell and see if he has any updates from your mother," Sasha said at last. "It might change our thoughts on gowns and crowns."

Ilaria laughed at the rhyme the two had used to describe formal events and their expected fanfare over the years. At least Sasha could give her that small relief.

"Yes, thank you. And don't worry yourself over me." Ilaria caught her hand. "I'll be fine. *We'll* be fine."

Sasha nodded, squeezed her fingers and then slipped from the room. The boat was rocking a bit harder, and she slid her fingers along the wall to balance herself as she twisted and turned from the family part of the ship's halls to the one where the servants were housed. Dashiell Talbot's cabin was first in the line there, and she knocked lightly.

"Enter," he said from within, and she did so to find him seated at the escritoire near the porthole, writing neatly despite the tossing seas.

"Do you ever stop working, Dash?" she asked, reverting to the playful nickname Dashiell had gone by in the years since he had been promoted to Queen Giabella's private secretary. Even Her Majesty, herself, slipped from time to time and called him that, though she always corrected herself.

He smiled as he turned toward her. "You know the answer to that, Sasha. Come in. May I get you something to drink?"

"I'll cast it all back up thanks to these waves," Sasha said as she entered the room. "I wondered if there were any updates to the family schedule now that this new announcement has been made."

Dash's expression grew more serious. "Talked to you about it, did she?"

"It is my job, isn't it, to hear the princess's concerns and try to be helpful and supportive?" Sasha said it with as much enthusiasm as she could, but Dash's wrinkled brow told her she had not exuded the correct level of lightness.

"You aren't merely a servant, Sasha," he said gently. "You know you are loved like a sister by all of the family, and as a daughter not only by the queen, but by myself."

Sasha moved closer and took his hand. For a moment they were quiet together and then she sighed. "I know I am loved, yes, but that doesn't mean I'm not a servant. It's such a strange thing, Dash, to be welcomed into the inner circle, but also be outside its boundaries. I'm never truly accepted into either their world or the one of the servants."

He nodded slowly. "I know a little about that. Is that what makes you so restless as of late?"

"I think we've all been a little restless since the death of King Alastair and the ascension of King Grantham. That kind of change is difficult on all in the household." Dash arched a brow and she laughed. "You see too much. At this particular moment, I can admit that I am more directly concerned about this plan to marry Ilaria off to a title. She is not happy."

"She made that very clear," Dash said. "I may have even written it in my notes about the exchange."

"Of course you did, you are too fastidious to ignore such a thing." Sasha shook her head. "When her life changes, so will mine. And it will be no more my choice than it is hers."

Something about Dash's expression changed, grew faraway. "When we care for those we serve, it is always more complicated, Sasha. The changes to their lives touch our hearts as much as our day-to-day existence."

"That is true. And I know that I must be there for Ilaria, to support her and to guide her if she desires it. To give her a place to spill her pains when she cannot share them elsewhere. I know my place, you needn't worry."

"I would *never* worry about that," Dash said, and smiled at her gently.

She returned the expression. "It's always been you and I, hasn't it? On the inside looking out, on the outside looking in."

He shook his head. "I've never been on the inside, lovey. I can't be."

There was something in the way he said those words that made Sasha come up short. She stared at him, saw the tightness of his mouth, the slight whiteness to his knuckles as he gripped the back of the chair he had vacated a moment before.

"Dash—" she began.

He cleared his throat. "I don't think you came in here for nonsense. You said you are looking for an updated schedule, yes? I have just finished with it and I do have a copy for you."

He turned away from her and her questions and swept up a heavy sheet of vellum from the desk. He handed it over and said, "You will note the changes from the last schedule here and here." He indicated with his forefinger where she should look. She did and nodded. "Though you know all this is bound to change."

"Yes, of course. But it gives me a place to adjust in my planning for now." She folded the paper and tucked it into the pocket of her smock. "We dock in the morning?"

Dash nodded. "Indeed and then a very busy day for us all after that. Including the welcome ball."

She leaned up and kissed his cheek, eliciting a light blush and a quick smile from him. "Thank you, as always, for the chat. I love our time together, even when it is brief."

He waved her off, but she could see he felt the same even if he didn't say it. She was warmed as she left him. Dash had a way of doing that, especially for her, and he had been a source of comfort for most of her life. When she heard the word *father*, it was never

King Alastair who came to mind, though he had taken her in. And it was rarely her own father, long buried and so hard to picture.

It was Dash. Always Dash.

So she danced along the corridor back to the chamber, ready to face the future and whatever came her way. Ready to support Ilaria and help her through this difficult transition. She could do it. She knew she could.

CHAPTER 2

Thomas had been the Earl of Bramwell for four years and the title had never rested comfortably on his shoulders. Perhaps that was because his good-for-nothing bastard of a father had destroyed their financial prospects through endlessly selfish behavior and abject cruelty. Perhaps it was because Thomas had always preferred a good book to a night at a club or a dance at a ball.

Either way, he felt constrained by expectation as he stood in his mother's parlor, awaiting her arrival so they could head out to what seemed like the hundredth party he had attended since the Season of 1817 had launched just a week before.

"Don't you look very handsome," Lady Bramwell said as she entered the parlor. She crossed to him and slightly adjusted his cravat before she patted his cheek. If his father had been a curse, at least he had been blessed with a fine mother. The countess was kind, amusing and always seeking out those she could offer compassion. She was well liked by all those in her circles and beyond.

"Thank you, Mama," he said, bussing her cheek. "And you are divine in that green, which I think you already know. What house of horrors will we be visiting tonight? I have forgotten already."

His mother pursed her lips and crossed to pour him a sherry. She handed it over with an arched brow of both judgment and pleading. "Lady Gregson."

"Ah yes," he said, sipping the drink rather than swigging it in one fell swoop as he wished to do. Mama would make a worried face if he did that, and then they'd have to have a long talk about subjects best unmentioned.

"She always does invite too many people," his mother admitted with a sigh. "And so it's difficult to see friends or make new acquaintances."

He arched a brow in her direction. There was one of those subjects now, cloaked in subtlety. "I suppose you are as interested as ever in my...making new acquaintances this Season?"

"We've had this conversation so many times," Lady Bramwell said with a shake of her head. "My answer hasn't changed, love. You are of an age to marry, don't you agree? Hasn't seeing your sister so happily settled with her new husband given you reason to hope that a union could be a positive thing?"

"Her first union was enough to put anyone off marriage, wouldn't you say?" Thomas asked.

Mama shifted. His sister, Aurora, had been initially matched with a viscount who had made her miserable, thus separating her from a man their father had not approved of. But after she had been widowed, Aurora had reconnected with her childhood love and the two had been married and blissfully happy for nearly a year now.

"I wasn't talking about *that* marriage," Lady Bramwell said.

"Probably for the best. Hateful man. And yes, it is a good thing to see Aurora so in love and so loved in return," Thomas said at last, giving his mother what she desired. "Though I cannot be happy with the suffering she went through to reach this happiest of endings. Nor can I ignore that her path to becoming Mrs. Nicholas Gillingham created more scandal for our sadly damaged name. One that might make such a happy union less possible for me."

"Thomas," his mother said softly, sadly, but she couldn't deny the truth of his words.

He shook his head. "I would never say that to her, of course. But the facts are the facts and you and I must be mindful of the past and its consequences as you are making exalted plans to marry me to the daughters of dukes or marquesses or even squires."

Lady Bramwell pinched her lips. "And what of a princess?"

He stared at her. "What?"

"I know you care little for gossip, but even you must know that the royal family of Athawick are expected in London tomorrow."

He nodded slowly. "I am not daft, Mama. Yes, I am aware of the impending arrival considering it has been splashed in every paper for the last week. The new king is meant to be shown off during the Season, yes? And I'm sure new treaties will be signed and trade deals will be made. Good for all parties, but how will it affect us? We'll be casual observers at best, nothing more."

"I have heard it from more than one good source that the family is seeking to arrange a marriage here in England for their daughter, Ilaria." She nodded her head once, eyes sparkling, and waited as if Thomas should have some grand response to this news.

But he shrugged. "Bully for them?"

Lady Bramwell huffed out a breath. "Thomas James Mackenzie Martindale, earl or not, I shall box your ears for being so obtuse. You must know that I wish to see if *you* might be a good match for her highness."

"Me?" he repeated, the world going rather distant as if she had dunked his head beneath water. "You cannot be serious."

"Why not?" she asked. "This could be the perfect solution to all our problems."

"Problems…" he said slowly. "That's a kind synonym for scandal, ruin and debt. Why would the royal family of any country wish to align themselves with *that*?"

His mother gripped her hands at her sides and paced away, standing before the fire, her shoulders rolled forward and trembling. Guilt stabbed at Thomas's chest. He was normally not too blunt with her, but her suggestion had taken him aback. His future wife was always discussed in general terms, like a dream, but this was a real person. One who could be hurtled into his path and his life within days. That made the concept all the more tangible...all the more troublesome.

"Whether you wish to see it or not," the countess began quietly, "we have a name. One that was once very strong, one that you have worked hard these last few years to make strong again. Yes, Aurora's romance with Nicholas caused some setbacks, but he is a war hero and well respected in his own right. People have all but forgotten the...the other circumstances."

"Is a slightly tarnished name enough for those with Highness as part of their honorific?" he asked.

She shrugged. "It is what is claimed that the Athawickians desire. To marry their daughter to someone with clout, but not so much that it outshines her own. To someone who gives their family a strong link to the power structures of our country, without the amount of direct influence that might put the Regent off the idea."

Thomas bent his head. So they were looking for connection by proxy, power in name only. "Well, then I suppose we do fit the bill," he murmured.

"We *could*." She sighed. "And if we did, then when those in our acquaintance spoke of the Earl of Bramwell, they would first mention that he married a princess rather than..." She trailed off with a pained wince. "Well, it would bring a great deal of influence...and money...back to our coffers. Enough to erase the problems of the past, even."

He saw the desperation flicker in her eyes. The pain his father had caused had landed most often on his mother's shoulders. She had borne it all and had spent the years since his death trying to make things better for her children. For herself. Recovering some part of the family name and respect was important to her.

And when he was honest with himself, it was important to him, as well.

"Then it sounds as if there is some chance of this being a mutually advantageous situation for all parties," he said, forcing a smile.

It was worth it when his mother's dark brown eyes lit up with excitement and relief. "So you will try?"

"Of course," he said. "And you may spend the ride giving me all the details you have clearly collected about the family."

He took her arm and let her launch into a list of facts about both Athawick and its royal family, though he felt not even a fraction of enthusiasm for the idea that she did. Perhaps that would change once he met the princess in question. Perhaps there would be a spark that would make this mercenary concept more palatable... even enjoyable.

One could only hope.

~

Sasha had once been a normal girl, not wrapped up in the intrigues of court or the whirlwind of royal scheduling. Sometimes she tried to remember those long-ago days. Tried to picture what her life would be like if she weren't the adopted daughter of a most unusual family.

She had to assume that regular citizens, when arriving in London after a long trip aboard a ship, were not greeted by honor guards and screaming crowds. And likely they did not rush almost immediately to a welcome ball in their honor. No, they probably got to do normal things like have a nice, quiet supper. Or take a long rest in a comfortable bed.

She wouldn't know, of course, because that life had been slipped from her fingers the moment she had been asked to join the royal family of Athawick. She had received all the benefits therein...and all the disadvantages.

Including the fact that she was dressed in an uncomfortable, if beautiful, ballgown that matched Ilaria's perfectly, and heeled slippers to make her the same height as the princess. All part of the illusion, all meant to make her the perfect double if, God forbid, something went wrong and Ilaria needed to be protected.

She fiddled with a loose thread on the couch arm as she and Ilaria's maid, June, teased with the princess. Tried to ease her concerns about the path Ilaria did not wish to take. Of course, it seemed that every time Sasha got Ilaria to relax, she would immediately become concerned about some other part of the plan.

"It is only that we haven't been in London a damned day," Ilaria huffed at last, the anxiety she would later not be allowed to demonstrate clear in every line of her body. "I apologize for the language, June, but there it is. And already I am being expected to exhibit for what will surely be a parade of disappointing potential grooms."

"And the Prince Regent," Sasha said, biting her tongue so she wouldn't become sharper with Ilaria. "And virtually every other titled and important person in London. This isn't entirely about you, you know."

She had hoped that point would land, and it did. Ilaria's expression softened and she shook her head. "You are…right, of course," she admitted. "I know tonight is about Grantham being recognized in his new role as king as much as it is about me. More, even. Did you see him after we arrived?"

Sasha's own face fell. She had once been as close to Grantham as she was to Remi or Ilaria. She had called him brother long before she called him king. And she could see that he was drowning. "The weight of all this is enormous."

Ilaria sighed. "Fine, then I will not protest out of respect for Grantham. And I will dance and shake hands and behave myself."

Sasha almost laughed at the idea of Ilaria behaving herself, but managed to keep it in. "An excellent notion. You do look the part of proper princess in that dress."

Ilaria moved to the full-length mirror to examine herself and then waved Sasha over. "Come stand by me, let's compare."

Sasha pushed herself from the settee and did so. Together they looked at their reflection. The gown they each wore was blue, with alternating paler blue stripes and highlights of gold. Atop Ilaria's head was the sea crown with its sparkling blue stones that matched the gown to perfection. Sasha's hair was down at present, but June would match Ilaria's style after she had slipped away and place a paste version of the real crown atop her head.

From a distance no one would be able to tell they weren't the same person. At least no one ever had. That was Sasha's place, after all…to be seen from a distance.

"You are prettier in it," Ilaria said, and drew Sasha back to the image before her.

Sasha snorted. "Unlikely. Anyway, no one will see me."

"Unless there is suddenly grave danger," Ilaria said, and then rolled her eyes. "Nothing is going to happen to me."

Sasha glanced toward the clock on the mantel. "Except that you are late and your mother might murder you."

Ilaria followed her gaze and yelped. "Oh, damn. Yes, I'll be off. I will see you later tonight with a full report on whatever wretched suitors they throw into my path. Good night! And thank you, June!"

She hurried from the room, leaving Sasha and June laughing as she went. Sasha followed to close the door and then returned to the spot Ilaria had abandoned. She settled in and smiled up at June. "How can I help?" she asked.

June brushed some of her hair up and said, "Hold this."

Sasha did so, and they chatted about London and upcoming events as June repeated the same style she had just created for Ilaria on Sasha's dark locks. When she was finished, they sighed together at the reflection.

"You really do look like you could be blood sisters," June sighed. "Will you go look in at the ball?"

Since Sasha had begun playing double for Ilaria after her coming out, she sometimes slipped to terraces or balconies to watch the festivities that Ilaria attended. She missed being part of gatherings, even if she understood that when it came to bigger public events, it was best for her to be silent and secret for Ilaria's potential protection.

But this was the first event of the family's arrival in London. There would surely be loads of pomp and circumstance to dissect and mock with Ilaria later. Sasha did want to see it and any of the gentlemen Ilaria might be matched with in the end, if only to gently guide her, if she could, to the best one for her.

"I will step out onto the terrace and see if it is safely empty, then peek through the windows, I think," Sasha said. "I can position myself to where I can slip into the shadows if need be."

"If you come back up, see if you can sneak a glass of madeira for us," June whispered, as if full voice would bring down the hounds of hell.

"You are wicked!" Sasha giggled as she caught June's hand and squeezed. "But I'll do my best."

June was still smiling as she began the process of tidying up the room, and Sasha slipped into the hallways. She didn't have to be careful in the family wing of the house. Everyone on staff knew her role—none behaved differently, except when they mistook her for Ilaria, and then there was bowing and the rest. Tonight, though, everyone was busy with the arrival and the ball, so she saw no other person as she made her way down the back servant stairs.

She turned through twisting halls, trying to find her bearings in this new home. In a few days, it would all be natural, but for now she felt a little lost and not just because of the new environment. There was something just...off lately. Something she couldn't place. But she would have to get herself together and soon, because she had a duty to perform here, and it wasn't moping around feeling melancholy.

CHAPTER 3

Thomas entered the foyer of Bleaking House, the state residence that had been loaned to the Athawick royals during their stay. His mother's hand gripped the inside of his elbow a bit tighter, and she was all but vibrating as they moved along toward the receiving line to greet the family.

"Steady now, Mama," he teased in a whisper. "Or else they will guess your mercenary thoughts."

His mother glared up at him, but there was a sparkle in her eyes. "Oh, you hush, Thomas. I am excited for the ball, that is all."

He snorted his derision, but they had reached the receiving line and he was forced back into propriety as the courier announced him and his mother to the King of Athawick.

"Lord Bramwell, Lady Bramwell," King Grantham said. He was of about Thomas's years and as handsome as the papers had been rambling on about for weeks now. They spoke for a moment and then were moved down the line to meet the queen, then the younger prince, Remington. Finally they reached the princess.

"The Earl and Dowager Countess of Bramwell," the courier behind her said softly, and she lifted her gaze to him.

Princess Ilaria was beautiful. There was no denying that. She had dark hair and eyes and wore a stunning blue striped gown. She wore a tiara in her curls, and for the first time Thomas really took in the truth of the matter: she truly was a princess. And his mother was determined that she might also be his wife.

An odd thing when he looked at her and felt...nothing.

His mother was chatting with her, and the princess was kindly responding. And then the exchange was over and they were shuttled toward the ballroom.

As they entered, his mother squeezed his inner arm again. "There you have it. She is even more lovely than she was described."

He forced a smile. "Indeed, she was very pretty. I'm sure if your belief that she is to be paraded out for the marriage mart is true, she will be swarmed with suitors. I hope you will not be crushed if your dreams for a match are unrealized."

There was a flash in his mother's stare. Something...desperate. But then it was gone and she smiled up at him. "You've said you would try with the lady, what else can I ask you to do? Now I see your sister and Nicholas across the room. Will you join us?"

"I'll say good evening to them later," he said. "I'll take a moment with a few friends of my own, if you don't mind."

She nodded and slipped away, leaving him alone. And alone he stayed, for he had no desire to truly speak to anyone in particular. He actually already felt exhausted by this entire endeavor and wanted a few moments of peace before there was not another chance for them during the ball.

But he had not stood by the side of the ballroom floor for two minutes when he was approached by Captain Jonah Crawford. He had met the man through his brother-in-law. The two had known each other thanks to their years in the war, though Nicholas had served in the King's Army and Crawford in the Royal Navy.

He'd actually encountered the man recently and talked to him about the Athawick family. Crawford knew them before, it seemed, though Thomas had gotten nothing from the captain about them beyond a slightly bad attitude.

So he was surprised to be greeted as warmly as he was by Crawford.

"My lord," the captain said as he stepped up, a hand extended. "Good to see you again."

Thomas shook the offered hand and smiled. "It is good to be seen. How is your night so far?"

Crawford's lips thinned. "Unexpected."

Thomas might have asked for more details on that answer, but before he could, the Athawick royal family entered the hall. They chatted together for a moment and then they all separated. The king went in one direction, Prince Remington another, and the queen and Princess Ilaria surprised him by coming his way. He straightened slightly as they reached him.

"Your Majesty," Crawford said first, which made sense since he knew the family better. He executed a bow and gave Ilaria a quick glance even though he was addressing her mother.

"Captain Crawford, let repeat to you what a pleasure it is to see you again," the queen said, then shifted her attention toward Thomas. "Ilaria, you met the Earl of Bramwell in the receiving line."

"Good evening again, my lord," the princess said.

He inclined his head. "Your Highness." His mind felt like it was entirely blank. What in the world did one discuss with a princess? "How are you enjoying London?"

God's teeth, he sounded like a bore. He felt like a bore, but what else was there to say?

"Not much so far," Princess Ilaria admitted. "We only arrived earlier in the day. This is a whirlwind, I'm afraid."

Thomas shifted, still at a loss of anything to say to this woman. "Well, then I hope you will have a chance to settle in and see our city to its full potential in the next few weeks and months."

"Perhaps you could be her guide, my lord." Queen Giabella leaned closer as she said those words, and he realized there was the same glint in her eyes that he'd earlier seen in his mother's.

Which resulted in the shocking realization that she was actually considering *him* for her daughter. How was that possible? He'd thought this all his mother's fantasy, but now it was reality and it hit him in the chest.

They were waiting for him to speak, to answer. He could see it on all three of his companions' faces. His mouth felt dry as he choked out, "I would be honored to give you some version of a tour if you would like that." Another loaded silence that could not have lasted ten seconds but felt like ten years stretched between them. "And perhaps you would honor me with a dance?"

Princess Ilaria hesitated a fraction of a moment and then nodded. "I would very much enjoy a dance, my lord."

He took her hand then, and off they went toward the dancefloor. This meant something, of course. Being chosen as the first gentleman to dance with the princess would pull him to the top of the crowded field that would soon be chasing her heels. Perhaps he should have been happy for that, but instead he was numb.

The music began and they turned into the steps. Thomas once again searched for a topic to broach when Princess Ilaria didn't seem fully there with him. She kept glancing away, as if distracted. "The entire country is aflutter about your visit, Your Highness."

That brought her back, and she smiled slightly. "It seems so. They are all watching us dance, after all. The interest will not let up...unless someone else does something shocking and turns their attention."

He laughed at the observation. At least she wasn't entirely dull. "I suppose we can hope."

She returned the smile, and as they continued the dance, the lack of connection faded a fraction. They talked of nothing serious, but of music and books. She was clearly a very clever person, which was a point in her favor. He hoped he seemed the same to her. If they were to even consider a future, he would like for them to be able to hold an intelligent conversation.

Of course, when he'd bothered to picture marriage at all, it had also included passion. Desire. If he was lucky, even love. But as he stared down into the beautiful face of his companion, he felt none of the stirrings of any of those things. There was no spark there, none of the instant tension that made a man's stomach flutter and heart race.

So as the dance ended and he executed a bow and led her back to her mother, he couldn't help but feel a sense of discontent. One that didn't fade as they said meaningless platitudes and then the princess slipped off into the crowd.

He paced away, restless as he took a drink and tried to fade into the gathering. He was suddenly out of sorts, he didn't want to see friends or make small talk about roads or weather or anything else. But that wouldn't do.

He set his half-empty glass on the tray of a servant who passed by and then moved across the room toward the terrace doors. A trumpet blared as he did so, but he ignored it and pushed out into the relief of the cooler night air.

He had to get himself together. He was expected to behave a certain way and he needed to find his way back to that behavior before he created problems for himself. More problems than he already faced.

∾

Sasha stepped out of the darkened parlor that had access to the wraparound back terrace overlooking the garden. She hovered near the door for a moment, letting her eyes adjust to the moonless night.

The music from the ballroom and the murmur of the crowd drifted over from her left, and she edged her way around the terrace, staying close to the house as she kept her eye out for wayward guests outside enjoying respite from the stuffy ballroom.

There were none, and as she reached a place where she could peek into the windows, she saw why. The Prince Regent had arrived and was dancing with Queen Giabella while the crowd looked on, enchanted. How could they not be, though? Giabella was so utterly beautiful and she was a graceful dancer. Just as she had cool grace in all things, really. An admirable quality Sasha had never been able to replicate, no matter how she tried.

Sasha scanned the floor for the rest of her family and found Ilaria first. She stood off to the side of the dancefloor with Remi. They had their heads together and were talking. Sasha shook her head. No good could come of that, Remi was never a suitable influence...and she adored him for it. As for Grantham...she lifted on her tiptoes and darted her gaze all around the room, but didn't see him.

She sighed heavily and backed away from the window, moving toward the shadow again. She leaned against the terrace wall's stone edge and gazed up at the stars. The English had their own constellations, but she saw a few of her favorite Athawickian ones like the butterfly, the sailing ship and the crown. She sighed in pure pleasure, and for a moment all was calm and right in her world. She had no duties or fears or anything but the sweet connection to the sky above.

"Your Highness?"

She froze at the words coming from behind her and all good thoughts fled. She'd thought she'd hidden herself well enough, she'd thought that no one would wish to miss the end of the dance between the Regent and the Queen of Athawick.

She was apparently mistaken, and now she had created a situation that could go very wrong, very quickly if she didn't use her wits and manage the intruder. She only hoped she was capable of doing just that.

Sasha turned slowly and lifted her chin, trying to put herself in as much shadow as possible. The stranger, on the other hand, was fully lit by the ballroom window, and she caught her breath. He was uncommonly handsome and put her to mind of Paris from the ancient mythology of Troy. The only man beautiful enough to pair with Helen, the one who would start a war to have her. This man had thick dark hair, full lips, a jawline that could cut through metal and warm, kind brown eyes that widened as he moved closer.

"Oh…I beg your pardon, you are not Princess Ilaria."

Sasha wasn't certain that his observation made this situation better or worse. She cleared her throat. "Er…no. But I thank you for the comparison."

His brow furrowed a little and he came to a stop, tilting his head. "You are wearing the same gown."

Sasha's eyes went wide. Here was the perfect excuse. "Indeed, I am. I was embarrassed by the fact and slipped from the ball to keep from further humiliation."

He arched a brow and she could see his disbelief on his face. "But you are also wearing a copy of Princess Ilaria's crown. And your hair is styled in the same way. You mean to look like her. For what purpose?"

She folded her arms. "If I am to be interrogated, I would expect to know the name of my inquisitor. Who are *you*, sir?"

"The Earl of Bramwell, madam."

Sasha's breath caught. Earlier in the day, before their disembarkation at the port, she had stumbled upon a list on Dash's desk that included this man's name. A list of potential suitors for Ilaria. Her heart sank a little when she ought to have no reaction at all.

"And I think you will find that I cannot be so easily put off, even by one so lovely as you," Bramwell continued, his eyes locking with hers. "Do you dress like the princess for some nefarious purpose?"

She shifted. Only the royal family and staff knew of her role. She had never been so reckless as she had been tonight to reveal it to someone who was unaffiliated with the Crown.

His jaw tightened and his lips thinned when she was silent too long. "I will fetch someone from inside, do not move."

He pivoted as if to march back to the ballroom and she stepped forward. This entire situation could easily escalate in a very bad way if she didn't end his curiosity. "No, wait. My lord, I *can* explain myself. But first I will need to know that you can be discreet."

He hesitated and turned back, his gaze flitting over her from head to toe in one smooth motion. "It depends upon your answer. I will not do anything that would put someone in danger."

"Especially the princess?" she asked, searching his face. "You have a stronger drive to protect her?"

His brow wrinkled. "You are styled like her, so she is my current concern. But I would feel the same if it were any person. Though I'm not sure why you ask."

He seemed unmoved by Ilaria, and that threw Sasha off even further. After all, men were always drawn to her even when she didn't notice them at all.

"Have you met the princess?" Sasha asked.

He tilted his head. "Yes, earlier this evening. We danced."

She blinked. So he had met Ilaria and yet seemed unaffected. Very interesting. "You must see that a lady of her position and her beauty attracts a great deal of attention. Sometimes attention that is unwanted or even dangerous."

He nodded slowly. "I can imagine that is true." He examined her a little closer, and then he drew in a sharp breath. "You are a double."

She drew back a fraction. Here she had been trying to find a way to describe her role and he had guessed it without any additional help. "Er..."

"Of course," he mused, almost more to himself than to her. "In her role, she would not always be available or safe in public. To have someone who looks enough like her to wave from a balcony or carriage...to step in under duress..."

Sasha let out her breath gently. "I admit no one has ever guessed the truth. Though I suppose not many see me dressed as her. When I am in my own clothing, when my hair is different, they just see me as..."

"Sasha Killick," he finished for her. "That is who you are, aren't you? The adopted daughter of the family, the princess's companion."

She wrinkled her brow. "You certainly seem to know a great deal about Ilaria and the family, my lord."

He shrugged. "At my mother's behest, it seems I do. God, what have I become?"

There was something about his tone that she couldn't help but laugh, and when she did so, he smiled. Her breath was all but sucked from her lungs. Great God, but he was not just handsome, but beautiful. Utterly, perfectly beautiful. She had never met a man his equal and she hated herself for being so drawn to him in this moment.

She cleared her throat. "I think you are no worse than dozens of other men in that ballroom who have been gathering intelligence about the family since their impending arrival was made public."

He pulled a face of utter disgust. "And here I was trying to be better than dozens of men in the ballroom." He sighed. "So what are you doing out here? Laying in wait for any moment of danger?"

She laughed. "Nothing like that. I enjoy watching the parties that I'm not able to attend because of the potential need for my services as a double. Normally I'm a little more aware of what is happening around me, but I was distracted by the beautiful night sky."

He glanced up with her. "It *is* beautiful. You can see more stars in the countryside, of course, without the lights and the dirt in the air to block them."

"It's the same in Athawick, though we certainly don't have the same kinds of huge cities like London. But I do love to go out away from the buildings and look up at the sky."

She turned her face and realized he was watching her rather than the aforementioned stars. She bent her head, feeling the heat rush to her cheeks under his suddenly focused regard. It had obviously been far too long a time since a handsome man had paid her attention, because she was like a schoolgirl in her reactions. Entirely inappropriate, especially considering that the man was far above her station *and* potentially intended for Ilaria.

Taking a long step back, she forced the palace smile she had so long practiced back to her lips. "It has been a pleasure making your acquaintance, my lord, but I think I should go back into the house before I find myself caught in my costume by more than just you." She inclined her head. "I hope you will keep your promise not to reveal my role to anyone else."

"I will, Miss Killick," he said. "Good evening."

He executed a slight bow as she slipped away, back into the dark shadows toward the parlor. She fisted her hands at her sides as she moved, unable to keep herself from thinking of the man and his extremely handsome visage. As the terrace curved, she peeked back over her shoulder and found that he remained where she had left him, watching her go.

Heat filled her cheeks and she scurried to the parlor and let herself back inside. Her heart was racing almost out of control and her hands shook as she latched the door behind her. But she could not lock out the truth and the truth was that she had been very attracted to the Earl of Bramwell.

Despite the fact that nothing could ever come of such a silly thing. Despite the fact that he likely forgot her the moment he went back into the ballroom and was surrounded by ladies far more fitting to his station, his life and whatever plans he had for the future.

CHAPTER 4

Thomas stepped back into the bright, loud, hot ballroom, but he hardly saw any of it. His mind kept turning to the moment when Sasha Killick had laughed on the terrace and his stomach had done what he'd waited for it to do when he danced with Princess Ilaria. It had made the strangest flip.

How in the world could he feel such an attraction to her when he felt absolutely nothing for a woman who looked so remarkably like her, at least from a distance? Up close, of course, there was no comparison. Miss Killick had brighter, livelier eyes and a more engaging smile. Fuller lips.

He blinked to clear those thoughts from his mind. It was all just incomprehensible and mightily inconvenient.

"Do I catch my brother woolgathering?"

He pivoted at the playful teasing of his sister and turned to watch Aurora step up beside him. She was a beautiful woman, always had been, but the last year of blissfully happy marriage had made her glow. Those around them couldn't miss it and many a male gaze flitted her way. Not that she gave a damn. She only had eyes for Nicholas Gillingham and always had.

Another thing their arse of a father had very nearly destroyed.

She linked an arm through Thomas's and smiled up at him. "Fancy a dance with your little sister?"

He pushed unpleasant thoughts away and nodded. "Always, Aurora."

They made their way to the dancefloor and, when the next song began, stepped out together. He marveled a moment at how graceful his sister was. She danced rarely in public. Nicholas's permanent injuries after the war made him self-conscious about it in public, though they often took a turn together in private and were always deeply connected when they did.

Still, watching her do an elaborate turn with a bright smile was warming. It was a country dance, so it gave little chance for conversation. A fact that had never seemed to bother Aurora. The next time they came together, bobbing up the line, with only their fingers touching, she said, "When I found you, you were staring off into the distance at a certain princess. And you seemed quite engrossed. Does that mean Mama's plans to catch you a princess bride are not as distasteful to you as you feared?"

They parted, pivoting around other partners. Thomas was just as happy for the moment to think about what he would say in return. When they returned to each other, he said, "She is quite something, that is true."

He waited for his sister's gaze to brighten with pleasure, excitement, but it didn't. Her brow furrowed a fraction in concern and then she pivoted off, spinning around before she returned to her place across from him. It would be a few beats before he did the same and then they skipped up the line together, so he had no escape from her evaluating stare.

"Did you see her dancing with the Regent?" Aurora asked.

"She did?" Thomas cleared his throat and did his turn, then they clasped hands and skipped farther up the line before retaking a place across from each other.

Aurora's question pinned him. He'd seen Queen Giabella with the prince earlier. If afterward Princess Ilaria had danced with the

Regent, as well, that was certainly a moment the entire ballroom would have been engrossed by. And yet he had been on the terrace and hadn't seen because he'd been with someone far more interesting to him.

Aurora stared at him. "Are you attempting a...joke, Thomas?"

"Well, no. I...er...was outside, I believe, when that happened."

Her eyes went wide, and when she pivoted away and back again, she shook her head. "That was the moment of the Season, Thomas. People will be talking about it for ages."

He frowned. "Then I suppose you will have to tell me all about it later so I can aptly pretend that I was attending to the dance."

She glared at him as he took his turn away from her and when they came together to skip closer to the end of the line, she said, "You know I will do just that. But what on the terrace could have so bewitched you that you didn't even notice what was happening inside? The crowd watched them dance together without moving. They gave thunderous applause when it was over. You noticed none of that ten feet away on the terrace?"

He had been more distracted by Miss Killick than he had realized. Even now he tried not to replay the moments with her. The music came to an end and the couples acknowledged each other and then began to leave the dancefloor, laughing and chatting as they did so.

Aurora clasped his arm, and together they moved toward her husband, Nicholas, who was standing by the edge of the dancefloor now, leaning on his cane and smiling at Aurora.

"You two are always lovely to watch dance," Nicholas said as he caught Aurora's hand and lifted it to his lips.

There was an electric connection between them, and Thomas dropped his gaze because it always felt like intruding when he was near them.

"Tonight my brother was distracted," Aurora said, and arched a brow at Thomas. "Though he is avoiding telling me why."

Thomas let out a sigh. "And you will bulldog it out of me, won't you?"

"Indeed, I shall," she said brightly. "So you might as well stop fighting me."

"As a regular victim of her bulldogging—" Nicholas began.

She burst out laughing. "Not a victim!"

He leaned back and speared her with a look. "Of course not, love. I meant *grateful recipient*." She rolled her eyes with another easy laugh as he continued, "As a highly grateful recipient of your sister's bulldogging, I would suggest you just tell her what she wants to know because she will needle it out eventually."

"Don't I know it," Thomas said with a playful look in her direction. Then his smile fell. "I went out on the terrace to get some air. And there was…a person outside who interested me. Distracted me."

Aurora's eyes went wide. "A lady."

"A lady," he admitted. "And now you know it all."

She snorted her derision. "I doubt that is true."

"At any rate, it doesn't really matter."

"It will to your mother," Nicholas said with a gentle chuckle. "She is gunning for your union before we see the end of the Season. Princess or no."

"Yes," Thomas said softly. "I am well aware. But I think the lady on the terrace would not be a good fit. She was a fine companion for a moment, but I know the expectations for my future. So does she. There are some paths that will simply never diverge."

"Thomas—" Aurora began, her tone truly concerned now. But to Thomas's great relief, Nicholas took her hand and gently shook his head.

So they were all silent, and it was impossible for the collective gaze of the group not to turn to Princess Ilaria, who had just been spun out on the dancefloor by yet another interested party.

His errant mind took him right back to Sasha as he watched the princess from his slight distance. Only he had to cease those thoughts. An instant attraction in the starlight was all well and good, but he was on another path now. And so was she.

And that was, unfortunately...that.

~

It was the wee hours of the morning, late enough that it could actually be called early considering the sun was beginning to rise in the east and cast light on the drunkenly departing guests. Sasha sat on the terrace at a table overlooking the garden, still in the gown that matched Ilaria's. In the distance she could see her sister standing, clearly trying to escape whatever farewells were being said within the ballroom.

Sasha should go to her, she knew. Begin discussions of Ilaria's night, head back to their chamber where they would giggle and gossip until they fell asleep, just as they had been for years. Only at present, she didn't really want to do that. Because she couldn't stop thinking about the Earl of Bramwell and their brief encounter.

She'd been around handsome men all her life. Many with power or title like the earl had flocked to the palace on Athawick and tried to catch the attention of anyone there who they thought would advance them. From time to time, a gentleman would smile her way. She always turned up her nose. She wasn't about to be used because of her proximity to power.

If she developed an interest in a man, she wanted it to be for his wit and his kindness, not because he wished to manipulate her in order to get closer to the king or a prince or princess.

But Bramwell hadn't struck her as any of those things. He'd been nothing but genuine during their exchange and honest. Those were very attractive qualities in an equally attractive man.

She sighed. "He is meant for Ilaria, though," she muttered. "So you should clear your mind of any other thoughts about him."

She pushed to her feet and started to cross the terrace to gather Ilaria, but before she reached her, she watched as the princess was approached by another man. One Sasha knew. It was Captain Crawford, who had joined the Prince Regent on a diplomatic trip to Athawick before the previous king's death. Ilaria had been drawn to him during his visit, and even from a distance, Sasha felt the connection between the pair.

She hesitated, watching their brief exchange for a moment before he pivoted and strode away, leaving Ilaria to watch after him, her hands flexing at her sides. As she approached, Sasha said, "Is that who I think it was?"

Ilaria jolted a fraction, as if she had lost track that others might be around. She looked down the terrace and Sasha was taken aback by the expression on her face: pained and empty.

"Who do you think it was?" Ilaria asked softly.

"Captain Jonah Crawford," Sasha said, arching her brow. "Or was I seeing things?"

There was a long pause before Ilaria responded. "You weren't. It was, indeed, the esteemed Captain Crawford. He was an attendee at the ball and we were just saying our farewells."

"Ilaria, you forget that I am your confidante and friend. I know you...well, you *liked* the man during his visit to Athawick, what was it...three years ago?"

"Two," Ilaria corrected. "It's been two years, and yes, I thought him very handsome when he visited me...the family back then."

For a moment they reminisced about those days, and Sasha could see that Ilaria was brought back to the brief time she'd shared with the captain. At last she shook her head. "But you can see by the way he walked away without so much as a backward glance that he thinks nothing of me. And I can think nothing of him, thanks to my family's plans."

Sasha flinched, for those words made her think of the Earl of Bramwell. He was part of those plans, potentially. He had mentioned he'd danced with Ilaria when he encountered Sasha on the terrace. What had she thought of him?

"Ilaria—" she began, but the princess lifted a hand.

"I'm simply tired. With the travel and then this huge event. I'm tired. Come, we'll have little chance for rest before the next event this evening. Let's go before I fall over or my brother and mother find ten more men off the street for me to meet."

Sasha inclined her head. There would be time enough to press Ilaria on the subject of Bramwell...and of Captain Crawford. For now she clearly needed a break. So Sasha wrapped an arm around her waist and together they walked back toward the parlor where they could sneak into the house without being seen by excited guests or interfering family members.

As they slipped up the back stairs together, toward the chamber they were sharing during their time here, Sasha squeezed her gently. "Were there any men who caught your eye?"

Ilaria snorted. "Of course not. I was surrounded by nothing by buffoons and popinjays from the moment I entered the ballroom. And these are my mother's chosen suitors." She shook her head.

Sasha bit her tongue to keep herself from asking directly about the earl, who was neither a buffoon nor a popinjay as far as she had seen. But that was treading into dangerous territory—and potentially revealing her own attraction. No good could come of it.

She pushed her thoughts away and smiled as they entered the chamber. "Come, let's get out of these uncomfortable gowns. It will all seem better after a good sleep."

But as they moved into the chamber and began the job of unfastening and taking each other's hair down, Sasha wondered if that were true. She still felt a sense of...dread at this trip. And it had not been made easier by her introduction to a man she most definitely could not have.

CHAPTER 5

Thomas stood along the edge of the crowd gathered for Lady Questington's afternoon tea, worrying the handle of his cup as his mind took him in directions it ought not. It had been four days since the welcome ball for the Athawick royal family and though he had other things to do, people to see, duties to attend to, his errant mind kept bringing him back to one place: the terrace with Sasha Killick.

He'd found out a bit more about her in that time. Easy enough thanks to his mother's interest in the family. If he asked about Sasha, she took it to mean he had sparked an interest in Princess Ilaria and she was happy to share facts about *her*. If Thomas had gleaned tidbits about Sasha...well, his mother seemed none the wiser.

Facts like that Sasha had been adopted by the family at a young age. That she and the princess were like sisters. Vague details, never enough, but always taking him to memories of her bright smile and soft laugh at the ball.

As if conjured by his thoughts, the Queen of Athawick and Princess Ilaria stepped out onto the sunny terrace with the rest of the group. He clenched a hand at his side. From a distance the princess really did look like Sasha—he could see how those unacquainted with them might be fooled. But she was like a shadow of the other woman, really. There was none of the spark to her, none of the brightness that had drawn him to Sasha so suddenly.

Immediately the gentry in attendance swung forward, desperate for a look or a word or a story to share and exaggerate later for those not lucky enough to be here.

Lady Questington made an announcement of some kind, but Thomas paid her no mind. He was looking behind them, trying to see if Sasha was part of their party. When she didn't materialize, he scowled.

Lady Questington stepped away, and Queen Giabella and Princess Ilaria both began to scan the crowd. Ilaria looked off away, but Giabella caught a glimpse of him. Her face lit up and made it clear she wished for him to join them. He stifled a sigh and made his way toward her. At least his mother would be pleased, as he was sure she was watching from the throng.

Princess Ilaria didn't even look at him as he reached them. She still seemed to be focused on someone else. But Queen Giabella beamed at him. "Lord Bramwell, how lovely to see you again."

"Your Majesty," he said, inclining his head toward her. "And Your Highness."

Princess Ilaria still did not acknowledge him and her mother squeezed her inner elbow a bit tighter, finally forcing her daughter's attention. "Ilaria, you recall Lord Bramwell, do you not?"

Ilaria smiled, but it did not quite meet her dark eyes. "Of course I recall you, my lord. How nice to see you again."

Thomas executed the expected bow. "Your Highness, the pleasure is all mine." He searched desperately for some topic to broach with the women, but then realized his mother was watching them from a distance. And there was his escape. If she was brought into the mix, she would very much dominate it and he could stand to the side and just wait for all this to be over. "I wondered if I might introduce you ladies to my mother.

The dowager countess is very anxious to make your acquaintance."

"We met so very briefly in the receiving line a few nights ago, but I have longed to make her acquaintance," Queen Giabella said. "Please, won't you lead the way?"

Thomas did so, smiling as his mother's face paled a shade at the impending introduction. She smoothed her hands along the skirt of her dark pink gown and gave a dazzling smile that had warmed more than a few hearts over the years.

"Queen Giabella, Princess Ilaria, may I present my mother, Lady Bramwell, the dowager countess."

He watched how his mother's gaze flitted over Ilaria and warmed. The countess liked her, it seemed—she had always been able to make those instantaneous judgments. And sometimes she was even right in them.

Not in her choice of husband...but he refused to hold that against her.

Her warmth seemed to affect even the queen, herself, for they quickly fell into a genuine conversation. Queen Giabella's smile became more real, more frequent. Ilaria even joined in as they spoke, though her gaze kept moving toward the crowd, as if she were looking for someone there.

"Your Majesty," Lady Bramwell said after a short time. "I wonder if you have ever played cribbage?"

The queen's expression brightened. "Oh my, yes. I often play with my private secretary, Dash—Mr. Talbot."

"That is excellent news," Lady Bramwell said. "Would it be too impertinent to ask you to join me in a little tournament a group of ladies plays twice monthly? It is nothing formal, but it is high fun."

Thomas's eyes widened. A bold suggestion, considering his mother was talking with a queen, not just another titled lady. But the expression of Queen Giabella was temporarily lined with... longing. But then it was gone.

The princess must have seen it, too, for suddenly her attention was entirely on the queen. "I think you should, Mama. It sounds like grand fun."

Queen Giabella slowly nodded. "I would very much appreciate the invitation. And I'm certain we can make the time and place work. Mr. Talbot is very good at managing my schedule."

"Wonderful. Why don't you come with me, then?" Lady Bramwell said. "A few of the other ladies who come to our group are in attendance today. May I introduce them to you now?"

Thomas's heart sank. So *that* was why his mother was so pointed in her request. The acceptance meant she could drag the queen away and leave Thomas alone with Princess Ilaria. Her direct stare at him left no question about those intentions.

The ladies moved off together, chatting as they went. Ilaria looked back at him and she shifted slightly. "It was kind of your mother to offer. Sometimes the queen finds it hard to indulge in pleasures due to the reverence people hold to her title."

"Well, she will find both reverence and companionship in my mother," Thomas said. "The countess has never met someone she didn't consider a friend. She can do nothing but welcome all comers."

Ilaria examined him a bit more closely. It was the first time she'd really seemed to see him, despite the fact that they had danced together a few nights before. "That sounds like a very nice quality."

"It is," he agreed. "She is the best of women." And with that, Thomas ran out of anything to say to this woman. So they stood in awkward silence while he searched desperately for some other topic to fill the space. "I-I think she is a bit taken in with all the court intrigue. My mother."

Princess Ilaria sighed. "I suppose there is some of that. Though in comparison to the intrigues in this country, I think we are staid."

At that, he chuckled and his traitorous thoughts returned him to the terrace when he had realized exactly why Sasha was dressed identically to Ilaria. "I don't know. I've never met a lady who had a double."

At that the princess's smile slowly fell. "I-I'm not sure what you mean."

He tilted his head. She seemed upset that he would say such a thing, but he didn't understand why. It seemed benign enough a topic. "I met her at the ball. Miss Sasha Killick, yes?"

"You met her?" Ilaria repeated. "How?"

"I went onto the terrace to get a bit of air and saw you standing at the wall, staring up at the stars. I thought I would come speak to you, but as I approached and the woman turned, I realized she was not you at all, but someone dressed and styled as you. It didn't take long to figure out the rest."

"Did you speak?" she asked, her tone sharper.

He stared at her, his questions turning to concerns that perhaps he had caused trouble for Sasha with his inquiries. "We did. For a moment."

Princess Ilaria shook her head. "Sasha never said anything to me."

That shouldn't have caused a reaction in him. Miss Killick owed him nothing and their encounter had been so brief. But the idea that she had said nothing still stung. "Ah, well, perhaps I did not make much of an impression."

Ilaria didn't deny that suggestion, but looked him up and down a moment before her attention was drawn over his shoulder. "Ah, it seems my mother is coming back to us. I suppose she will wish to introduce me all around."

Relief cascaded through him that this encounter was over. It hadn't been unpleasant, of course, but he felt no desire to keep her at his side. He executed a bow. "Indeed. It was a pleasure seeing you again."

"And I'm sure it will be a pleasure we will soon repeat."

Her tone was bone dry, and for a moment their eyes locked. He saw that she knew exactly as he did what the intentions of their families were. That she was just as unmoved by those plans as he was. They were both trapped, it seemed. And it made him feel worse to be stuck with another person, rather than better.

"Good day," he said, and stepped away. He felt numb as he moved through the crowd and found his mother standing with their hostess. Lady Questington glanced his way, said something to Lady Bramwell and then hurried into the crowd as he made his final approach.

"How did it go?" his mother asked softly.

He arched a brow at her. "You could not have been more obvious in your intentions when you two raced off and left the princess and me alone."

She blinked up at him in false innocence. "Intentions? I couldn't possibly know what you mean. I was only trying to be polite to a stranger."

He snorted out a laugh. "You might as well have pinned a card on my chest that read I had been claimed by the princess. Or she by me. No one could be confused about your desire to see us matched, or the queen's."

Lady Bramwell turned toward him, and her gaze was filled with concern. "You make it sound like that is a bad thing. Isn't it positive that both our families may desire the same outcome? That we could mutually benefit each other?"

He drew a long breath. He *should* have been happy about that fact, of course. He'd been struggling to rebuild all that had been destroyed by their father's imprudence and this union would erase almost all of that pain and harm and humiliation.

And yet…

"I suppose," he muttered.

"Not to mention that she isn't the most terrible match for you when it comes to temperament. She is an intelligent woman, that is evident when one speaks to her for even a moment. She will challenge you, I think, and you are a strong enough man to like that."

Thomas looked off into the crowd toward Princess Ilaria. She was standing with Prince Remington, who had apparently arrived during Thomas's conversation with his mother. The siblings had their heads close together and seemed to be engaged in serious discussion.

She was, at least on paper, a very good match for him. His mother was right that he'd never desired a simpering bride who had been taught to nod at anything her husband said. He liked a lady with spark, with desires of her own, opinions of her own. And then there were those additional benefits of the match.

"Plus, she is beautiful. Which is a nice bonus, I think, for most gentlemen," his mother continued softly.

He pursed his lips. Of course the princess was lovely. Every man in every room she ever entered marked that fact. And yet when he looked at her, he now only saw who she wasn't. He saw the subtle difference in the fullness of her lips, the comparison of the curve of her jaw...he saw Sasha Killick instead of Princess Ilaria of Athawick.

And he liked Sasha more. That was all there was to it. A frustrating thing considering how tightly bound the two women were. How he would not be able to forget the one because of the other.

"I'm sorry," his mother said softly.

He drew his gaze away from Ilaria and her brother and focused it on the countess. "Sorry?" he repeated. "Whatever for?"

"I would have very much liked it if you had been able to find the great love that your sister has with Nicholas." She worried her hands before herself and tears leapt to her eyes. "I hate to be like your father—"

"Now just a moment," he said, guiding her away from the crowd so they could speak more privately. "You are nothing like Father, I assure you of that."

She tilted her head. "He guaranteed that your sister would marry a man she did not love for his own gain. How am I not exactly like him in that regard?"

"Mama," he said, and caught both her hands, squeezing gently. "Father tore Aurora away from Nicholas because he judged him to be unworthy, that there was no gain, and threw her into a marriage with a man she did not love…she did not even like. She suffered and we all hate that. But that is not this situation. Firstly, you are not separating me from some great love."

His mind flitted traitorously to Sasha once more and he firmly pushed those thoughts away. He had talked to the woman once, for five minutes. That was not a great love. It was attraction to a lady who he most certainly could not have. And he hadn't even made an impression on her, for she hadn't told Ilaria about their encounter.

"But—"

He held up a hand. "No buts because you are also not *forcing* me to do anything. I am the Earl of Bramwell, I will remind you, and if I wished to marry someone…anyone…I certainly have the power to do so without your consent or permission."

"I suppose," his mother said softly, though he could see her relief at his statements.

So he offered one more. "Ultimately, though the damage that was created by my father is not my fault, it is my duty to clean it up. I know that. You have worked very hard to offer me a fine solution and I am not petulant about it, I assure you. I'm grateful you care enough to offer assistance rather than simply take to your bed and wail about your circumstances."

She laughed. "I've never been much of a wailer."

"No," he agreed. "You've been nothing but careful and caring. And I appreciate both those things more than you know."

She patted his hand and then shook her head. "And now you and I have spent far too much of this party discussing maudlin family matters. You have friends here, I know, and I'm sure you'd rather be talking to them than your mother."

He smiled at her and lifted her hand for a kiss before she shooed him off toward the handful of friends that were in attendance. But as he moved away from her, that smile fell.

He talked a good game when it came to accepting the path that was laid out before him. But walking it still brought a sense of dread. One he would very much have to quash, because he owed it to his family and to his title to do as was expected of him.

～

Sasha looked up from her book and smiled as June finished helping Ilaria into her nightrail and then gathered up the clothes for washing.

"You don't need anything else, Your Highness? Miss Sasha?"

"No, I'm going to force Sasha to brush my hair out before I do hers. We're fine. Good night, June," Ilaria said.

As the maid departed, Sasha tilted her head and looked at the princess a bit more closely. There was something troubled around her eyes, something faraway that had been there since her return from the tea earlier in the afternoon.

She tossed the book on the settee and got up, motioning Ilaria to the dressing table. Ilaria sat and fiddled with a loose string on the lace of the nightgown. "How is the book?"

Sasha opened drawers looking for a brush. "Excellent, but I'm almost finished and I'll need something new."

Ilaria glanced over her shoulder at the novel on the settee. "I'll read it next, I suppose, and we can talk about it. Oh, and someone at the tea mentioned a bookshop in the area they call Cheapside."

"Cheapside," Sasha repeated, and made a face. "That isn't a very nice name."

"No, they can be such snobs here. But the area is supposed to be very nice, with plenty of shops, including...oh, I've forgotten the name. Mulligan, Mittingham...Mattigan's! It was Mattigan's Bookshop."

Sasha arched a brow. "You want me to go."

Ilaria nodded. "Mama is making a huge fuss that I shouldn't go do such things by myself."

The strain was clear in her voice, and Sasha nodded. "Of course I'll do it. I suppose even if you were allowed full freedom, it would be difficult for you to find time. Aren't you all attending that afternoon reception with the Regent and his estranged wife tomorrow?"

Ilaria groaned. "Don't remind me. I am dreading it—he is such a bore."

"But the possibilities for an outburst are legion!" Sasha said, hoping she could lighten the mood a little. "They say Princess Caroline lives to humiliate her husband. Anything could happen!"

"I don't like the world to function as if anything could happen. I want to know what is going to happen so I can fully prepare for it," Ilaria said, but she was laughing.

Sasha joined in. "I don't know, I think I would like to observe a situation where anything could happen."

Ilaria's smile fell. "Mama and Grantham wished to bring you, as well. It wasn't their choice."

A little sting worked through Sasha but she pushed it back, just as she always had. She'd been forced to, especially over the last few years. "I realize that most people don't see my role as anything but elevated servant."

"But *we* don't see you that way," Ilaria said.

Sasha shrugged. "At any rate, I might like an English royal family drama for a short time, but in the end the bookshop will likely offer a longer entertainment. So I shall happily go and pick out a few new tales for us."

She began to brush Ilaria's hair. It was so comforting to do so. They had been doing this for each other for a very long time. It was one of her earliest memories after she'd been taken in: Ilaria brushing her hair.

"You have been very quiet about the garden party earlier today," Sasha said at last. "Do you want to talk about it?"

"My mother misses no opportunity to shove me into the faces of any eligible man of a certain rank and situation." Ilaria sighed. "This afternoon it was Lord Bramwell again."

Sasha faltered in her strokes. "The Earl of Bramwell?"

"The very one. He seems a nice enough man and he's not unpleasant to look at, but there is no…no *spark* there whatsoever."

Sasha felt her eyes go wide at that statement and had to control her facial expression. No spark? How was that possible? The man was nothing but spark! "That's too bad," she said mildly.

"He said the funniest thing, though. He said that he saw you on the terrace the night of the welcome ball."

Sasha gasped at that statement and the brush fell from her fingers. As she bent to pick it up, Ilaria pivoted in her chair. "Are you well? You are pale."

"I'm fine. Just tired, I suppose."

"Well, sit down," Ilaria said, waving her toward the settee. As Sasha took a place there, the princess joined her. "Is it because I mentioned Lord Bramwell?"

"Of course not," Sasha said, wishing she were not so easily read on this subject. "I have no connection to the man. He happened to come outside the night of the welcome ball and found me there. I tried to put him off the idea that I might be your double, but he is too clever for his own good. We talked for but a moment—there was nothing else to it."

"If you say so."

"I do," Sasha said. "And *you* are changing the subject."

"Was I?" Ilaria asked, and her gaze darted away much as Sasha had felt her own gaze moving when they discussed Bramwell. "I thought the subject was the garden party this afternoon."

Sasha tilted her head. "I've known you since we were girls, Ilaria. I can see you're holding something back. What is it?"

Before Ilaria could answer, there was a light knock on the chamber door. Sasha pursed her lips. That was bad timing. She got up and moved to see who was there and found one of the family servants waiting. Darby was his name, a short man with a mischievous air to him. Also the one all the royal children, including Sasha herself, went to when they needed information off the record.

He winked at Sasha. "I have what the princess was asking about earlier." He handed over a folded paper. "She better be careful now. Some fires burn hotter than others."

With that confusing statement made, he practically skipped away. Sasha returned to Ilaria and handed over the items. "From Darby."

Ilaria's eyes went wide and she snatched the papers away as she jumped to her feet. A blush brightened her cheeks as she read.

"Do you want to tell me what's going on?" Sasha asked.

"Nothing."

It was an obvious lie. "I grew up the same way you did—you know," Sasha said. "I *know* Darby is the servant all of us turn to when we want discreet information for a price. And your expression gives you away even if I didn't know that. What are you up to, Ilaria?"

Ilaria met Sasha's gaze. "Do you swear you will not tell another living soul what I am about to share with you?"

That was a concerning question. "I...suppose."

"Remi told me about this wicked club here in London, the Donville Masquerade. I wanted to know more, so I asked Darby for the information." She handed over the papers.

Sasha took them and read for a moment. Various phrases jumped out at her.

Private club. Backroom affairs. Nudity and public pleasure.

She gasped as she jerked her head up. "Ilaria, this is a...a sex club. Where people can have masked...encounters."

"Yes," Ilaria said, and didn't look shocked or embarrassed by the situation. "Which makes it a perfect place for me to visit, as I'll be masked as well, and no one will ever recognize me."

Sasha's own problems when it came to her encounter with the Earl of Bramwell fled immediately at Ilaria's casual statement. "You're going to go to this place?"

Ilaria nodded.

"*Why?*" Sasha asked. "Masked or not, it is a great risk to take. Why do you feel you need to do such a thing?"

"Because..." Ilaria bent her head and her exhaustion was clear. "Because I'm not so foolish to believe I will be able to escape my family's plans. I can fight all I want, but they will win and I'll end up leg shackled to Bramwell or some other man just like him."

Sasha flinched. It must be serious indeed if Ilaria was feeling so trapped that she'd want to risk herself in this way. She really thought she'd marry Bramwell. Which meant Sasha would have to see him all the time. She'd have to pretend like meeting him hadn't moved her.

Ilaria was still talking, and Sasha forced herself to attend as she said, "I want to...I want to go there."

"For what?"

"Just to see. And maybe to have one last little moment that is just for me. Just about me."

Sasha drew in a long breath. Ilaria had never been all that tied up in the idea of protecting her innocence. On Athawick, the concept of virginity just didn't matter that much, so long as one was careful. Still, there was a huge difference between having a discreet lover to pass the time and going to a public club in a country where innocence in ladies was the rule of the day.

"Is that wise, Ilaria? In your position—"

"My *position* should not be any different from that of my brothers, who are allowed to do such things, provided they are discreet about it."

"You're right." She caught Ilaria's hand. "And yet this is not the way of the world, especially this one. What will you do if you're caught? Or threatened? Or..."

"I won't be caught," Ilaria said. "I'll be sure of it. And you read the information. The owner of the club is named Marcus Rivers, and he seems to be a highly cautious man and protective of his business and clients. There is not even one report of bad behavior in his walls. It is likely safer than walking through a park in London."

Sasha had known Ilaria almost all her life. She knew when her stubborn streak had taken over. Once it did… "You can't be talked out of this, can you?"

Ilaria smiled. "No."

"Then how can I help?" Sasha asked on a heavy sigh.

Ilaria rushed to her and enveloped her in a hard hug that told Sasha, yet again, how desperate her friend was. "First, we have to find something for me to wear that won't be recognized. And a mask. Oh, and a carriage."

Sasha forced a laugh at her enthusiasm, but as she began to work on putting Ilaria's hair back up, her heart sank. The princess was being marched down a certain path and it seemed she would go kicking and screaming the entire way. Which made Sasha wonder how happy any marriage she was forced into would be.

Even to a man as fascinating as Bramwell.

CHAPTER 6

S asha stepped from the carriage and smiled at the footman who assisted her down. She had invited June as her chaperone for the trip and the maid looked positively elated as she stepped out. Together they gazed up at Mattigan's Bookshop and Sasha's heart soared. It was a beautiful shop with brightly decorated windows filled with books.

"Lor', you'll have books aplenty to choose from," June breathed. "Even Prince Remington would have to be impressed, and he's no great reader."

Sasha laughed and waved off their driver, who moved the rig so as not to block the way. "I think Remi may be only half the thoughtless rake he pretends to be. I would wager he has a few books hidden beneath his pillows."

June opened her mouth as if she were going to retort and then stopped herself. "I think I ought not hazard a guess as to what he has hidden under his pillows."

Sasha laughed even more loudly then and guided them to the door. A bell jangled when they entered and a kindly faced older man behind a high counter just beyond the door smiled at them. "Good afternoon, ladies," he said. "Emery Mattigan, at your service."

"Good afternoon, Mr. Mattigan," Sasha returned. "And may I say what a remarkable shop you have here."

The shopkeep puffed up a little as they looked all around the cozy, warmly lit shop with its row after row of bookshelves. Between them in the back she could see comfortable-looking seats facing a roaring fire. A very inviting prospect where one could browse before they bought.

"Enjoy yourself, and if there's anything in particular you're looking for, don't hesitate to ask."

She nodded at the gentleman, and then she and June moved into the stacks. For a short time they stayed together, but eventually June was held up by a tome on Roman history, a pet subject of the maid's. Sasha took the opportunity to browse off alone, running her fingers along the leather spines and tilting her head to look at the embossed titles along them.

She was utterly lost and completely charmed. So much so that she forgot her surroundings entirely. Until, that was, the bell at the door rang again. She heard Mr. Mattigan greet the newcomer, but it wasn't until the person answered that she was yanked from her happy cloud of distraction.

"Mr. Mattigan," the male voice came. The Earl of Bramwell's voice, to be more specific.

Sasha nearly dropped the book in her hands as she skirted her way closer to the stack to...hide? Was she hiding? From a man she had only met once and then only in passing? That was utterly ridiculous!

Bramwell was speaking again in that low, resonate tone that she'd been trying to forget for days. "How nice to see you. And I was directed to ask if my mother's order had arrived."

"Indeed, it has, my lord," Mattigan responded, all jolly warmth, as if there wasn't a woman trying to shrink to nothingness in the stacks just a few strides away. "Just this morning. I'll wrap it up for you to take to her when you go."

Bramwell thanked the man and they made a little more small

talk. Then she heard his footfalls coming toward the bookcases. He seemed to turn up the one just next to where she stood and then stopped, like he was searching out the books on the shelf.

She let out a low breath. She was being ridiculous and she knew it. There was no reason to hide from the man or feel awkward about meeting him. They were not friends or even acquaintances, and if she found him attractive...well, she was allowed to do that, wasn't she? She found a great many men attractive on their surface.

None of them haunted her dreams, but that meant nothing. Absolutely nothing. Less than nothing, and...

She let her thought trail away. Bramwell was moving again, going farther down the aisle on the other side of the bookshelf. She moved in the opposite direction and then slipped around to the next bookshelf down the aisle so that if he came around the corner he wouldn't find her. Why she was cowering, she didn't want to analyze too closely, but it seemed the best decision.

Except that as she came around into the next aisle, there he was. She stopped short, caught her breath as he lifted his gaze from the book in his hand and looked right at her. The moment stilled, lengthened as they simply stared at each other, and it felt like a lifetime. It felt like the blink of an eye.

"M-Miss Killick," he said, and the book in his hand began to slide away. He grabbed for it and it bounced from one hand to another before he finally stilled it. "I didn't expect to see you."

She couldn't help but smile. "I seem to have interrupted your juggling practice."

He glanced at the book he'd been awkwardly bouncing and laughed softly. "I fear I shall never be able to join the circus."

"An earl it is then," she said.

Some of the pleasure left his gaze. "I suppose so, yes. What are you doing here?"

She looked around. "Well...er..."

His dark eyes shut and he shook his head. "Looking for a book. I am doing exceptionally well, aren't I? Perhaps I should simply put back the book I manhandled, go outside and have a lay down in the carriage for a while, then come back and try again."

"I could pretend to be surprised to see you again if it would help," Sasha teased.

"It might at that."

She moved a little closer, imprudent as that felt when everything between them was so light and easy. "I don't think you should leave, my lord. Why don't we try something else?"

She smiled and darted away from him. She hustled down the next aisle and came around to approach him from the other side. "Lord Bramwell," she said, feigning surprise as he turned toward her. "Gracious, I didn't expect to see you here today."

His eyes danced and he executed a slight bow. "Why, Miss Killick, what a pleasure to see you this fine day."

"Much better," she teased, and loved the laugh it elicited. He really was very handsome when he laughed. Or smiled. Or just stood there with that jawline that looked like it had been carved from granite.

She cleared her throat. "All jesting aside, I finished my latest book and the library at Bleaking House is…well, it's not good. So here I am."

"And an excellent choice you made for your patronage," Bramwell said. "I have been coming to Mattigan's since I was little more than a boy. It is my favorite shop in all of London."

"I can see why." Together they looked around the large bookshop, filled with the smells of paper and ink and leather-bound spines. She gave a happy sigh. "There is a bookshop in Athawick that is lovely. I do miss it."

"I'm sure. There's something so comforting about having a shop whose shelves you know."

She nodded. "Exactly."

He hesitated and then cleared his throat. "Perhaps I could be your guide in this one."

She stared up into his face. Warning bells were going off in her head. Reminders that this man was meant for the woman who was practically her sister. Was definitely her employer in the eyes of most. And with every word she exchanged with him, her attraction to him grew.

And yet she didn't want to walk away. Not yet. Not now.

"That would be lovely," she croaked out.

"What was your last book?" he asked.

"A very scandalous gothic tale," she said. "With madness and ghosts and shadows."

"Oh, nothing wrong with that. Do you want something similar or something different?"

"Perhaps fewer ghosts?" she said.

He chuckled, and for a while they browsed together, comparing favorites and new authors alike. When Mr. Mattigan had swept away the huge stack the earl had gathered for her, promising to wrap it up at the front, Bramwell smiled at her.

"I feel as though we've put you to rights for at least a week in your reading," he said.

She shook her head. "At minimum a day. It will depend on what Ilaria steals for herself whether I'll get to a week."

His expression fell a little at the mention of Ilaria. "I do have to say you don't look much like her today."

"It's the clothing. When I'm not done up in her fine gowns, I just look like a normal, boring person. Not a princess in sight."

"I would not categorize you as either normal or boring, Miss Killick," he said, his dark gaze sliding over her in a way that made her toes curl in her slippers. "If anything you are lovelier in your own gown and with your hair styled this way." His brow wrinkled. "And shorter."

She burst out with another laugh, this one filled with surprise. "Most people don't notice that. Yes, Ilaria is taller, so I wear slippers with a heel when I'm…" She looked around. "Er, playing my role."

"I think I might owe you an apology, though."

She shook her head. "For what?"

"I told the princess that we'd met, that I guessed exactly what your role was. I hope I didn't cause you grief."

"You didn't," she assured him. "The family is my family, after all. And none of them are cruel. They were surprised I'd been uncovered; I'm usually more careful, but there was no censure or anger. And Ilaria is a force of nature, she would have uncovered the truth herself if you hadn't told her."

She wrinkled her brow as she thought of how distracted Ilaria had been since their arrival. When she'd returned from the Donville Masquerade the night before, she had been very coy about her activities and then almost sullen all morning.

"I find myself wondering then why you didn't tell her yourself," Bramwell said, interrupting her thoughts.

She blinked at him, brought back to the present in an instant. "What do you mean?"

"When I encountered her at the tea and accidentally spilled the secret, she said you hadn't told her about me. I wondered why."

A million reasons flooded her mind in an instant. Because she'd already said she wasn't in trouble for their meeting, she couldn't lie and say her furtiveness was out of fear. Which left the truth in its wake.

She hadn't told Ilaria or anyone else about meeting Bramwell because the instant connection she felt for the man, a connection that had only grown thanks to this playful encounter at the bookshop, was wrong. And dangerous. And could lead to nothing but heartache if she wasn't careful.

But as she looked up into warm brown eyes, she couldn't say that. She could never say that to him or else she'd look foolish. Or worse, have him say he felt the same and then where would they be?

She cleared her throat. "I think it might be best if I don't answer that question, my lord."

His lips parted and she could see he understood her meaning perfectly, whether she stated it aloud or not. He edged a little closer and his hand fluttered at his side, his fingers brushing hers. Even through both their sets of gloves, the feeling of that touch was electric and powerful.

She stared up at him and wanted more than anything for him to bend his head and kiss her. And then perhaps more than kiss her, right here in the stacks of books where anyone could find them.

She shook her head, breaking eye contact with difficulty. "I think it might be better if I...if I left."

He swallowed hard and then stepped back to offer her space. "I understand. It was wonderful seeing you again, Miss Killick. And I think we will do it again soon. My mother and I have been invited to supper at Bleaking House tonight."

She blinked. No one had told her that, though why would they? Ilaria had probably forgotten, she thought so little of this man. And no one needed Sasha's permission.

"Yes, we will," she said. "As this is a family supper, I will be part of it, not laying in wait for an emergency where I might have to play the part of a princess. I will...I will see you tonight."

He nodded and did not call her back when she hurried away. June was gathering the parcels at the counter and gave Sasha a strange look as she rushed up.

"You are pink as can be. Is it too warm in here?" she asked, smiling as Mr. Mattigan bid them farewell.

Sasha pushed out into the cool spring air, but it did nothing to soothe her. Even if she lied and said, "Oh yes. I think I stood too close to the fire."

"Well, you must be careful," June said, waving to their driver up the lane. "You wouldn't want to get burned."

Sasha almost laughed. "I fear that is still a distinct possibility," she said as the carriage arrived and they were whisked away. Back to the home that wasn't hers, the family she didn't entirely belong in and away from the man who she could see standing in the window of the bookshop, watching her as she left.

CHAPTER 7

"I cannot believe your sister," Queen Giabella huffed as the family lined up in the foyer to greet the guests who were beginning to make their way to the door for the small supper.

Sasha glanced at her, smiling a little at how easily the queen treated her like a daughter. And if Grantham's main courtier Stephen Blairford hadn't been watching her every move with a scowl on his face, she might have called Giabella *Mama*, as she had for many years. At least when the old king and his staff weren't looking. Blairford was always very insistent that she know her place. She rather hated him and his pinched expressions and dark glares.

"How can she not be here?" Giabella huffed. "I told her six-thirty sharp. *Sharp*. After a day of moping around and glaring daggers at everything and everyone, now this?"

Sasha shifted into the role she'd been playing far longer than double for Ilaria: she became her protector. "She readied herself on time," she said. "Perhaps she merely forgot. She has been a little...distracted."

"Well, she already missed the entrance of Captain Crawford," Giabella said, shaking her head.

Grantham leaned down from his place at the head of the line. "To be fair, Crawford was here abominably early. Said something about naval time. I sent him to the parlor to have a drink."

Sasha shifted. She knew Ilaria's attraction to Crawford. It was written all over her face any time she spoke about or saw the man. She could only hope the princess would not do something foolish. Something that could hurt her...or hurt Bramwell in the end.

As if conjured by those thoughts, Greenly opened the door and Lord Bramwell and his mother, themselves, entered the foyer. She saw how his gaze immediately flitted over her, just as it had earlier in the day at the bookshop. But then he was distracted by saying his greetings to the king, and that allowed her to breathe.

She really had to stop with all this nonsense surrounding the man. He was not for her, full stop. Mooning over him was unseemly and foolish and...

Her thoughts trailed away as he moved down the line to the queen and she caught a faint whiff of his scent. Sandalwood and a hint of leather that made her breath come sharp and heavy for a moment before she retained her calm.

"Lord and Lady Bramwell," Queen Giabella said. "We are standing a bit out of order so that I might introduce you personally to Miss Sasha Killick, my adopted daughter and Ilaria's companion during our trip."

"Translation: she did not trust *me* to introduce Sasha when Ilaria didn't show up for the welcome line," Remi muttered. Sasha elbowed him in the side not particularly gently and then focused on Lady Bramwell.

"Miss Killick," the dowager said. "I have heard so much about you."

Sasha blinked at that unexpected comment and glanced at Bramwell. "You...you have?"

"Oh yes. Thomas and I have a vested interest in your family visit and have been keeping up with all the papers. Though I'm sure some of their breathless recounting of your history must be untrue."

"A bit is exaggerated, yes, madam," Sasha said, trying hard to concentrate on formulating words and not on the fact that Bramwell's given name was Thomas. *Thomas.* It rolled around in her head like a caress and she longed to whisper it just to know what it would sound like in her own voice. Somehow she managed not to do something so telling or foolish.

"Well, it is a pleasure to meet you," Lady Bramwell said, and squeezed her hand gently. There was such kindness in her eyes, such genuine warmth that Sasha couldn't help but instantly like her.

A feeling that didn't lessen when Thomas…Bramwell, she had to keep thinking of him as Bramwell, stepped up to her. "Miss Killick," he said, the corner of his mouth twitching. "What a pleasure to formally meet you."

She shook her head, feeling the heat of a blush warm her cheeks. "Indeed, I suppose this is our first official introduction."

"And from a queen no less," Bramwell said, leaning a little closer to whisper the last.

Good Lord but he was impossibly handsome. Why did he have to be so attractive? Why couldn't she just dismiss him as she'd dismissed every other man she'd ever met during her twenty-three years on this earth?

He caught her hand then and lifted it to his lips. There was nothing untoward about the greeting, of course. Many a man had kissed her hand over the years—it was an option for a formal greeting. And yet she felt like the world slowed on its axis as she watched him bend slightly, his lips pucker, and then the warmth of them spread through her glove, into her skin, tingling through her bloodstream until she felt off kilter and a little dizzy.

"Miss Killick," he said softly, and released her to move down the line to say good evening to Remi. She might have eavesdropped on their conversation, but her ears were ringing too loudly to focus on anything else. She was hardly present as the rest of the welcoming line moved through and she met the handful of additional guests invited to supper.

At last they broke and the crowd moved toward the parlor for a drink before supper. Remi stepped up and caught her arm, tucking her hand into the crook of his elbow as they walked behind the queen and Grantham. "Look at you, all a-sparkle," he said, winking.

She glared up at him. "I'm not a-sparkle. That's not even a word."

"Aflutter?" he suggested. "Akimbo?"

"Stop," she groaned.

"What makes you so very happy to spend an evening with—" Remi glanced behind them to make sure none of the party guests they were leading could hear and dropped his voice to a whisper. "—with what will surely turn out to be the most boring collection of people to ever grace the cold and rainy shores of England."

"Stop," she repeated, unable to stop from giggling as they entered the parlor. But her laughter faded a little as she saw Ilaria was there already, alone with Captain Crawford. And judging from her expression as she stepped away from him and toward the entering group, they had been engaged in intense conversation.

Sasha glanced over her shoulder, trying to find Thomas—no, *Bramwell*, he had to be Bramwell—in the group. The earl made up the final guest in the line entering the parlor and he wasn't looking at the princess.

He was looking at Sasha. Directly. Firmly. Unmistakably.

She found herself squeezing Remi's arm a little harder as she glanced away from Bramwell, her face burning like fire.

"Oh," Remi said softly, his tone no longer playful. "I see."

She pulled away from him and glared up at him, hoping she could pull herself together enough not to make a scene in front of Remi, of all people. A man who cared little for propriety. If *he* was judging her...well, she'd fallen far, indeed.

"I don't know what you think you see," she said. "But if you care about your sister, you might want to rescue her from our...your mother's wrath. She needs it more than I do."

She gave him a little shove toward Ilaria, who was now standing next to the queen, stone-faced as her mother whispered close to her ear. Remi gave Sasha a look as he walked away. "I wonder if she's the only sister who needs saving," he said.

Sasha ignored him and moved to stand against the wall, as far away from Bramwell and the others as she could. She needed a moment to gather herself. A moment to remember herself.

She had to do that. It was all that mattered.

Supper was almost over and Thomas was certain it had been delicious...he simply couldn't recall the flavor of even one dish. He'd eaten them, of course, ohhhed and ahhhed with the rest over each one. He'd engaged in conversation all the while, politely nodding at observations, laughing at jokes. And yet he wasn't really there.

No, his attention was always at least partly at the opposite end of the table, on Sasha. He'd watched as she chatted with the king, who she was seated beside. It was clear the two were truly as close as siblings. Grantham even smiled here and there when she spoke, and that seemed a rare enough occasion.

Across from her was another gentleman...Thomas couldn't recall his name. A squire perhaps, or perhaps he was a vicar? At any rate, he was clearly enraptured by her.

And too old for her. He was definitely too old for her.

"Thomas," his mother whispered as she leaned closer. "You might wish to ask Princess Ilaria about her favorite authors. You two share a love of books, her mother says."

He fought the urge to let his eyes fall shut. Ilaria was just across from him and yet he'd felt no connection to her tonight, just as he hadn't during any night they'd spent time together. And the mention of her love of books only put him to mind of seeing Sasha in the bookstore earlier in the day.

"Pushing," he muttered softly, and watched his mother's lips purse.

"Only because you are stuck in one place," she whispered back.

He sighed and did as was expected. He shoved aside his thoughts about Sasha and focused instead on Ilaria. They chatted amiably enough, though her gaze sometimes slipped to the other side of the table as his was. He followed it eventually and realized she was either staring at the same vicar who was ceaselessly flirting with Sasha...or at Captain Crawford.

And considering she'd been alone with the second man in the parlor earlier, he had to guess her interest was in the captain. An interesting development. He'd talked to Crawford a handful of times, once even about Ilaria. To say the man seemed defensive of the princess was putting it far too mildly.

So they had a connection. Was it one he could encourage, if only to get himself out of his own turmoil? Perhaps it was worth looking into. Only as his gaze shifted to his mother and he saw how excited she was, how pleased, his hopes fell. She was pinning so much on him marrying this woman and having their own problems all but erased with the signature on the marriage documents.

Supper ended and the party made their way to a large parlor in the back of the house. Thomas had escorted his mother, and as he released her arm and looked around, he realized the room connected to the terrace. Was this the same parlor Sasha had come out of days ago in order to spy on the party in the ballroom?

"Seems you, my lord, are being primed for a position of great interest."

Thomas turned and found the same gentleman who had been ogling Sasha earlier at supper. "Have we met?" he asked, trying to keep his tone calm when his immediate dislike of this man was far too telling.

"We have, but I'm sure a man of your stature meets a great many people." He extended a hand. "Sir Richard Benson, my lord, at your service."

"Sir Richard." Thomas shook the offered hand and shook briefly. "A pleasure to see you again."

"You and the princess then," the man said, elbowing Thomas's side as if they were cronies. "If you can pull it off, the possibilities are endless, aren't they? The Athawick royals are the most discussed topic of the Season and anyone who pins their star to them will go far." He chuckled. "Even the ones without a title will do in a pinch."

At that Thomas pulled his entire focus to the man at his side. "Am I to assume you are referencing Miss Sasha Killick? I saw you speaking to her and the king tonight at supper."

"A good eye, my lord. Yes, I did talk briefly to the lady. In a different circumstance, I suppose one would think her too low to consider, but this situation is rare. Although she is a companion, and so little more than a servant, she is also the adopted daughter of the family. To connect to her would be to connect to my own little corner of this world and all it entails."

Thomas fisted his hands at his sides. He would not throttle this man, no matter how much he might deserve it. "I would be careful, Sir Richard, at how you position yourself. As you said, Miss Killick seems to be greatly loved by the family and I suppose some of a mercenary bent might wish to use that for their own purposes. But it also follows that if the royals found out about a person's unsavory interest, they could destroy as easily as they could assist."

Sir Richard leaned away, his face lined with confusion now. "And...how would they know?"

"Someone could tell them," Thomas said as calmly and succinctly as he could manage. "*Someone* would."

Sir Richard's nostrils flared slightly. "You speak as if you, yourself, were not using a potential connection to this family to save your own from ruin. How is that any different?"

Thomas winced. There *wasn't* any difference. That was part of what he hated so much about this situation. He was not a person who used others, who tried to advance himself in this way. But he was not the architect of his own fortune. Not since he took the title and surveyed the damage that had been done to his future at the hands of a man who didn't give a damn.

And so here he was.

"Perhaps you are correct, Sir Richard, and I should not judge. Excuse me."

He pivoted and walked away. Sasha was standing at the fireplace with Prince Remington, and Thomas could feel her gaze on him as he moved. Felt the hopelessness of it all, and suddenly he needed to get out of this room, out of this house, just...out. But there was no way to do so without causing a scene, so instead he stepped to the terrace door and stepped into the cool night air, hoping he could manage to collect himself.

Knowing he couldn't.

～

Sasha knew she shouldn't follow Thomas. It was entirely imprudent to do so, but she'd seen the expression on his face as he talked to the utterly awful Sir Richard and then as he went out on the terrace. He'd looked...lost. How could she not help him? How could she not follow?"

She smiled up at Remi. "Your mother is staring at you, you know."

Remi's eyes widened ever so slightly and he glanced over his shoulder toward the queen. "God's teeth, I wonder what I did now."

Sasha laughed. "She might just want to tell you how handsome you look."

"Of course she'll tell me how handsome I look." Remi glanced down at himself. "I *am* remarkably handsome. But you know she will then follow with some directive about slouching or staying out too late or some other sin."

"And you'll tease her and you'll both love it." Sasha said. "You can pretend her attention drives you mad, but we all know you two adore each other and it's all part of some game you play."

"Perhaps." Remi's eyes narrowed. "Is everything well with you?"

Sasha drew back a fraction. "With...with me?" she asked.

He nodded. "You've been distracted as of late. I see it, you know."

"You see a great deal more than anyone gives you credit for," Sasha said. "But I'm very well, I promise you. Now go speak to your mother."

She shoved him gently and he gave her one last long look before he strode off toward the queen with a broad smile on his face. Sasha sighed and looked toward the terrace doors again.

Thomas hadn't returned. No one else had gone out to find him. Which meant…

Well, it meant nothing, but she found herself moving toward the double doors anyway, glancing over her shoulder before she slipped out into the night and toward a foolish attraction she ought to be denying, not feeding.

He was standing at the terrace wall, staring up at the night sky, just as she had been the night they met. She stood there for a moment, just watching him. Tonight there was moonlight and it moved across his face, casting him in an intriguing combination of dark and light.

She drew a deep breath to calm her suddenly racing heart and moved toward him. "It seems our positions are now reversed, my lord," she said.

He stiffened slightly and then slowly turned toward her. His expression was dark as the night, clouded with emotions that he swiftly erased. But she'd seen them, seen his conflict and his pain. She would not easily forget any of it.

"How is that, Miss Killick?" he asked, and his voice was strained.

"I've found you on the terrace this time," she said, and smiled. It took him a moment to return the expression and she folded her hands before herself. "It seems I've interrupted you in deep thought, though. Would you like me to leave you to it?"

She found herself holding her breath, hoping he would say no. She didn't want to leave him, not like this. When she was honest with herself, not at all.

His expression softened slightly. "No."

A thrill worked through her that was utterly foolish, and she crossed the rest of the way to him and stood beside him at the terrace wall. They were quiet for a short while and then she nodded toward the garden below. "Have you taken a turn around the gardens yet?"

He shook his head. "No. I've heard Bleaking House has beautiful plantings, though."

"They're wonderful. I've enjoyed exploring them. There is the most beautiful statue of Venus near the gazebo."

"The goddess of love," he said softly, and brought her up short.

She nodded, wishing her hands hadn't started to shake. "Yes. Are you a student of the classics, the gods?"

"I enjoy a good tale of a god meddling with a mortal. I can relate, at any rate."

She tilted her head. "You feel as though your life has been meddled with?"

He choked out a laugh that did not sound light or happy. "Most definitely."

"How so?" she asked.

He turned toward her slightly and his dark gaze snagged hers. In the dim light from the house behind them and the sliver of a moon above, his eyes seemed to glint. She swallowed hard. It would be too easy to get lost there.

"Let us just say that the gods have found great pleasure in creating an environment where I have few choices."

She nodded. "I think I understand that."

"I'm sure you do."

There was so much more to be said. She wanted so much to ask him more about his past, his life. She wanted to tell him about her own. But if that happened, she knew that a bond would be formed. Something that would only hurt when it was ultimately broken.

She wanted to avoid that pain at all costs.

"Were you enjoying the party?" she asked, switching to a topic she hoped would be more benign.

A soft smile tilted his lips, as if he knew she was retreating from everything that could have been and back into safer territory. "Yes," he said. "The meal was wonderful."

"It was. I do miss our cook at home, but the one here has been a marvel. And what of the company?"

He arched a brow. "I'm very much enjoying the company now."

Heat filled her cheeks and she ducked her head, desperately searching for a way to keep from making a cake of herself. "I saw you talking to Sir Richard before you came out on the terrace."

To her surprise, his expression hardened and she saw a hint of anger there. "I believe we were both the recipients of the man's attention. He was seated near you at supper, wasn't he?"

"He's harmless," she said. "He talks and talks and says nothing. But that is not unlike a dozen other men who have tried to impress a king and failed."

The earl's nostrils flared just a fraction and his hand fluttered against the edge of the terrace wall, as if he wanted to reach for her but stayed his own hand. "Perhaps you are correct. I would...I would only advise you, though it is not my place, to be careful with Sir Richard."

She blinked. "Careful?"

He nodded. "The man said some things to me inside that led me to believe he wishes to use you for your connections."

She let out a long sigh and tried to ignore the sting of those words. It wasn't that she cared about Sir Richard—on the contrary, she thought him dreadful. But what she said next was true and painful. "I suppose I am accustomed to such things. *Everyone* uses me for my connections, my lord."

For a moment their gazes merely held there in the moonlight. And then he moved closer, closing the small gap that remained between them. Now they were so close that her skirts tangled around his boots and she could feel the warmth of his breath on her lips.

"Not everyone. Not me," he said softly.

He was looking at her mouth and she knew he wanted to kiss her. It wasn't a shocking realization even if it should have been. More the culmination of days of tension and attraction and forbidden desires she'd been trying to control. Now it seemed it was all for naught, because her hands trembled as she reached for one of his. She had not put her gloves on after supper and he was also not wearing them, and for the first time their skin touched.

She wanted to memorize every rough groove of his fingers, every warm brush of his palm. She wanted to capture the way he looked down at her, gaze filled with desire and longing and kindness and regret. He shut his eyes briefly, but when he opened them again he did not pull away, but lowered his head toward hers.

She leaned up, God help her, yearning for what he would give, for what she could take and keep just for herself, just this once. Ilaria would never have to know. Ilaria probably wouldn't care, at least not now when the earl was nothing more to her than a terrible inevitability.

But in a year or two or three? When they were married, when they had children of their own...wouldn't a kiss with this man come between her and the friend she loved as a sister? Wouldn't it color every part of her world and make everything worse?

The thought tore through her and she ducked her head before he could brush his lips to hers. Her breath was shaky as she released his hand and took a long, painful step away.

CHAPTER 8

Thomas had never been the kind of man who beat his chest and made demands. He'd been raised by one of those, he'd seen people he loved suffer for it. He had vowed to never be anything like him.

And yet, as Sasha stepped aside without the sweet moment where their lips could meet, he wanted to catch her in his arms. He wanted to claim her mouth and feel her soften beneath him. He wanted to tell her she was his and then show her, even if it wasn't true.

Instead, he ran a hand through his hair. "I'm sorry."

She had been staring at the ground since she stepped away, her hands opening and shutting at her sides, but now she glanced up.

"You shouldn't be. My lord..." She trailed off. "*Thomas*."

He shuddered at her use of his given name, so perfect when her lips formed it.

She continued, "I would very much like to kiss you. You cannot know how much I want that. And if you were just some handsome, wonderful, interesting man on this terrace, I would do so with abandon."

"But I'm not," he said.

She shook her head. "You *are*. God, you are very much all those things."

"Sasha..."

"But you are also being pushed into the path of a woman I consider my dearest friend, my sister." She sighed and the pained sound seemed to come from deep within her soul. "Even if neither of you has feelings for the other, I couldn't be a barrier to what is best for her and for you. And I would be if I let you touch me. I would hate myself and you would eventually hate me." She took another step away. "So I can't."

He couldn't form words for what felt like an eternity. His disappointment, his frustration at the situation that had brought him here, his absolute hatred for the future she described washed over him in a long wave. And then he pushed it all aside, as he had always done, as he would always be forced to do.

"I know," he said.

There was nothing more to say. She had a strength he didn't possess but would have to find somehow. He owed it to himself, to Ilaria, if that was the path he had to walk, and to Sasha to do that.

"I shouldn't have come out here," she said. "I knew it was imprudent the moment I did so. I should go back inside."

He saw the hint of tears sparkling in her eyes as she spoke. Wished he could reach for her and offer comfort. Only his touch would only make it worse. His words would ring hollow. The best he could do for her was just...nod.

So he did. And she smiled, though the expression didn't reach her gaze. Then she turned away and left him on the terrace, wishing he could be anyone else. Wishing he could change things.

He had but a moment alone with those thoughts when there was a sound from off to his right. "I think you and I should have a chat."

He glanced toward the voice that had spoken those words and watched in pure horror as Prince Remington stepped from the shadows at the edge of the terrace. From that distance, he might not have been able to hear every exchange between Thomas and Sasha, but he certainly must have seen the near-kiss. Seen the tension between them.

"Your Highness," he said with a small bow of his head. "I didn't realize you were out here."

"I would wager neither of you did. I slipped out from another room a few moments ago and stumbled upon you two." Prince Remington stepped closer. "You were so wrapped up in each other, you didn't notice."

Thomas's mouth suddenly felt very dry. He straightened his shoulders and held the gaze of the man across from him. The prince had blue eyes, the only one in his family who did, and at present they were focused very intently on Thomas.

"You believe I owe you an explanation," Thomas said when the prince didn't say anything.

"I'm not sure if you do or not. I suppose that depends on your intentions with my sister."

"Ilaria and I—" Thomas began.

Prince Remington shook his head. "Not Ilaria. Sasha."

Thomas was brought up short and stared at him. "Oh."

"That surprises you. I suppose it does anyone who hears it. But I *do* consider her my sister, Lord Bramwell. I hardly remember a time when she was not. And since Ilaria has a dozen people who would race to defend her honor, I choose to focus my attention on protecting Sasha." Prince Remington leaned in closer. "Do I need to do so against you?"

Thomas actually had to consider that question for a moment. *Was* he a danger to Sasha? He didn't want to be and yet his imprudence kept making things more difficult. He could hurt her, he knew that. He was already hurting himself.

"I met Sasha accidentally, the night of your welcome ball," he explained. "I was charmed by her, for she is delightful, as you know."

"I do," the prince agreed softly. "And?"

"I know what is expected of me," Thomas said. "I know the things I cannot change, even if I could. Even if I would give *anything* to change them. What you saw tonight, what nearly...*happened* between us...that was an anomaly. I would not hurt Sasha. I would do my best never to hurt Ilaria if what our families desire is what comes to pass."

Prince Remington searched his face, seemed to judge his character with a brief look. "I hope that is true," he said at last. "You do seem a decent fellow on the whole, though I am perhaps not the best judge of character, having very little of it myself."

"Somehow I doubt that is true, Your Highness. A man with no character would not be standing on a terrace interrogating me about my connection with your sister. Sisters."

The prince shrugged as if to concede the point. "One way or another, I do have some experience in trying to live up to impossible standards. In having to walk a path that you would not choose. I am truly sorry that you must do the same. But understand this: I will take Sasha's side *every* time."

"Good," Thomas said, and meant it. "I would be happy knowing she had such a staunch ally, even if it is against me."

Prince Remington's brow lowered, and for a moment he seemed to see into Thomas's very soul. Then he sighed. "We should go back in," he said. "Back to expectations."

"God help us both."

Remington laughed and nudged his head toward the door. "I'll buy you a drink."

Thomas couldn't help but laugh in return at the joke, and together they reentered the parlor where the rest were gathered. Including the woman he couldn't have...and the one destiny seemed to be pushing him toward.

The guests had gone, the family had said their goodnights, and together Sasha and Ilaria made their way to their shared chamber, arms linked. Ilaria seemed miles away, lost in thought, and for that Sasha was happy. She couldn't stop thinking of Thomas, after all, and the near kiss. God, how she wished she'd let him take her mouth with his. At least then she'd have that memory to warm her and to…

To spoil everything. It would have spoiled everything. She had to remember that one pertinent fact when her mind tried to tell her stories about what she could have.

They entered the chamber and Ilaria paced away to the window. After a beat, she spun back. "I-I need your help."

Sasha stared at her, her troubled thoughts fading for that moment. She had to focus, because there was no mistaking the wildness to Ilaria's expression. The determination. "Ilaria—"

"Don't say my name that way!" Ilaria gasped. "Please don't."

"How can I not?" Sasha asked with a shake of her head. "How can I not express my worry to you when you're standing by the very window you snuck out of days ago and promised me it would be the only time?"

"Jonah said he would help me."

Sasha blinked. "Jonah?"

"Captain Crawford." Ilaria held her stare. "He's going to meet me behind the garden in just a little while."

Sasha thought of Thomas, thought of that kiss again and how she had stepped away because she didn't want to interfere with the future her sister might have with him. And yet Ilaria was dancing close to a dangerous edge with another man. Not thinking of her future at all.

"Captain Crawford, who you can't stop mooning over," she said, her tone sharper.

Ilaria's face crumpled. "I know it isn't forever," she whispered. "I know it can never be forever. That's why I so desperately want it for tonight. If you don't want to help me, I understand. But perhaps you could just go downstairs to the library for a few moments, just so you can say you didn't know. *Please.*"

Sasha saw the lines of worry and fear on Ilaria's face. She pushed aside her own thoughts of Thomas and sighed. "I would never refuse to help you, even if I don't think this is a good idea. What do you need?"

Ilaria almost buckled at her agreement and then lunged forward to embrace her. She was shaking as she did so, and Sasha held tight to support her.

"I need to change," Ilaria said. "One of your gowns, perhaps."

"The last time you came back with a tear in my gown," Sasha said, but she was already moving to the wardrobe and trying to find a piece that would allow Ilaria to fade into the crowd.

Ilaria's gaze darted down. "I know. I still don't understand how it happened. But I'll be more careful. Oh, what about the blue there?"

She motioned toward one of Sasha's plainer gowns. Not something fit for a princess in public, certainly, which was probably the appeal. Sasha took it from the wardrobe, and together they helped Ilaria from her fancy gown. The tiara was removed from her curls. Sasha brushed them out and wound her locks into a staid fashion.

When it was all over, Ilaria stared into the mirror and smiled as she smoothed her hands over her skirt. "I don't look like royalty anymore."

Sasha pursed her lips. "But you are."

Ilaria looked at her over her shoulder. "What?"

"You *are* royalty, Ilaria, no matter how you try to minimize it. No matter how you try to pretend otherwise. You are who you are, just as I am who I am. You can't pretend away the future and I do worry that you might destroy it in the process."

Ilaria's face fell. "I'm not trying to destroy it," she whispered. "I promise you, I'm not. But right now what I'd love to do more than anything is to run, Sasha. I want to run away and never come back. Since doing that would hurt everyone, the only thing I can think to do is to pretend that I'm not me for a little while. And purge whatever it is that is driving me to feel so lost. If I do that then when I come back, I can surrender to the inevitable and maybe even find some happiness in it."

Sasha squeezed the bridge of her nose gently. She did understand where Ilaria was coming from. If she didn't know Thomas, didn't have some connection to him, she might have more easily supported Ilaria's desire to do as she wished just a little while longer. And yet all she could think about was *his* potential pain. *His* potential loss.

And she hated what that meant for herself, for her future.

She cleared her throat. "Just be careful."

Ilaria seemed uncertain about that, but she nodded anyway. "I will."

"Are you going out the window again?"

"No, Jonah made me promise to go through the garden instead."

"At least we can thank him for that. Come, I'll walk you down," Sasha said, and moved to the door to peek out and make certain no one would see or hear them in Ilaria's great escape. It was all she could do to protect her.

And if she were honest with herself, to protect Thomas too. She only hoped that was possible as the spinning wheels of fate seemed to be ready to steer them all to ruin and despair.

CHAPTER 9

Thomas had been listening to his mother chatter on about the Athawick royal family for at least fifteen minutes and his head was beginning to ache. It also did the thing it did any time that family was mentioned: it drew him back to moments with Sasha on the terrace a few nights before. He'd been able to feel her breath soft on his lips—that's how close he'd come to heaven.

Only to have it torn away, leaving him with only memories and longings for what if.

He pushed to his feet when she paused and he looked toward the clock on her mantel. "It has been a pleasure seeing you, Mama, but I am meant to be at my club soon and I best be off." He had no official meetings at Fitzhugh's, but he could use the escape, both from the dowager and his own churning thoughts.

She blinked as she rose. "Of course, darling. I didn't mean to keep you. Let me escort you to the door."

He offered her an arm to soften his departure and let her know he wasn't irritated by her. In truth, he wasn't. Her enthusiasm grated, but that was more because of him than her. He understood why she wanted him to accept her desires and the future she was attempting to carve out for him.

As they reached the foyer, her butler, Vickers, turned away from the door. "Ah, my lord, my lady, what good timing. A missive has arrived for you, Lady Bramwell, from the Queen of Athawick."

He held out the message with its gilded paper and the swirling *A* to seal the fold. Lady Bramwell looked toward him and she was practically bouncing as she took the missive. "Thank you, Vickers."

He stepped away, and she turned to Thomas. "Take a moment and let me read this. I'm certain it has to do with you."

He pursed his lips. "Of course."

She broke the wax seal and swiftly read what appeared to be a short message. When she was finished, she pressed the pages to her chest and looked up at him. "Thomas!"

He smiled slightly at her enthusiasm. She had been so troubled since his father's death, it was nice to see her excited, even if he didn't love the reason. "What is it?"

"Come to the parlor and let me read it to you," she said, motioning him back to where they'd departed a moment ago.

It was evident there was no escape, so he followed as she wished. She pushed the door shut and leaned against it as she read, "*Lady Bramwell, I have been considering our conversation from two days past, and I agree. Princess Ilaria and I will be attending the opera tomorrow evening and I would like to extend the invitation to include you and Lord Bramwell. As we have discussed, I believe the time has come. Please do let me know. Warmly, Giabella of Athawick.*"

Thomas stared at his mother, his ears ringing at the message. "You and the queen have clearly been spending a great deal of time together, that you are arranging these machinations," he said at last.

His mother nodded. "Queen Giabella joined my cribbage group two days ago. She is wonderful, Thomas, you will like her very much as you grow closer to her. She's formal in public, of course, she must be, but privately she is warm and witty. A pure delight."

"I'm certain that is true," Thomas said. "But what in the world have you two arranged for me and her daughter?"

He heard how sharp his tone was, and by the way his mother

jumped, she was just as aware of it. "Thomas," she said slowly. "You must have known this was coming. If we are serious about the courtship between you, you would have to have a public outing with just you and the princess, and chaperones, of course. This is a logical culmination of all the work we've put in to build a relationship."

"Relationship?" he repeated. "What relationship, Mama? I have talked to the princess all of...three times? Two? Four? I cannot even recall, that is how little an impression they left. I have never been alone with her, I have never been interested in doing so. Nor has she, I might add. We have no *relationship*."

Her eyes went wide at his outburst. "What would you have me do, Thomas? What is your solution to our problems, if not this?"

He hesitated. "I...I don't know."

"But you do know we have problems."

"Of course," he said, running a hand through his hair. "I see the ledgers. I've made progress in alleviating some of the strain, but the properties are a drain. They are not quick to recover from bad management and the use of the funds they did produce when Father was still alive. And I owe them..." He trained off. "I owe them to do better."

"And this will allow you to do so," she said. "The princess's dowry is unheard of, Thomas. It will repair all wounds. And she is such a revelation, such a desired addition to any gathering, that she will greatly raise your esteem and that of your sister. Think about no more whispers about your father. No more side glances. Would that not make it easier for you? For those you care for?"

He realized she was talking about herself. It was easy to forget sometimes, what his mother had endured at the hands of his father. What his sister had lost and thankfully found again, though at what cost?

"Is there some other reason you are reluctant?" his mother asked. "Is there someone else that keeps you standing aside?"

He squeezed his eyes shut. There was such a strong desire to say yes. To tell her about Sasha and what he knew he could share with her. To say out loud something of the feelings he'd been trying to wish away almost from the first moment he saw her.

But he couldn't. Not unless he wanted to crush the dreams of everyone he loved.

"No, there is no one," he said. "And I'm not reluctant. This evening at the opera will be a way to get to know Princess Ilaria as I wish to do. I will be open to it. I will be everything you wish me to be."

His mother reached for his hand and squeezed it gently. "You already are. I will respond to the queen and tell her we are available for the opera. And if you try with the princess, perhaps you will come to care for her as much as you desire to."

He nodded and they returned to the foyer. He said his goodbyes and mounted his horse, but all of it felt like it was coming through a dream fog. A nightmare.

Somehow he managed to maneuver his way to Fitzhugh's, the club that belonged to his brother-in-law Nicholas's half-brother. As he entered the smoking room, he saw the two of them talking at the bar. They had not always had the closest relationship, but right now both men were smiling. When Nicholas saw him, he waved and Thomas made his way across the room to them.

"Good to see you, Bramwell," Fitzhugh said.

"And you," Thomas replied, shaking the man's hand. "Business appears to be brisk."

"Turns out a little scandal can do wonders," Fitzhugh said. "But it also creates a great deal of work and I would very much like to get home to my wife at a decent hour. So I'll leave you two to catch up." He smiled at Nicholas. "We'll see you and Aurora for supper on Tuesday next?"

Nicholas agreed and Fitzhugh stepped away, leaving them alone. Nicholas pushed his drink over. "You look like you could use this more than I could."

"I could use the bottle," Thomas said, and slugged back the whisky in one gulp. "Christ, that's good."

"My brother only has the best smuggled in," Nicholas said with a smirk. "So what has your face looking so pinched?"

Thomas shook his head. If he told his brother-in-law about his problems, he would certainly find a supportive friend with a kind ear. But Nicholas was married to Aurora, and his tales would absolutely find their way back to her. He didn't want to concern her.

"You don't want to know," he said, and hoped his tone was light. "How are you, how is my sister?"

"Very well to both those questions," Nicholas said. Then he looked past Thomas's shoulder. "I see Crawford over there. Should we say good afternoon?"

Thomas winced. Nicholas had to be referring to Captain Crawford, for the men were friends. But he was not in any mood to speak to the man who might have an interest in his potentially future wife. Still, there was no way to avoid the situation, so he merely followed as Nicholas made his way across the room.

Crawford saw them when they were near, and his gaze flitted over Thomas with a scowl before he lifted a hand in greeting. After hands were shaken, the men all sat together. It was all very benign for a while, and though Thomas felt the tension in their companion, no one brought up the inevitable. It hung in the air between them, like a guillotine waiting to fall.

And then it did.

"It seems like it's been an eventful Season thus far," Nicholas said. "My brother, the Duke of Roseford, tells me he hasn't seen anything like it. But you know, Thomas—you are at the heart of this royal family situation."

Christ, why did he have to bring that up? Thomas tried to force a smile. "Yes. Every party is truly a crush and half the people in attendance have snuck in just to get a look at the Athawick party's gowns and hair. And the rumors run rampant. I think I've been featured five or six times in barely blind items in the *Scandal Sheet*."

"Are the items true?" Crawford asked.

"Some of them, yes, but you know that rag. It's nonsense more than half the time." Thomas rolled his eyes, thinking of the various stories that had been written. "I shudder to think what they'll say after tomorrow."

Immediately he wished he could take it back. He didn't want to discuss what was about to happen with anyone, but most especially this man.

And Crawford's reaction made that all the clearer. He straightened up, his expression hardening almost to steel. "What is tomorrow?"

Thomas exchanged a quick glance with Nicholas, and then he said, "The opera. My mother and I will be sharing our box with Princess Ilaria and Queen Giabella."

He tried to play off the importance of that as he rambled off something about the potential appearance of Queen Charlotte, but he could see from the expression of both his companions that the meaning of this was as evident to them as it was to him.

A public outing along with the princess and her mother meant they were seriously courting. Serious courting could only lead to an engagement. And with a princess, an engagement would not be broken. It couldn't be.

"You're really going to do this, are you, Bramwell?" Crawford asked.

"Do...what?"

"Marry her." It came out through Crawford's clenched teeth.

At that, Nicholas slid to the front of his chair. He was ready to intervene, it seemed.

Thomas bent his head. "I suppose the intention is not a secret, especially since you are so close to the family, I've heard. There are overtures being made in that arena, yes."

A heavy silence fell between them. Nicholas's attention was now focused entirely on him. "Is that what you want, Thomas?"

Thomas couldn't find words. He didn't want to agree. He

couldn't disagree. So how could he answer and not make things worse? "I...sometimes what we want cannot be taken into account in these situations. We must do what is right. What is beneficial to both her family and my own."

That seemed to break Captain Crawford. His expression grew wild. "Ilaria is a person. You understand that, don't you? A woman with desires and dreams, not just a political pawn. Would you crush that for the benefit of your precious title?"

Thomas stared at the man and saw reflected in his gray eyes all the pain and heartbreak he felt in his own. He understood him then, perfectly clearly. Crawford was in love with Ilaria. It was evident in every line of him, every flinch, every dark storm in his gaze.

"Why do you want to know so much about it, Captain Crawford?" Thomas asked, almost hoping this might devolve into a fight. Maybe that's what he needed: the clash of fists. Maybe it would make Crawford stake his claim and that would end all this the way Thomas, himself, couldn't.

Only Nicholas intervened. He pressed a gentle hand on Crawford's chest to hold him back. "Steady now, both of you," he said softly. "We are not in some private hall where you two could spar over...over what we both know this is over. We're at Fitzhugh's and half the men of the ton are watching you."

Crawford blinked, as if he'd forgotten that. Then he got up. "My lord, Gillingham, please accept my apologies. I am out of sorts and I clearly need to take some air. Good afternoon."

He left without waiting for their farewells, and for a long moment Nicholas and Thomas sat together in silence. At last Nicholas turned to him. "That's why you're drinking? Because of the match?"

"I suppose so," Thomas admitted.

"Because she might love him, as he loves her?" Nicholas asked.

Thomas shook his head slowly. "Whatever is between them clearly predates me. It is none of my business. No, I drink because I don't care if she loves him. I will *never* love her."

Nicholas's expression softened and filled with understanding. Of course it would. He had been separated from Thomas's sister thanks to the manipulations of their father. She had been forced into a loveless marriage, Nicholas into service for the king that had nearly taken his life and left him permanently maimed.

"What can I do?" Nicholas said softly.

"Nothing," Thomas said. "No one can do anything, can they? After tomorrow, all will be written in stone."

He said it and for the first time he truly heard those words. After tomorrow night, the world would see the intentions of the two families. And he would never have another chance to see Sasha alone again, to touch her again, even in passing. He would not be able to allow himself that pleasure because then it would be a betrayal for them both.

Which meant he needed to see her just one more time tonight. One last time before they would need to look away from each other, not toward. Before nothing could be changed.

Nicholas seemed troubled, but he nodded nonetheless. "Then let me buy you another drink," he said, and waved to the steward.

Thomas let him, but all the while his mind was turning and planning out a final meeting with the woman he had come to care for despite how desperate and unfair his errant heart was.

CHAPTER 10

O ne thing Sasha had learned from growing up in a royal
family was that there was very little quiet to be found. There
were always meetings and balls and teas and clucking tongues of the
courtiers who herded their charges from place to place. It could be
exhausting.

So the rare night when there wasn't something to be done was a
treasure that they all gathered close to their chests and cherished.
Tonight that freedom was offered to Ilaria, Remi and Sasha, as the
queen and King Grantham had gone out to some state affair. Remi
had been entertaining them with tales of his bad behavior, another
narrow escape from consequences. Though she laughed at his
hijinks, it was impossible not to worry about her adoptive brother.

It seemed she was not the only one, as Ilaria said, "You must be
more careful. Honestly, Grantham might not have you murdered,
but imprisoned in a tower is a good possibility."

"God, he'd love that, wouldn't he? To tuck us all away while he
goes about being kingly." Remi sighed. "I suppose that is unfair."

Ilaria nodded. "It is. As I was reminded not that long ago, he has
a great deal to carry. Perhaps more than we even know."

Remi frowned. "If that is true, then he should tell us. We're his siblings, after all, and I include Sasha in that assessment."

Sasha shifted. She did love them all desperately, even if she knew she was not as much a part of the inner circle as they believed. But that outside-looking-in view sometimes gave her greater knowledge then they had. "I think Grantham feels it is his burden—he doesn't want to place it on any of us."

Remi shook his head. "Well, I hear Ilaria has a wonderful time ahead of her at the *opera* with the Viscount Blamewell," he said.

Sasha frowned. He was trying to tease, but she was in no mood for it. Ilaria had told her earlier in the evening that her mother had planned a more intimate outing with Thomas and his mother. Something that would make clear the intentions of the two families.

Even now her chest hurt. "It's the Earl of Bramwell," she said softly, trying not to think of his smile or his eyes or the scent of him when he was close to her.

"It seems there is no escaping it," Ilaria said.

Remi winked at Sasha. "Sasha will go in your place if you don't want to. She seems to like Bramwell well enough."

Sasha caught her breath. Remi was grinning, but he was always grinning. Sometimes he used that playfulness to cover up what he knew or didn't know. What he saw or didn't see. His role as jester was just that...a role.

She pushed to her feet and glared down at him. "What do you mean by that?"

There was a moment's hesitation where she saw a flash of seriousness in her brother's eyes. "I saw you two on the terrace at that little gathering...what, three nights ago? Four? I lose track with all the nonsense we are expected to perform."

She pivoted to walk away. Remi said those words like they weren't daggers, like they weren't bombs. "You want to talk about nonsense, there it is. I was just talking to the earl outside, nothing more."

She felt both Ilaria and Remi staring at her, but refused to look at them.

"Very well, as you say," Remi said at last. "My apologies."

"Well, I *wish* I liked him," Ilaria said, and if the topic hadn't been equally painful, Sasha would have thanked her for drawing the focus of the room away. "I *wish* I could feel something for the man when he is being thrown in my path so obviously, and now it will be so publicly."

Sasha faced the pair as Remi moved to sit beside Ilaria, to offer her comfort and solace.

"I realize it was silly to think I could marry for love," Ilaria whispered. "That any of us could, given our positions."

"Sasha can," Remi said with a conciliatory smile for her.

Another arrow slung straight into her heart. Marry for love? She'd never considered it until she met Thomas. Never wished for it. But now...now the concept was like fire in her soul. She cared for him. She could probably more than care for him with just a tiny push, though she could not dig further into that truth because it would only make the future that much more unbearable.

"No. I will never marry for love," she said softly. "You may call me sister, but I am not and we both know that. I will spend my life as Ilaria's companion and occasional body double. And I'll...I will do my best to help her be happy if I can."

She could see the impact of her statement on both Ilaria and Remi. She could see their potential arguments to the immovable facts on their lips, but before any of them could be hatched, the door to the parlor opened and Greenly entered.

"I'm sorry to intrude, Your Highnesses, Miss Killick, but there is a message that just arrived for Princess Ilaria and it was given with some urgency."

Ilaria took the note from the servant and rushed across the room to read it as he left, which gave Sasha a moment to gather herself. She couldn't have this conversation with Ilaria or Remi, no matter how much they pried. If Ilaria knew about the connection between her and Thomas, it would make things even harder for her. And she was suffering in her own way. Sasha didn't want to make it worse.

Sometimes duty came before personal pleasure. That was what Giabella had been gently reminding all of them for years. It was a code that was valiant and honorable, that would hopefully make the pain worthwhile in the end.

Ilaria had said nothing since receiving her unexpected note, and now Sasha looked at her. She had lost all color to her cheeks, her hands shaking.

"Who is it from that you go so pale?" Sasha asked.

Ilaria flattened the note to her chest and looked at Remi and Sasha. "I...I have been spending a little time with Captain Crawford. Sasha knows that."

Sasha hurried across the room and snatched the letter without thinking. She read Crawford's words, a desperate plea for Ilaria to meet with him one final time. His desire for her sister was clear in every shaking pen stroke, in every heady word.

He was in love with her. That was so evident, he might have written it in his own blood. And for a moment Sasha hated them for it. Hated Ilaria for being able to take her final encounter with Crawford if she chose while Thomas and Sasha...well, it was more complicated.

"Ilaria," Sasha breathed.

"Well, it's not fair that I don't get to see it," Remi grunted, and took the paper next. He read it and said his sister's name with much the same tenor that Sasha had.

"Oh, please don't take a serious tone. I get that enough from Grantham and Mama." She snatched the note back. "I know I'm being a fool, but this is my last chance to be so. Tomorrow everything will change, won't it? Within a few days, perhaps a week or two, my life will be set in stone and I'll never have the opportunity to do this again." She held up the note and shook it. "I'll never have the ability to see...to see him again."

"This is far more serious than I thought," Sasha whispered.

"Will you help me? Or at least not thwart me?"

Remi sighed. "I won't stop you. But I'm going to go down with you."

"You're playing protective older brother then?" There was no mistaking Ilaria's surprised tone.

He shrugged. "I have the costume, I might as well since there's no one else to do the duty." He looked her up and down. "Are you wearing that?"

Sasha looked at her. Ilaria was wearing a rather plain gown. Sasha wondered what she would have wanted if she knew she would be seeing Thomas for the last time. She would want to be pretty and polished. She would want to burn a memory on his mind that he would never forget. She would want to steal one glorious moment from time to keep.

Didn't she want the same for her sister? After all, they would *all* lose thanks to the circumstances.

"No, she's not," Sasha said, grabbing for her hand. "If this is your last hurrah, you're going to have it in all your glory. I'll help you."

She dragged her from the room, intent on giving Ilaria what she, herself, would not be able to have. It was all she could do.

～

After a rushed toilette, Ilaria and Remi had gone down so she could meet Crawford, which left Sasha alone in their chamber, staring at the mess of discarded clothing and tossed about ribbons and jewels. She would have to tidy this up before June's arrival in the morning to help Ilaria, but at that moment, the task seemed too daunting.

She was restless, her thoughts continually trying to come back around to a place they should not be. She clenched her hands at her sides and left the room. She needed air, that was all. A walk in the garden would set her to rights.

She moved down the hallway toward the stairs but before she

could reach them, Dashiell stepped from the queen's quarters. "Good evening, Sasha."

She stopped in her tracks, not daring to meet his gaze. If he looked too closely, he would see her turmoil, her torment. She didn't want that.

"Dash," she said with a false smile. "I didn't see you there."

"I was just making a few last alterations to the queen's schedule for tomorrow. I wanted to go over them with her when she returns home shortly. I thought you and Ilaria had gone to bed already."

Sasha shifted. She'd never liked lying to Dash. Often she wasn't successful at it.

"I was restless and thought to take a walk in the garden."

"Why restless?" He arched a brow at her. It had been seventeen years since he first brought her to the queen and changed her life forever. He was a little grayer than he had been in those days, but he was just as handsome. Just as sharp. Just as kind as he had ever been.

She cleared her throat. "A great many things, I suppose."

He reached for her hand, and she smiled. He'd stopped holding her hand when she was a very little girl, but it was still such a comfort. "Come in and talk to me," he said gently.

She followed him into the antechamber, which was set up with Dash's desk and a seating area so he and Giabella could hold meetings. Through one door was the queen's dressing room, the other her bedchamber.

But right now it was just Sasha and Dash. "What's troubling you?" he asked.

She swallowed hard. If there was one person she could pour her troubles into, one person who would understand and love her just the same for them, it was this man. And yet she also feared he would be disappointed in her. The moment she knew Thomas was meant for Ilaria, she should have backed away. Dash would say that, certainly.

So she had to be careful.

"You...you served the late king when you first came onto palace staff," she said slowly.

Dash's brow wrinkled in confusion at what certainly must have sounded like a change of subject. "Yes. I worked within the offices of his head courtier, Mr. Blairford, for nearly a decade."

There was just a hint of distaste around his mouth as he said the man's name. Sasha didn't blame him. Blairford was much maligned by the staff and the younger members of the family, alike.

"How did you come to work for Giabella?" she asked. "I don't remember. It was as if one day you were simply there."

His expression softened. "I have you to thank for that, Sasha."

"Me?" she repeated in confusion. "How did I have any influence? I was just what...twelve or thirteen by then?"

He smiled. "The queen and I often talked privately about you over the years. It helped us form a..." He hesitated. "A...a bond of sorts. A strong enough one that when she required a new private secretary, she offered me the position. A much better fit than what I had done before." When she didn't speak, he examined her closer. "Why do you ask me about this, Sasha?"

"We are alike, I think," she said softly. "I see you with Giabella. You are more than a servant to her—you are her friend. Her confidante."

He flinched ever so slightly. "I have tried to be both those things over the years, but make no mistake, I am still a servant. I know my place and I know what it is not."

"But it's not the same," she said. "We both know it. And I am somewhat similar. I was raised by the family, they embrace me. But I'm not theirs. The king made sure of it before his death, didn't he?"

For a brief moment, Dash actually looked angry, though not at her. But then he wiped the expression from his countenance. "He made things difficult, I know. I wish I could have protected you."

She shook her head and pushed her hurt down. There was a reason they never broached this topic. She shouldn't have let it rise to the surface in her upset. "No one could protect me from him, not even Giabella. Because of him, I belong neither in all their spaces nor in the spaces of the servants. I'm outside looking in and inside looking out."

He held her stare for a beat. "You are in a unique position, yes."

"Lately, I suppose I have had to ponder my future more. Ilaria will likely marry soon." She had to choke out those last two words. "And I'm sure the rest of the children will follow swiftly behind. And where will I be? How will I fit?"

"It's a fair question," Dash said slowly. "What do you picture that future looking like?"

"I always thought I would stay with Ilaria. Help her all her life. Only now..." She trailed off.

"Now?"

"I think it would be difficult to be part of her household." She bent her head. "Please don't ask me why."

Dash was quiet. "Then what about a life of your own? When we return to Athawick, I'm sure the queen would be happy to pull you from any duties. You could be introduced to some men of an appropriate station."

"I have nothing to offer," she whispered.

"You have yourself. A prize worth more than rubies, in my estimation." He reached for her hand again. "After what King Alistair... did...I set aside a little to offer as your dowry if you wished to pursue a marriage."

Tears filled her eyes and she stared at him. "You...you did?"

He nodded. "You could marry and have a family of your own."

She flinched at the thought. "I don't know that I'd want to marry."

He stared at her, and then his expression softened. "Ah. I think I might see."

She hoped that wasn't true. "Please don't ask me questions," she repeated.

"If you don't want me to, I won't." They were both quiet for a moment, and then he cleared his throat. "Perhaps a better answer to your predicament would be to find you a position on palace staff that would not be with Ilaria. Once she marries, it will be likely she will spend a great deal of time in England with her husband. You could take an elevated place on the queen's staff, perhaps, if you would like to continue to serve the family. I can always use the help, and it would groom you to one day take a position as the next queen's secretary, should Grantham's future wife have a need."

She had never considered that option before. The idea of being parted from Ilaria was painful, of course, but so was the reality that if she stayed with her, she would be forced to watch her with Thomas for the long years of their life. Ilaria would eventually love him—how could she not? They would have children, beautiful children. It would crush Sasha in the end.

"I would like to think about the possibility. Can you begin to feel out what the queen would think of such a thing?"

"I will, if that is what you need," Dash said.

Sasha took a breath and realized it was the first deep one she'd taken since she first saw Thomas on the terrace that long-ago night that had changed her life forever. "I know you're busy," she said. "I'll leave you to it and go take my walk."

He nodded, but before she could exit his space, he caught her hand. She moved toward him, and to her utter surprise, he folded her into his arms in a hug. He hadn't done that since she was just a little girl. She went limp against him, allowing him to be her strength when she felt so weak.

"It is hard to…to care for someone you cannot have," he whispered. "I would never wish that for you, Sasha. And I will spare you all the pain of it that I can."

She drew away from him and he let her go. She wanted to tell him that she didn't care for Thomas, but it wasn't true. She did care for him, more deeply every time they met. She wanted him, she liked him, she dreamed of him. Despite who he was and who he was meant for. All she could do was run from those feelings.

"Thank you," she said, offering no other explanation, him asking no other questions. "Good night."

"Good night," he said softly, his eyes sad as he turned away from her and went back to his work.

Sasha's feet felt heavy as lead as she trailed her way through the house. At last she exited the house onto the terrace from a parlor. The night air was cool, and she sucked it in with a deep breath, as if it could cleanse her of all her problems. Of course it couldn't, but at least she had taken steps to ease some of them tonight.

She focused on her breathing for a while, noting the sounds in the night air. The scuttling of small animals in the garden below, the occasional burst of song from a nightingale, the hum of the city. She was beginning to feel more centered, calm, when she heard a new sound, one that forced her eyes open.

It was a tap, off in the distance, toward the window to the set of chambers that she and Ilaria shared. She wrinkled her brow, straining to hear the sound again. It came in short measure, a tap and then a faint clatter, as if something was falling.

She leaned forward over the terrace wall, looking toward her window in the distance. She heard the sound again and drew back. The lamp in the bedroom was still lit, and she could have sworn she saw a small pebble hit the glass and then fall.

"I say," she called out. "Is someone there?"

There was a hesitation, and then Thomas's voice answered, "Sasha?"

"Where are you?" she asked, peering through the darkness to try to find him amongst the shrubbery.

There was movement there, but she couldn't see him. "I'm down here. Where are you?"

"On the terrace."

He barked out a laugh in the dark and then she didn't hear him anymore.

"Thomas?"

He burst through the bushes, brushing himself off as he looked up at her. Her breath caught. The moonlight hit him, framing him perfectly in that beam, and all she could think was that he was beautiful. Absolutely beautiful with his tousled dark hair and sharp jawline. His expression was so filled with the same longing she felt and her heart began to pound so loudly, she almost couldn't hear over it.

They simply stared at each other for a moment that felt like a lifetime. She could no longer think of all the good reasons she had to stay away from him. No longer tell herself the stories where she had to be good and decent and sacrifice herself.

No, in that moment all she could see or think or feel was that she needed him.

She held up a hand. "Wait there."

She slipped off toward the stone steps that led to the garden, to a man she should not touch, to a future she couldn't have. But she did it anyway, because she knew it was the last chance.

CHAPTER 11

Thomas could hardly breathe as he watched Sasha come down the steps. She was gloriously beautiful, her dark hair pulled back loosely, her pale green gown clinging to her curves. But mostly it was the fact that she was focused entirely on him as she glided toward him, her hands clenched at her sides.

"What are you doing here?" she whispered.

He tilted his head. "Well, I *was* making a romantic gesture and throwing pebbles at a window."

She worried her lip. "Trying to find...to find me?"

"Of course," he said. "Of course you."

Her face lit up with a happiness she couldn't hide. "Why?"

A thousand answers to that question raced through his head. That he wanted her so much he could hardly think of anything else; that he was a bastard and selfish; that tonight would be the last time they could do this...

But instead he said, "I needed to see you."

She glanced back up at the house, her expression growing guarded again. "My lord—"

He shook his head and lunged forward, catching her hands so that she couldn't run away. She wasn't wearing gloves, neither was he, and the warmth of her seemed to seep into every part of his heart, his soul, his body.

"I don't *want* to be Lord Bramwell," he said. "Not tonight. Please, Sasha."

Her eyes fluttered shut and he saw the struggle on her face. The same as his own, and that was what was so desperately unfair about it all.

She exhaled at last. "Come, then. I promised you a walk through the garden before—let's take it now."

His knees almost buckled with relief, but he somehow managed to keep them firm as he tucked her hand into the crook of his elbow, and together they stepped out onto the path.

For a little while, they were both silent, just walking together farther and farther from the house, back into the darkness where only the moonlight reached. A dangerous place and yet it was where he wanted to be with her.

Still, he wasn't satisfied as she led him to a small gazebo beside a gurgling fountain. She released him and paced away, her hands trembling at her sides. He needed to speak, to say something, though he didn't know what.

"Sasha," he began.

She turned back, and he realized her dark gaze was glittering with tears. "Oh, please don't," she whispered. "Please don't say anything. We both know it will make this too difficult."

Her pain was so palpable and he longed to ease it. To make her happy, even though it wasn't his place, would never be his place.

"What can I do, then?" he asked.

She stared at him, her entire body vibrating with tension and pain. The silence stretched between them, the longing. She took a small step toward him. "Thomas..."

He moved without meaning to do so, closing the distance in a few long steps. He caught her in his arms, drawing her against him, feeling her mold to him with a gasping breath. God, she was perfect in his arms, like every dream he'd ever had.

He dropped his mouth to hers, reveling in the softness of her lips, in the way they parted beneath his in this first, heady kiss. Control flew away as she gripped his lapels and lifted into him. He buried one hand into her hair, tilting her head for better access as he tasted her mouth, drove his tongue into her and felt her respond. Her little moans were like music to his ears, the way she rubbed against him, reaching for more, was like heaven.

He backed her across the gazebo slowly and gently pressed her against one of the pillars. He leaned into her, loving her softness where he was hard, loving how his legs tangled in her skirts. He wanted her so much, it coursed in his veins with his blood, driving him to do more, take more, ask for more than perhaps was fair to either of them.

Fair to her.

That thought brought him up short. If he were only torturing himself, he would have surrendered without hesitation. The pain would be worth the pleasure. But to hurt her?

He broke the kiss and rested his forehead against hers as they panted together in the dark. "You—you know what happens tomorrow," he said.

The grip of her fingers tightened on his forearms and her voice broke as she answered, "Yes."

"It will change everything," he said, and drew back just enough to look down into her eyes.

"I know." She sighed and leaned up to brush her lips against his one more time, then paced away. "This is a dream, a fantasy."

"No, it's a punishment...and one I did not earn, but have to live with."

She turned to look at him. "Will you tell me why? I've heard whispering and implications, but I don't fully understand why."

He shifted. To give her that answer was to open up his chest and expose the most desperate part of himself. A part he kept private... hell, he'd even tried to keep it from his sister for a while. Gossip didn't know the whole story, whispers had never captured its essence.

But he somehow wanted Sasha to know. He wanted to open his heart like that so she would understand, so she would have a piece of him that he would not ever give to anyone else. Even if it was the worst part, he trusted her to keep it safe.

And if she knew then she would understand that the future was out of his hands. He could not veer from its course.

He motioned to the bench that was placed in the middle of the gazebo. She sat and he joined her, shivering as their legs touched. She stared down at that place where their bodies met and then said, "Would you put your arm around me?"

He blinked at the quiet request. How could he deny it, deny her? He put his arm around the back of the bench and she leaned in to rest her head against his shoulder.

For the first time in years, a sense of peace worked through him, settled into his blood, made the ceaseless anxiety that plagued him stop. It was a stunning thing, to not hear the constant click of worry for even a moment. It made him realize just how loud it had been and fear how much louder it would become when she wasn't there anymore.

"You don't have to tell me," she said, her voice a little muffled against his arm.

He glanced down at her. "No, I want to. I want you to know, to understand. I'm just...just trying to find the words."

"I understand that. The pain is often wordless, so it's hard to find a way to explain it."

He sighed. "And when that pain is part of your life from a young age, it's hard to pick it away from the rest of your own story."

She nodded. "Yes."

They sat in silence again for a moment, both knowing exactly what the other meant because they had both felt it. It made the stark unfairness of the situation all the clearer.

"My father was..." Thomas trailed off. "Horrible. He was a

pompous bastard who thought his title made him better than anyone around him. He was cruel to those who worked for him, to those who lived in his domain and to his family."

"I'm sorry," she whispered. "Physically cruel?"

"On occasion," Thomas said. "But mostly he liked to toy with emotions, to feel he could control them. He would manipulate for fun and for profit. You loved something or someone? He could convince you it was folly or that it wasn't what you thought it was. You wanted something? He would keep it from you for sport. And if your desires interfered with his? Well, that was a battle you could never win."

"It sounds terrible," Sasha said.

"The best example of his abject cruelty was my sister," Thomas said. "Aurora had been in love with Nicholas forever. They wanted to be together, but Nicholas's father was my father's steward. Not good enough for the daughter of an earl because my father would gain nothing from the match."

Sasha pinched her lips. "I have seen your sister and her husband —they are perfectly in tune. She is happy with him, that is very obvious. I understand the way of the world, that unions are often based on gain, but could her heart have truly meant nothing to your father?"

"Nothing at all," Thomas said with a shake of his head. "Worse, he lied to her and to Nicholas in order to separate them. He created a situation where they each believed the other to be uninterested and shattered them both to pieces. Then he forced my sister into a very unhappy first marriage. And Nicholas went into the army, where he was nearly killed. They were kept apart for years, almost a decade because of his machinations."

She lifted a hand to her lips. "That's terrible. But they found each other again."

"They were very lucky," he said. "I watched him do these things, watched him hurt my mother, watched him hurt anyone who got in his way or just would entertain him if he crushed them. And I knew

I would *never* be like him. I promised myself I would be better, that I would fix anything he'd damaged that I could."

"A fine desire," Sasha said. "And not surprising. You are a good man, Thomas. That is clear from speaking to you for two minutes."

He bent his head. "I try to be. I fight to be because I know that bastard's blood runs through my veins and I never wish to surrender myself to it." He sighed. "But I *am* living with the consequences of his actions, Sasha."

She turned in her seat toward him slightly and her dark gaze was fully focused on him. "Such as?"

"His selfish cruelty extended beyond manipulation," he said. "What he wanted, he took. He never thought of the estates in entail or the duty he held to those who worked in them. Every one of his holdings was deeply in debt at the time of his death and even more in disrepair. The money he could touch was all..." He hesitated. When he talked about this, his throat closed. "It was all gone. As was a portion of the money he ought not have been able to touch, because it was set aside for upkeep."

"Oh, Thomas," Sasha breathed. "How terrible."

"The situation was, and is, desperate," he admitted. "And worse, if there is a way for this to be worse, is that my father sullied our name in the process. When I inherited, I found tenants who hated us thanks to his behavior, merchants who would not deal with anyone connected to the earldom because they knew they would be left unpaid. It has taken me years to reform those bonds. Some can never be repaired."

"That is desperately unfair. I'm so sorry."

So many people over the years had said they were sorry to him when they knew some of the circumstances of his life. His mother, his sister, even a few of the creditors who loomed over him seemed apologetic. Seemed to know he was not at fault, even if he was responsible.

And yet when she said those words, they meant so much more.

"I am the one who is sorry," he said. "Because it puts me in a situation where I must move from a place of desperation. I must marry for benefit, not..." He stared down into those beautiful eyes. "Not because I care for someone. And I must do it now, because the fact is that I've rebuilt this name as best I can, but if I do not find a way to refill the coffers through a dowry, to rebuild the reputation through a decent marriage, there will be a point where it will all slip through my fingers again."

"Hence, Ilaria," Sasha whispered.

He nodded. "My title is of no threat to the Crown, but it is...or was...a good enough name to make it a powerful link to England. Your family erases my problems, I ease theirs. And in theory, everyone wins."

"Except us," Sasha said.

"Except us."

Their gazes met and she smiled at him sadly. "If I could hate you for this, it would make it easier, I think. But how could I? You are trying to fix something that you had no hand in breaking. And I know a little about that."

"How?" he asked.

She opened her mouth and seemed to consider sharing a piece of herself as he had. Then she shook her head. "Perhaps it's better if I don't. It's not that I don't want to tell you about my life or my past. I do. But you're going to have to focus on Ilaria after tomorrow. If you have me in your head, you won't be able to do that so easily. And you should, she's wonderful. She will make a good wife for you."

He flinched at the idea. "But you now know about me."

"I'm allowed to—" She cut herself off with a blush. "I won't be married to someone else, so it won't matter as much. You need me to be some woman you kissed in a garden one night, nothing more. And I plan to make that as easy for you as I can, as easy for her."

He wrinkled his brow. "What do you mean by that, Sasha?"

She glanced up at the house. "I should go in. Grantham and Queen Giabella will be home soon, if they aren't already, and I wouldn't want to create questions." She looked back at him. "And if I don't go now, I fear I won't be able to."

He rose with her. But as she turned to walk away, he caught her hand and drew her back. She leaned into him, staring up into his eyes. He memorized every angle of her face, every sparkle in her stare, every tremble of her lips. And then he leaned down and kissed her one last time.

She opened to him instantly. He wanted to devour, to claim, to burn some part of this night into them both so they would never forget. Only if he started down that road they would end up making a decision that could not be undone. So instead he forced himself to be gentle, exploring her lips, drowning in her taste until she at last drew away.

"Goodbye," she whispered, pulling from his arms.

He let her go. He had no choice but to do so. Her choice of the word *goodbye* was like a knife to the gut. Oh, he'd see her again. Quite a bit, considering her role alongside Ilaria. But they would never be alone like this again. He would never touch her again. They would both do their level best to avoid that, because they each knew their place.

But he also knew something else. An indelible fact that tore him to shreds.

He loved her, even though he hardly knew her. It was as if from the moment he saw her, his soul had known they belonged together. And in his final acts of cruelty and selfishness, his father had created a scenario where Thomas could never be with her. Something that would probably please the old man to no end.

Thomas sighed and made his way to the gate in the fence where he'd snuck in earlier. His hands shook as he exited it, walking away from her, walking away from the future he would have chosen for himself.

And hardening himself for the one about to come.

CHAPTER 12

Sasha could scarcely breathe as she entered the house. She stood in the dark of the parlor and bent at the waist, choking on her sobs as she relived every beautiful, wonderful, terrible moment with Thomas in the garden.

If she had built a man out of everything she had ever desired, he could not have lived up to Thomas. He was everything she had ever dared to dream about when she thought of falling in love. And the universe was so cruel as to make him the one man she could not have.

She shook her head and forced herself to stand up straight again, breathe deeply to regain some control over herself. She might care for Thomas—she would allow herself nothing more than that admission—but that didn't mean she had to be destroyed by losing him.

Dash had offered her a way out earlier. A way to separate herself from what she could not have and return to Athawick for a real life, a real future. It might not be what she wanted, or perfect, but she could fight to be happy even without Thomas in her life.

She pushed her shoulders back. Dash would still be up. He had wanted to wait to speak to Giabella. She could go to him right now and discuss his offer, perhaps even seal the bargain with the queen, herself.

She nodded and smoothed her gown, wiped the tears from her cheeks. She exited the parlor, but as she headed toward the stairs, she heard pounding at the front door. She stopped and pivoted toward it.

There was talking in the foyer, though she couldn't make out the words, then louder talking, and now she moved toward the commotion.

A stranger with short-cut dark hair was standing in the foyer with Greenly. "I'm telling you, I must speak with the king immediately. It's a matter of great importance."

"Sir, you cannot simply barge in here in the middle of the night —" Greenly began, widening his stance as if ready to fight, good man.

"I work for a man named Marcus Rivers," the intruder interrupted.

At that, Sasha gasped. She knew that name—it had been in the notes for the Donville Masquerade, the wicked club Ilaria kept insisting on visiting.

She rushed forward. "Who are you?" she asked.

The stranger's gaze moved to her. "My name is Paul Abbot," he said.

"And you say you work for Mr. Rivers. At his…his club, I presume?" she pressed, ignoring Greenly's annoyed expression.

"Yes. Tonight Princess Ilaria was…she was attacked there, and I've been sent to collect the king."

Sasha nearly deposited herself on her backside as shock flowed through her. "Ilaria was attacked."

"You are lying, sir, though I do not know for what end," Greenly said. "The princess is safe and sound in her bed and I am calling for the king's guard."

Sasha shook her head. "The princess is not safe and sound in her bed," she whispered. "Greenly, fetch the king immediately. I will find the queen."

Greenly pivoted to face her, cheeks bright with shock and surprise. "What?"

"You heard me!" Sasha snapped. "Go!"

He ran off, and before she moved to follow, she said, "Please wait here."

Mr. Abbot inclined his head but said nothing else as she raced away. Greenly had turned in one direction and was pounding on the door to Grantham's suite. She went the opposite direction and burst into Giabella's chamber. The queen was standing at the window, Dashiell close to her side. When the door flew open, they stepped apart and faced her.

"What is going on?" Giabella asked. "Why have you burst into my chamber, Sasha? Are you well?"

She looked back and forth between them. In her haste and upset, she realized she had gotten no more information from Mr. Abbot. Ilaria had been attacked, but what did it mean? Was she injured? Worse? She was about to hurt the woman who had served as her mother and she had no idea how to soothe it.

"Ilaria," she gasped out. "Mama...Mama, she has been attacked."

Giabella tilted, and Dashiell moved back to her side, catching her elbow and turning her slightly into him to support her. "What?" Giabella gasped.

"I don't know the details, but please, you must come with me. And Remi, Remi must be told."

They exited the chamber, and she found Grantham coming toward them, Remi and Greenly at his heels. "Remi was with me when I heard," Grantham said, having obviously overheard Sasha's shouting. "How could this have happened? What did Ilaria do?"

"Please," Sasha said, guiding them all to the foyer. "Let us listen to Mr. Abbot."

"What happened to my sister?" Grantham bellowed as he strode toward the man still waiting there for them. The king's eyes were bright with terror now.

Mr. Abbot seemed unbothered by the outburst and inclined his head. "Your Majesties, Your Highness. There was an incident at the Donville Masquerade tonight."

Grantham jerked his head toward Remi, who flinched. "The Donville Masquerade?" Grantham repeated.

"Yes, sir, it is a club—"

"I bloody know what it is!" Grantham shouted. "My sister?"

"She was attacked and though the attacker's intentions to kill her were thwarted, she hit her head in the struggle."

"No," Queen Giabella gasped, her hands coming up to cover her mouth.

"How badly is she injured?" Dash asked, grasping Giabella's elbow for support once more.

"When I left to fetch the king, she was...she was still unconscious," Mr. Abbot said softly.

"A carriage!" Grantham cried out to no one in particular. "Unmarked, with our fastest horses. I'm going to my sister." Greenly ran to fulfill the order.

"Not by yourself," Giabella said. "I'm coming with you. Dash, will you please ensure that a physician is ready for our return? The best in London."

"I'm going, too," Remi said.

"*You've* done enough," Grantham growled.

Remi moved toward him. "You're not in charge of me, Grantham. I'm not bowing to you when it comes to our sister."

Sasha could see the situation was about to dissolve into fisticuffs and wedged herself between them. "We will all go."

"No," Grantham barked.

"She might be dying," Giabella whispered. "We should all be there."

That soft statement brought all arguments to a halt as the three siblings looked at each other. Then Grantham moved toward their mother and folded her into his embrace. "Yes, we'll all go."

"The carriage is on its way," Greenly said, and opened the door.

Abbot departed first. "I'll give direction to your driver and meet you there."

In a few moments, the rig arrived and the family loaded inside. Grantham and the queen were on one seat and Remi and Sasha on the other. Greenly and Dash waved them off to their uncertain future. They had not gotten out of the drive when Grantham leaned forward and speared Remi and Sasha with a dark glare. "Tell me everything."

Sasha swallowed hard and exchanged a quick glance with Remi, who looked no more interested in telling this tale than she felt. "She's not happy," she whispered.

Grantham flinched. "As she makes us aware daily. How did that become her sneaking out of the house at night to go to a..." He glanced at his mother apologetically. "Sex club."

The queen's eyes widened. "Is that what it is? In the middle of London?"

"Yes," Remi admitted, his cheeks almost purple with rare embarrassment.

"*You* told her about it," Grantham said softly. "Just as you told me. Did you encourage her to go?"

"Of course not," Remi said.

Sasha couldn't help but think of Thomas with his mouth on hers in the garden such a short time before. "She has needs just as any man might. Why shouldn't she be curious?"

Grantham gripped his hands in his lap. "Because of exactly what happened. She put herself in danger, put her own future plans in danger. And now she might be..."

"Don't say it," Giabella whispered. "Please."

He stopped, and for a moment a heavy silence settled over the group of them. Then Grantham sighed. "I asked Captain Crawford to keep an eye on her. I wonder if he was there to thwart the attack."

Remi's eyes went wide and he exchanged a quick glance with Sasha.

Grantham glared at them. "What is that look?"

"Nothing," Remi said.

"Sasha," Grantham snapped. "I'm asking as your king, not your brother. What do you know about it?"

"That's unfair," Sasha said, shaking her head.

He looked guilty, but he folded his arms across his broad chest. "Tell me."

"Captain Crawford...escorted her there tonight."

Grantham went entirely still at that statement and a muscle in his jaw twitched. The carriage they were riding in eased to a stop and he shook his head as a footman opened the door. "I see," he murmured, climbing out. He reached back to help his mother. "It seems I have a great many conversations to have."

Sasha climbed down from the carriage. They were parked in a dark alleyway behind a tall building. Mr. Abbot was already off his horse. "This is the back entrance with a secret passage to Mr. Rivers' office, where Princess Ilaria was taken after the attack. Please follow me."

They did so, up a dim stairway. It was brighter at the top and music from the hall below drifted up, as well as...other sounds that made Sasha blush. Abbot motioned to a door there and Grantham did not wait to be led or announced. He burst through, shouting, "Where the hell is she?"

Sasha and the others crowded in behind him. She all but blocked out all the arguments as she searched the small office for Ilaria. But she was nowhere to be found. Captain Crawford was there, and a tall, handsome man Sasha assumed to be the infamous Mr. Rivers, but no Ilaria. Her heart throbbed with terror. She'd thought to help Ilaria, to give her relief.

Instead, she'd sent her to danger?

"I'm here." Ilaria's voice cut through the din of conversation, as if she had been conjured by Sasha's fears and worries.

Ilaria stepped from a room adjoining the office, a pretty woman in an expensive gown at her side. For a moment, the room froze. Although there was a bruise on Ilaria's temple, she looked none the worse for her ordeal. Grantham's expression all but collapsed in relief. Sasha saw the kind, loving sibling he'd always been to them all before he inherited. Before the weight of the world buckled his shoulders.

"Ilaria." The king crossed to her and pulled her into his arms.

They parted after a brief moment and Ilaria stared in horror at the entire group of them. "Why in the world would all of you risk coming here?" she asked. "You could be seen and the stir that would create is—"

Giabella silenced her by tugging her into her arms next. "As if I could hear that my daughter had been injured and not come to her."

Remi followed to hug her next, and then Sasha stepped up before her. Their eyes locked and she saw Ilaria's fear, her torment, her heartbreak. So much like her own as her gaze flitted briefly to Captain Crawford. Then she pulled Ilaria close.

"I'm so sorry," she whispered against the princess's hair. "It's my fault."

"Of course it isn't," Ilaria murmured back before they parted.

"You have some explaining to do," Grantham snapped, all his softness gone.

"I know," Ilaria said. "But please don't shout. None of this is anyone's fault but my own."

The woman in the room, who Sasha now assumed was Mr. Rivers' wife by the warm way they looked at each other, helped them settle into seats and make themselves as comfortable as one could be in such circumstances.

Finally Ilaria sighed and then launched into an explanation. Sasha couldn't help but notice that she lied as much as she could about Captain Crawford's role in her great escapes...to protect him, it seemed. She shifted her gaze to the man and found him watching Ilaria intently.

Captain Crawford loved Ilaria. She felt it radiating from him. Her heart hurt all the more at it. One more innocent person to be torn apart by the necessary sacrifices made for Crown and Country.

Ilaria cleared her throat eventually and her cheeks were bright with color. "This was my third time coming here."

Sasha dipped her head. Well, now it was out.

"Ilaria," her mother murmured, a hand coming up to cover her mouth.

"You may express your disappointment at length later, all of you. But perhaps I should first tell you what brought us to tonight."

Grantham folded his arms. "I think that's a good idea. Because it isn't every day that a princess of Athawick is attacked. I want to know who did this, I want to know why and I want this person brought to justice. I will do everything in my power to make sure that happens. So tell me."

Ilaria did so, recounting three nights at the infamous club and three times she had encountered what she had written off as simply odd behavior by a patron there. Only now it seemed she had been stalked by an enemy of some kind.

Sasha stared as she listened to the story. Ilaria had said nothing to her about any of this. Their sisterhood, which had always seemed so close, now felt pushed apart by the secrets. Ilaria's and her own.

The princess reached the details of her attack. "The same man I'd seen before came out of the crowd tonight," she said. She stopped and swallowed hard, like the fearful memories were too much.

"How did he attack you?" Remi asked gently.

Ilaria looked toward Captain Crawford instead of answering, and a world of communication flowed between them. His hand flexed as if he longed to touch her, and then he said, "I saw them struggling and Ilaria fell. I raced toward them to find the man raising a knife over his head to stab her."

"My love!" Giabella burst out, clutching Ilaria's hand tighter.

"I would not have reached her in time. Marcus Rivers was the one who saved her. He lunged at the attacker and sent him sprawling." Crawford reached into his pocket and pulled out a wicked-looking curved blade. "The bastard dropped this."

Sasha trembled with the utter fear of it all, with the realization of how close they'd come to losing Ilaria. And while this was happening, what had she been doing? Standing in the garden with Thomas, kissing him when she ought not to have been.

Guilt rushed through her.

While she was lost in those horrible thoughts, Grantham had taken the knife and was looking at it, tugging free a piece of cloth wrapped around the handle of the weapon. He held it out, and Sasha realized it was a reverse image of the beautiful flag of Athawick with its swan centerpiece and dancing whales to each side. Only instead of being blue and white, the background on this flag was black, the swan and whales red.

"*This* is the flag of the rebellion," he whispered.

Sasha's thoughts of Thomas faded as she stared at Grantham in shock.

"Rebellion?" Queen Giabella said. "What are you talking about?"

He turned away and tossed the weapon and the flag on the desk. He then turned to Rivers, himself. "I realize this is your establishment, Mr. Rivers, and that you saved my sister's life tonight, for which I am eternally grateful. But what I am about to say is highly sensitive."

To Sasha's surprise, Rivers didn't simper or bow to the king, but held his gaze evenly. "I assure you, Your Majesty, that highly sensitive is my business. I recognize your hesitation to speak of private things, but those private things have entered my club now and threatened more than just your sister. So I won't leave. There may even be a chance that I can help."

Grantham gave Rivers a long look. "How?"

"I have connections," Rivers said softly. "And I can find things that perhaps even your courtiers would find difficult to uncover. I will offer my assistance in any way I can. But I must understand what happened in my club tonight and why."

Grantham ran a hand through his hair and looked at his family, then back to Rivers. "Very well. If I have your word that nothing I say here leaves this club, I don't suppose I have much choice."

"I swear to you that nothing you say will ever leave these walls," Rivers said.

Grantham sighed deeply and turned back to the family. "There has been trouble since I took the throne, a trouble I...I kept from all of you. There is a faction of our people who do not wish to have a monarchy anymore. Apparently they would go so far as to murder my sister to make that point abundantly clear."

As Sasha's mouth dropped open in shock, Remi got up and crossed to the desk. "They want you to, what...abdicate?"

Grantham nodded. "I'm receiving regular reports of their behavior from home. My advisors keep telling me to squash them, do it swiftly and harshly enough that it will never happen again during my reign. I've resisted—I do not wish to turn brutality against my people. But I never thought it would go this far."

"It seems odd it would." Remi fingered the discarded flag. "Odd to leave a calling card like this when they must know you are being pressured to retaliate. It feels too obvious."

Crawford cleared his throat. "I don't disagree with Prince Remington," he said softly. "But I think the matter at hand is that Princess Ilaria's life has been threatened, not once but three times in a short period. She is the target, no matter what the purpose of the attacks is in truth. And she must be our focus. Your Majesty, you asked me to do a duty. To protect your sister. And I have a suggestion as to how that needs to be carried out."

Grantham glared at him. "You have a suggestion after you have failed three times? After you allowed her to come here *three damned times*? For what purpose, I can only imagine."

"She needs to be removed from London," Crawford said, ignoring the accusation. "Secreted away, even if only for a short time while you investigate."

Sasha's head was spinning and she glanced toward Ilaria, hoping to offer some support. But the princess's gaze was locked on Crawford, focused on him and him alone.

The queen got to her feet. "I don't disagree with Captain Crawford," she said softly. "My daughter must be protected at any cost."

"Then we should return home," Grantham said. "We could be on the boat by tomorrow."

"And destroy all your hopes for this visit?" Ilaria gasped. "Undo all you've built?"

Sasha watched them argue, but it all felt like it was coming from behind glass or under water. Distant as her own thoughts mobbed her. Memories, too, of the love this family had always shown her, the acceptance. She wasn't fully one of them, no…but they were still hers.

"And how do we explain a missing princess?" Grantham said, his tone laced with exasperation.

Sasha stared at Ilaria again, then Remi, Giabella, and last at Grantham. The path forward seemed painfully clear.

She reached out to Ilaria and caught her hand. "You don't." She heard the tremble in her own voice. "*I* will stand in her place."

CHAPTER 13

S asha had said those words, but they rang in her ears as if they'd come from someone else's lips. She meant them, but the danger that she was opening up for herself was new. She'd played double to wave out a carriage window before, to stand behind the old king on a terrace...but never had it been for such a desperate reason.

Never before had it truly resulted in a target being placed firmly on her chest.

The room was quiet—stunned, she thought. Grantham turned toward her, his eyes wide. "Sasha!" he gasped.

She shook her head. "Please don't pretend that this isn't exactly what my presence was always meant for. Ilaria's schedule includes many events where observers will not get too close to her. Even those who do, most of them only have seen sketches of her in the papers." She wished her voice didn't tremble so hard. "I look close enough to pass if need be."

"And what of the Earl of Bramwell?" the queen interjected. "*He* would know you weren't Ilaria, so he would have to be told the truth."

Sasha shut her eyes briefly. Thomas. She would have to stand in beside Thomas, pretend to be Ilaria. Be close to him as his future fiancée would soon be. Another torture on top of a torture. But by doing so, she protected his future, as well, didn't she?

"Yes," she whispered. "But I believe he and his mother could be trusted with this information. We could carry on just as you intended, only with me in the place of threat rather than Ilaria."

Ilaria shook her head hard. "No. That is too dangerous."

"*That* is what a double does," Sasha said, and touched Ilaria's face gently.

"You are more than my double," Ilaria declared. "For God's sake, you are my friend. My sister. Grantham, Mama, tell her this is outrageous. Unacceptable!"

Sasha didn't allow the king or queen to do that. "It is *because* I am your friend and your...your sister that I am willing to take the risk. Now that the danger is known, I will be well-protected, I'm sure."

Grantham ran a hand through his hair as he paced the room. "I don't like this. I don't like that we would endanger Sasha, nor that the rest of my family may be at risk. I don't like that Ilaria would go away with Crawford. God's teeth, this is a mess." He rested both hands on the desktop and leaned heavily there.

A silence stretched for a moment and then Crawford cleared his throat. "I can protect her, Your Majesty. I vow that to you now. I will die if need be to see her through this."

"Jonah," Ilaria whispered, heedless, apparently, at how intimately she said his name.

Grantham glared at Crawford, but finally let out long sigh. "*Fine.* I see no other choice at present. Sasha, you and Remi go back to the house. Gather some of Ilaria's things...quietly. She won't return until we all feel this danger has subsided. No one else in the household must know what is happening. If anyone asks about her, she has taken ill and only Sasha and her mother are seeing her. We will close off her room, we close off everything. Return in the unmarked carriage."

"Understood," Remi said, taking Sasha's arm. "Come."

Sasha followed him, for she had no choice but to do so. The plan had been agreed upon. For better or for worse.

∽

During the entire ride home and later during every moment they had rummaged through Ilaria's things, trying to find the best choices for days in hiding, Sasha had been holding her breath. Remi had opinions, she could see them all over his handsome face. But he was keeping them to himself, somewhat out of character.

Now they were back in the carriage, though, returning to Donville to deliver the small trunk and say their goodbyes, and he was just...*watching* her from across the rig.

She huffed out a breath of frustration. "I'd rather have you interrogate me than just stare at me like that. God's teeth, Remi, out with it."

He tilted his head. "I'm not the one who interrogates and we both know it."

She pursed her lips. "Fine, not interrogate, then. Share your lofty opinions."

There was a small hesitation before Remi leaned forward and took her hand. "Concerns," he said softly. "I have a great many concerns."

"Of course you do. Ilaria has been credibly threatened, even attacked. It's terrifying. And now she's going off with Captain Crawford, who we both know she's in love with and probably has been since he first appeared in Athawick all those years ago. It's an alarming situation."

Remi wrinkled his brow. "Of course I'm concerned about all those things," he said. "But what I was talking about is *you*, Sasha. Yes, Ilaria may have been the subject of threat in the past, but now it will be you in the crosshairs. Now it will be you forced to spend time in the company of a man you...well, perhaps I won't say *love* like you just did about Ilaria and Crawford. But you care for him and he for you."

She flinched. "I don't know what you're talking about."

"Don't you?"

"I can't," she corrected herself.

He glanced away from her. "I don't know why so many fools are so drawn in by love. It only seems to harm people, at least the people I care for."

She pondered that thought for a moment. "I think you malign the emotion."

He chuckled. "Love's champion even after it all. Should I call you Cupid now?"

To her surprise, she was able to smile even after everything that had happened. How she adored Remi for that ability to cut through tension and pain and bring levity.

"I have no desire to manipulate love with arrows, but I must defend it, yes. The people you care about must put duty before kinder emotions sometimes. I blame the constraints of that duty, not love."

"Well, you may leave me out of it. I'll continue to avoid it at all costs," Remi said.

"I hope that isn't true. I hope that you will one day get to experience the warmth of looking at a person you care deeply for. The sweetness of a kiss that is more than a kiss. The hope for when you see them next."

He tilted his head. "And what about the pain? Would you have me experience that, as well?"

"We will all experience pain in life, Remi. We already have." She squeezed his hand. "I would rather feel pain about something great, something wonderful, something meaningful. That pain is worth it."

His eyes darted away from hers and his discomfort was plain. She understood why. Remi had always dealt with painful emotion by retreating from it. By making it a joke or a lark. The very concept of embracing such a feeling, of the reward being worth the agony, was foreign to him.

The carriage stopped back at the Donville Masquerade and he sighed, almost in relief. "Know that I will do everything in my power to help you. To protect you both from whatever is out there trying to hurt Ilaria...but also from what you will lose."

Her eyes stung with tears at that simple statement. Coming from Remi, it meant a great deal. "Thank you," she whispered.

Then the carriage door opened and there was a bustle of activity to fill the time and space. She followed Remi back into the secret entrance to the club, but her mind was reeling as she did so.

She went through the motions for the next several hours as the family waited for the club to fully clear, the workers to go home. It also gave Ilaria extra time to recover from her head injury as the family doted on her. Sasha kept a close eye on Captain Crawford, observing how he never went too far from her side, even as he, Mr. Rivers, Remi and Grantham were formulating plans to uncover who had attacked Ilaria and how to keep Sasha safe.

At last dawn came and they moved down to the carriages. Each of the family members said their goodbyes to Ilaria, and then Sasha stepped up. They embraced, she clinging to Ilaria just so she could feel her warmth, her wholeness after this terrible ordeal.

"Be careful," Sasha whispered.

Ilaria leaned away and met her eyes. "You be careful. I cannot lose you."

Sasha's tears began to flow then. "I was about to say the same thing."

Ilaria kissed her cheek and then stepped away to Grantham, who was waiting to help her into the carriage she would take to the country with Captain Crawford. They spoke briefly and then he moved back to the family. "I'll be to the carriage momentarily. I want to speak to Captain Crawford."

The rest of them loaded into the vehicle. This time the queen sat on Sasha's side and wrapped an arm around her. Her dark eyes were filled with tears, but she did not shed them as they waited. "We will call Lord Bramwell and his mother to us tomorrow."

"Today," Remi corrected softly.

The queen flinched and looked out the window toward Ilaria's carriage. "Yes, I suppose this terrible night has turned to a new day. Then this afternoon we'll ask them to join us and tell them about the new plan. I do think they are decent people, and if Bramwell is serious about marrying Ilaria, he will want to keep her safe."

"He will," Sasha managed to whisper, ignoring Remi's pointed stare.

Before they could continue the conversation, Grantham joined them in the carriage, closed the door and tapped on the roof for the driver to take them home.

"Grantham—" his mother began.

He reached out and caught her hand. "Mama, I am exhausted, as I'm sure are all of you. I'm going to sit here in silence and try not to think about the terrible turn this entire visit to London has taken. And later we can discuss every single thing you wish to discuss. I promise."

Giabella didn't seem certain, but she settled back, tightened her arm around Sasha, and for the ride back to Bleaking House, all was silent.

But it was not well. And Sasha feared it might not ever be again.

～

Lady Bramwell was all but bouncing as the carriage made the last few turns to Bleaking House. She had been in this happy state for the last two hours, since they had received the message asking them to join the Athawick royal family for tea before the opera that night.

"To be called early can only be a good sign," his mother cooed.

Thomas nodded, but in truth he felt anxiety about the situation rather than excitement. The note that had been sent had a solemn air, in his assessment. Could it possibly be he was being called to the royal apartments so he could be taken to task over his night with Sasha? He hadn't thought anyone had seen them in the garden, but in a place like Bleaking House, someone was always watching.

It was possible everything was about to be torn to shreds before his mother. Strangely, he did not feel unhappy about that outcome, particularly. If Ilaria refused to have him…if the family was angry enough that they felt Sasha had been compromised…

But no, he couldn't think of the future that would make him so happy. It would only become a crushing disappointment if it worked out another way.

They arrived in the circular drive and were escorted to a parlor, where tea was already waiting. His mother went to look at one of the paintings near the sideboard, and Thomas shuffled to the window to look down on the bustling city below. No access to the back terrace from this room, and his usual escape with Sasha. Then again, that escape was no longer an option.

The door behind them opened and he turned, expecting to watch Ilaria and her mother enter the room. The queen did step inside, but following her was the king, and taking up the rear of their group was Sasha.

His breath caught. She was as beautiful as his favorite spot on his estate in Bramwell. Her pale blue gown with its scooped neckline and short, puffed sleeves clung perfectly to her curves and accentuated her luminous skin. Her hair was done in simple yet elegant style, with a few curls framing her cheeks. But her eyes, which were normally so bright and full of spark, seemed dull. She looked tired and worried.

And his own concerns about the nature of this meeting returned immediately. He stepped closer, squaring his shoulders for what might be the battle to come.

"Good afternoon, Lady Bramwell, Lord Bramwell," King Grantham said with a brusque nod for each of them as Thomas executed a bow and his mother a curtsey. "And thank you for coming."

"Your invitation was most welcome," Thomas's mother said, apparently oblivious to the mood of the room in her excitement. "It is always a privilege to see you, Your Majesties."

"Please sit," Queen Giabella said, motioning to the settee.

Lady Bramwell took a place there, and Sasha and the queen took a place on the settee opposite, but Thomas remained standing because the king did and was staring at him, his gaze unreadable.

"I'm afraid our reason for bringing you here today is not a happy one," the king continued. "It is in regards to Princess Ilaria and Sasha."

Thomas straightened his spine. And so he was correct. "Your Majesty, perhaps I should begin," he said. "Because I can see the issue written all over your face and I suppose it is time to address it directly."

Sasha's mouth dropped open and she stared at him, eyes wide. He met her gaze and she shook her head slightly, as if trying to put him off of the words about to fall from his lips. He appreciated the attempt to protect him, and perhaps herself, but if things had progressed so far as to warrant a meeting with the king and queen, certainly the confrontation could not be avoided.

King Grantham held up a hand. "My lord, I do not know what you wish to discuss, but I assure you it cannot be as important as the topic that brings us here today. What I am about to tell you is in the strictest confidence. Is that understood?"

Thomas wrinkled his brow. Now he was back to uncertainty about the topic about to be opened. He glanced down at his mother, who appeared as confused as he did.

"Y-yes," she stammered. "Of course, Your Majesty. We would each be the soul of discretion if need be. What is wrong?"

"You may notice that Princess Ilaria is not here this afternoon," the king said, glancing briefly at Sasha and his mother. "And that is because..." His jaw tightened and a flash of deep pain and concern moved over his expression. But then it was gone, controlled as this man controlled himself in all ways. "It is because she was attacked last night."

Thomas staggered back a step and his mother threw a hand over her mouth. "Attacked?" he repeated. "Great God. Is she well?"

"We are lucky that she escaped with minimal injury," the queen said, blinking at tears. "But it appears there is a continued threat against her."

"As such, we have removed her to a safe place while the danger is being investigated," King Grantham said.

Thomas stared. Though he felt no connection to Ilaria, the idea that she had been threatened, attacked, was still deeply troubling. And no wonder the family seemed so solemn. Even now, Sasha's head was bent, her shoulders slightly slumped. What a night she must have had. God, how he wished he could comfort her.

"I am so sorry," Lady Bramwell said. "Queen Giabella, is there anything we can do at all?"

King Grantham answered rather than his mother. "Since you ask, indeed there is."

He paced across the room, hands clasped behind his back, tension in every line of his body. "Right now we are very much in the dark about the nature of this threat. We have some theories, but not many facts. The best way we can determine those facts is to carry on as usual. The public must not be made aware that anything is different. And so we must carry on with our normal schedule of events."

Thomas shook his head. "A difficult plan when Princess Ilaria is not present."

"No, it isn't," Sasha said, the first time she had spoken since entering the room. She lifted her gaze to him. "You know why."

Queen Giabella pivoted to look at Sasha, her eyes wide with surprise. "How would Lord Bramwell know why, Sasha?"

She swallowed, her gaze still on him. "Lord Bramwell and I met the night of the welcome ball weeks ago," she said softly. "And he was clever enough to determine the nature of what I do occasionally for Ilaria. But you can see, he has never spoken of it to anyone, which proves his trustworthy nature."

Thomas flinched. He had no trustworthy nature, considering less than twenty-four hours ago he had been passionately kissing Sasha in the garden and longing to do so much more.

"What you do?" Lady Bramwell said. "I'm sorry, Miss Killick, I don't understand."

"Look at her, Mama," Thomas said, doing just that, drinking her in. "Do you not see how much she looks like Princess Ilaria? She would easily pass for her, especially to those who had only seen her from a distance or sketches of her in the paper."

His mother gasped. "I do see it. So you act as her...her..."

"Her double," Sasha said. "Yes. When it is needed. And I think this highly dangerous situation is the very definition of need."

"Sasha will join us at the opera tonight, styled to look like Ilaria," Queen Giabella said, linking her arm with Sasha's. "So that to the world, it will seem that all is well, that nothing has changed."

Thomas stared at Sasha once more, then to the queen and finally the king. What they were suggesting was becoming entirely clear to him and his chest began to burn with...with anger. Rage that rose up until he couldn't contain it.

"Bait," he bit out, fisting his hands at his sides. "You are making Sasha bait for a trap, aren't you?"

The king pivoted toward him, and there a fire in Grantham's eyes that matched Thomas's own. "I would mind your tone, my lord," he said softly. "And remember to whom you are speaking."

"Oh, I realize to whom I'm speaking perfectly well," Thomas said. "And I mean every word I say. How the hell can you all call

Sasha family—a daughter, a sister—and dare to put her in such danger? How can you put her into the firing line as if she means less than Ilaria? Answer me *that*, Your Majesty, and then we can discuss what I'm willing and not willing to do to participate in your scheme."

CHAPTER 14

S asha stared at Thomas as he stood toe to toe with Grantham, fists clenched at his sides, clearly ready to fight if need be. Fight for her. It was an experience she'd never truly had before.

Oh, her adopted family loved her, of that she was certain. But their position forced them never to show too much public emotion or make a scene. How many times had she heard Giabella gently remind her children that they represented an institution and therefore couldn't take things personally?

She'd taken that advice on herself, even though she represented nothing but herself and had never imagined she might have a knight ride up on a white steed to defend her honor.

And yet here he was, almost chest to chest with a king.

"You are overwrought," Grantham said, and it was evident he was only barely holding back from overreacting, himself.

"Thomas, dearest," Lady Bramwell said nervously, rising from the settee and holding out a hand as if she could steady him.

"I want an answer," Thomas said, ignoring her.

Sasha stood then, moved toward him because she couldn't stay away, no matter how it looked to the room. "They aren't asking me to do this, my lord. I offered."

Thomas's head pivoted toward her. "What?"

She met his stare, hoping he could see her, truly see her and understand her beyond his charming worry and defense of her. "Ilaria is my sister," she said. "This is my family. I love them. Normally I am not allowed any way to help them beyond standing at their side, offering support. My playing her double has only been for convenience, never truly tested in danger."

"And it never should be," Thomas said, running a hand through his hair. "If these people attacked the princess and you are going to be made to seem to be her, why in the world would you think they won't attack you?"

A frisson of fear worked through her, but she pushed it down and slowly faced the others. They were all staring at her and Thomas, with varying levels of understanding dawning. That was a problem to be dealt with on a different day, though.

"Do you think I might have a moment to talk with the earl alone?" she asked.

Grantham arched a brow. "What good would that do, Sasha?"

She moved toward the king and took his hands. He softened instantly when she did so, held her stare like her brother, not her sovereign.

"Please," she whispered, and explained no more.

He let his breath out in a huffy sigh. "Fine. I could use some air, and perhaps you can make the man understand what I don't seem capable of explaining. Ladies, would you join me? I can at least answer any questions Lady Bramwell has about this situation."

The queen and Lady Bramwell followed him from the room, though Sasha noticed that the dowager gave a long look over her shoulder at them before she departed last, leaving the door open.

Sasha sighed at the attempt at propriety and then crossed to shut it herself. She leaned against it for a moment, not turning back, because if she did, she feared she would launch herself at Thomas and only make things harder.

"Tell me what happened," he said when the moment had stretched out for too long.

She slowly looked at him. He deserved the truth. "Ilaria has been going to the Donville Masquerade with...with Captain Crawford."

His eyes went wide. "I will admit that of all the explanations I thought I'd hear about this, that was not on my list."

She cleared her throat. "Have you ever gone there, yourself?"

A flash of discomfort moved over his face. "Yes. Not often, but occasionally."

"What is it like?" she asked.

His nostrils flared and heat entered his stare. "I wish I could show you."

She blushed as she thought of the naughty details of the club that had been provided to Ilaria weeks ago. The ones Sasha could admit she had read over and over again, fantasizing. But always about Thomas. Probably always about Thomas, for the rest of her life, it seemed.

"Are you angry with her?"

He shook his head. "No. Although Ilaria and I have not discussed such matters, I have exchanged words with Crawford several times where she came up. It's obvious he cares deeply for her. I would not begrudge them their stolen moments." He did move toward her now and traced his fingers along her jawline. "I wish I could indulge in more of my own. Only the situation is different."

She nodded. "Yes."

"So she was attacked there." He dropped his hand to his side. "What is the rest?"

"Grantham fears it has to do with the rumblings of rebellion at home. Since Ilaria has been the focus of the attacks thus far, secreting her away for a short while seems best."

"With Crawford."

She flinched. "How did you know?"

"You looked guilty, even if you shouldn't. I have no feelings for Ilaria. I cannot be jealous. I don't care. If...when we marry, it would be different, of course, at least until heirs and spares were created. But the best I can hope for is to be her friend, to not resent her for what...what the circumstances of our union will take from me. And have her not resent me for what was taken from her."

Tears stung Sasha's eyes. "That sounds like a terrible future."

"I'm trying not to think about it too much," he admitted. "Instead I'm thinking about you and your safety. I've made myself clear, Sasha. I don't approve of you putting yourself in the line of fire for her."

"But it isn't up to you, Thomas. I'm making this decision on my own, for myself. I'm not asking you."

He blinked down at her, and then his expression softened. "I-I'm sorry. I'm being heavy handed, I know, and it isn't fair to you. You are entirely capable of making your own decisions."

The emotions she felt for him seemed to swell even higher at the thought that he would grant her such autonomy in her own choices, even the ones he disagreed with. She did not know a handful of men who would do so. Slowly she crossed the room, closing the distance between them so that they were close enough that their breath mingled as she looked up at him.

"You're afraid for me," she whispered.

He nodded, wordless.

"You want to protect me."

He nodded again. "I would do anything to protect you."

"And I would do anything to protect her," she said. "So yes, I'll put myself in danger. But Grantham and Mr. Rivers will ensure I am fully guarded. And...and you'll be there tonight at the opera, for my most public appearance."

He bent his head, and she watched his reactions ripple over his face. When he met her stare again, there was purpose there. Drive. She shivered to see it, to feel the hardness beneath the gentleness she'd come to know and adore.

"I will," he said. "And if protecting Ilaria is your primary goal, then protecting you will be mine. I will place myself between you and any danger. I promise you that, Sasha."

She lifted her palm to his chest and he visibly shivered at the touch. It was like electricity flowed between them, or that they were magnets, drawn together. She couldn't resist the current or the draw, and she found herself leaning up toward him.

His mouth met hers, and he let out a heady groan of desire and pleasure. She slid her hand up his chest, memorizing the feel of him beneath her palm, and cupped the back of his head. He deepened the kiss, slowed it as he seemed to savor the act for a moment. Then he broke away and they stood there, foreheads touching, her fingers tracing patterns into the back of his neck. Their panting breaths matched and she knew their desires did too.

She wanted him to lay her out on the settee and claim her. She wanted him to make it so that he could never face that horrible future with Ilaria. So that he would be pushed toward a happier one with her.

Selfish, she knew, and so she backed away just as the door to the parlor opened. Grantham led the mothers back into the room, his gaze dark as it flitted over her and Thomas. They were standing too close still, and she stepped away reluctantly.

"Have Lord Bramwell's concerns been appeased?" Grantham asked.

Thomas cast one look down at her before he said, "For the most part. Though I will ask for a full accounting from you, sir, as to how you intend to protect Miss Killick and my mother tonight."

Grantham appeared relieved that he would no longer be forced to argue. "I have a report on that in my study. If you want to come with me, I'll be happy to show it to you and discuss the finer points."

Thomas glanced at her one last time and then nodded. Before he and Grantham could excuse themselves, Sasha stepped forward. "If no one minds, I'd like to excuse myself, as well. I am still very tired after last night's excitement and must gather myself for the opera tonight."

Both those things were true, of course. But the real reason she didn't want to stay behind in the parlor was that she didn't feel strong enough to be grilled about Thomas by Lady Bramwell and Giabella, both of whom were watching her far too closely now.

"Of course, dearest," Giabella said after a brief pause. "Rest. Recover."

Sasha bobbed out a quick curtsey to the king and queen, then slipped from the room, somehow managing to stop herself from sending a last longing look toward Thomas as she went.

If she was going to survive this, in her heart as much as in her body, she would have to find a way to create a wall between herself and her feelings. A wall to keep them in. A wall to keep him out. And even though it felt impossible, she had to start now.

Thomas and his mother sat in their box at the opera, watching as the crowd filtered in below and all around in the other boxes. As of yet they had not been joined by the queen or Sasha, but the air was filled with electricity as the world awaited their appearance. More people were staring at him than had perhaps ever done so, even when his father's scandals had been at their height after his death.

It was uncomfortable to see them whisper behind their fans and know they were talking about him. It had been for years, though now there was less hostility in the responses. People who had been giving him the cut direct for years nodded to him. There was approval in the stares.

He bit back a sigh. *This* was why they were pushing the union, after all. This proof that he could be saved by Ilaria and her family. He would just have to let go of what he held most dear.

"Don't forget, my love, that you must refer to Miss Killick as Princess Ilaria tonight when she arrives, in case there are listening ears," his mother whispered.

He looked down at her to find her watching him closely. She worried her lip, and now he couldn't help the sigh. He was surprised that she hadn't brought up the topic of Sasha earlier, honestly. He'd tried to fill their drive away from Bleaking House with details about the night's security, but he'd felt her curiosity, her concern.

"I understand, Mama," he said softly.

She nodded, and for a moment he thought that might be the end of it. But then she cleared her throat. "It is only that you referred to her as Sasha a few times earlier today."

He shut his eyes. "Do you have something to say, then?"

"Just that I...I'm so sorry."

He jerked his gaze to her then. She did look utterly broken-hearted and guilty, and he leaned closer. "Why in the world are you sorry?"

"Because I know what it is like to face a future you didn't want. I hoped you might grow to care for the princess, that you two might see each other as more than a prudent match with benefits to both parties. I certainly never wished for you to...to grow to care about someone else. And I am sorry that protecting your family will lead to heartache for you in the end. And for her." She smiled sadly. "She seems a lovely person."

"She is," Thomas said softly. "I wish you could get to know her, come to like her as I do. I also wish things could be different. But they can't. And the only one who should be sorry about the pain I'm caused is me. The moment I felt..." He trailed off and shook his head. "The moment I felt any connection, perhaps I ought to have backed away, kept my distance. I could have protected us both. But I was selfish in the end. My father's son at last."

His mother caught his hand. "That, my love, you could never be. You are ten times the man he ever was. It is he who we should blame for all of us. He created situations that we must suffer through, that you must repair. It's unfair."

He smiled, appreciating her comfort, even though it wouldn't change anything for him. But having her support, having her understanding about not just his situation with the scandals but also with Sasha...it helped. He didn't feel quite so alone.

He would have told her that, but just then the curtain to their box was pushed back and Queen Giabella entered, followed by Sasha.

He caught his breath. She was styled to look like a princess, and she certainly did. The dress she wore was red with a bejeweled detailing along the apex of her body running from her bodice to the hem of her skirt. She had long, pale pink sleeves, but the shoulders of the gown were pushed slightly back, giving a tantalizing view of the curves there, along with a hint of décolletage. She wore a tiara, and it didn't appear to be a paste version like she had probably been wearing the first night he met her. This one was a halo style that sat gently amongst her curls. Diamonds all but dripped from it, along with pearls along each crest of the swirling gold.

But it wasn't all the pomp or circumstance or finery that drew him in. No, it was the way her eyes lit up when she looked at him. The way her full lips lilted into a slight smile. She was luminous, glorious, perfect, and he ached to pull her into his arms and show this leering crowd just how much he wished to make her his.

Of course, by doing that he would be claiming Ilaria in their eyes. And that dampened his spirits considerably.

He executed his bow and his mother her curtsey. "Queen Giabella, Princess Ilaria," Lady Bramwell said at full voice so that anyone listening would be further convinced of the subterfuge. "It is our great pleasure to be hosts to you tonight."

"And ours to join you," Queen Giabella answered.

She and Sasha stepped up to the balcony's edge, and the crowd roared its excitement as they waved. Thomas noted how Sasha flinched slightly at the enthusiastic greeting, her eyes darting around as if looking for any dangers that might lurk in the crowd. He had been doing the same since their arrival.

"How are you holding up?" Lady Bramwell asked Queen

Giabella, this time softer. The queen's expression gentled, and the two women stepped off slightly to have a private conversation.

"It is kind of her to offer friendship," Sasha said. "Giabella puts up such a strong face, sometimes those around her don't notice when she's in pain."

"It seems as if she raised you to do the same," he said gently.

Her expression crumpled slightly. "I suppose she taught us all. Her blood children, especially, have a great many expectations. They are raised with duty as the highest calling, and so was I."

A few of the lamps in the hall were lowered and candles extinguished, indicating that the opera was about to start. The queen and Lady Bramwell sat first, and Thomas's stomach clenched as he realized that he and Sasha had been positioned to be next to each other with their mothers on either side. He motioned her to her place and then took his beside her.

God, he was so close he could feel the warmth of her, smell the sweetness of her hair and skin. This was going to be torture.

CHAPTER 15

Thomas didn't know how long he and Sasha sat in the dark together, the music rising and falling in passion around them. In truth, he couldn't have even named what opera they were supposedly watching, not for all the gold in England. He was too focused on the woman at his side to pay attention to anything or anyone else.

For a while, he thought Sasha was much more attentive to the opera than he. After all, she stared straight ahead, never glancing at him as he was at her. He would have accepted that was how it had to be, that it was even better that way. There was no use for both of them to be tangled up in regret or desire.

At least that was what he told himself until her hand crept out and found his.

He caught his breath as their gloved fingers intertwined, the warmth of her blissfully seeping through him at last. She let out a little shuddering sigh as she stroked her fingers against his.

He glanced at his mother on his left, but she was entirely enamored with the show, as it appeared the queen was on the other side. That ought not to have mattered, of course. He ought to have simply held Sasha's hand in a chivalrous way or, better for both of them, gently set it back on her lap and tried to distance himself a little.

But there were so few chances left.

Because the sleeves of her gown were long, her gloves were short, and he was glad for that. It was far easier to carefully unfasten the little pearl button on her wrist. He felt the flutter of her pulse increase there when his fingers brushed the sensitive flesh.

She glanced over at him in the near darkness and he inclined his head. A question. She hesitated but then nodded. His answer, and he had never been so happy for consent in his life.

He slowly peeled her glove away, revealing her soft skin beneath. He traced the center of her palm with his fingertips, then the length of her fingers before he turned her hand over and trailed over her knuckles. He slid his thumb around to caress her wrist again, let it slide under the silky fabric of her sleeve briefly.

Her breath was very short now, and she looked at him again. His desperation to be closer was reflected on her face, and it took everything in him not to lean in and kiss her. No one else in the theatre might notice that, but the mothers certainly would. There were enough problems in that arena—no use causing them to react with advice and admonishment.

So instead he released her hand, gently setting it back in her lap. She bent her head and he felt her regret coming off of her in waves. She didn't want this to end any more than he did, which gave him that small thrill that drove him forward, duty be damned, propriety be damned. He needed this, he was going to take it.

He unfastened his own gloves and secreted them into his lap. She glanced up at him when he did so and her eyes went wide. He smiled, he knew a little wickedly, and extended his hand between them once again. This time there was no hesitation. She immediately returned her bare hand to him.

They both shivered when skin touched skin. Slightly rough on soft, body heat mingling even if it wasn't the sweaty, passionate joining of his every dream of late.

It felt like a lifetime since he'd touched her, despite it being less than twenty-four hours since he kissed her in the garden, less than twelve since the parlor that very afternoon. But it wasn't enough. It would never be enough, he feared. He would be chasing the feelings she caused in him for years, decades, his entire life. He doubted he would ever find a desire so strong or feelings so sweet and sharp again.

But he couldn't think of that now. Right now he just wanted to focus on the way her fingers curled around his, sliding up their length until his cock started to tingle. Jesus, this had been a bad idea. And the best idea.

Their hands warred, tangling and retreating, stroking and soothing. Her breath was short, his was even shorter. All he could think about was closing the distance between them, yanking her from that chair to the floor and making her come. God, he wanted to see that, to feel her flex against him as she moaned out his name over and over and over until it was the only word left, until nothing else mattered, until they were lost in each other, never to be found.

The orchestra below played one last triumphant note, and then the lights in the theatre began to rise, signaling the intermission. She jerked her hand from his, cheeks high in color.

"Isn't it a wonderful show?" Lady Bramwell said, leaning around her son to talk to Sasha and the queen.

"It truly is," Queen Giabella said. "I've always been such a fan of theatre." She glanced at Sasha, who was still sitting, her head bent and her cheeks flared with color. "Oh, dearest, you dropped your glove."

Sasha grabbed it from the floor near her feet. "Oh...goodness. Yes, I-I got overly warm," she explained, not looking at the queen, nor anyone else in their box, including him. "I removed one of my gloves in the hope I could cool off."

"It *does* get warm in these boxes, and when the passions of the presentations are so high, it's even worse," Lady Bramwell said. "You do look a bit flushed. Perhaps we should step into the vestibule."

They rose to their feet together, but Queen Giabella shook her head at the suggestion. "Unfortunately, I fear Sasha ought not to go into the crowd. Some people out there will have surely met Ilaria, and up close they will see the difference. But I should go out for appearances. And will you two join me?" she asked Thomas and his mother.

"Of course," Lady Bramwell said. She squeezed Sasha's bare hand, and she flinched ever so slightly at the motion. "We'll fetch you a cool refreshment, my dear."

"Thank you, my lady, that is so kind," Sasha said, her gaze flitting to Thomas at last.

They held stares for a brief moment, and then he offered his arm to lead the queen past the guards stationed at the door and away from the box, his mother close behind. As they entered the milling crowd and all the eyes turned on them, he straightened. He really needed to get himself together if he didn't want to cause a scene, or at least not have his mother realize what he was doing, how he was feeling.

Later he could resolve all the passion that touching Sasha had caused. Later, alone, he was most definitely going to do that.

∾

Sasha sagged against the balcony barrier with a sigh as the others left her alone. She felt flushed and overheated, and though the others had accepted her explanation of why, the truth still throbbed in her. It was pleasure. Deep, powerful, erotically charged pleasure that made her skin hot and her legs clench and her hands shake at her sides.

Thomas had done that not by kissing her, not by touching her intimately, not by taking her...but by stroking his fingers along hers in the dark. Just that simple act and she found herself on the edge of powerful release, on the cusp of humiliating herself by begging him to do more. To take everything. If the mothers hadn't been there, she knew she might have done just that.

A few women were watching her from down below the box, and she gave a weak wave that sent them tittering with glee. God's teeth, she had to remember her role here tonight. It wasn't as Thomas's paramour, it wasn't even as herself. She was playing Ilaria and she had to represent herself as such.

"Sasha?" Her name was said softly enough that it didn't carry to anyone listening. She turned back to find Thomas had returned from the assembly hall gathering and was standing watching her.

Their gazes held and she shook her head. "That was..."

"I know," he murmured, stepping closer.

She looked around. People were still watching from the other boxes, from below, even a few of those milling around on the stage were glancing up from time to time.

"Be careful," she gasped.

"Normally I am," he said, but he stopped coming to her. She was both relieved and disappointed. "Normally I am always careful, always prudent, always guarded. But with you...with you it's hard to be. You attract all my attention, make me forget everything else."

She swallowed hard. He couldn't know what those words meant to her. Perhaps she should tell him.

"My—my whole life I have not been the center of any world," she said. "The royal family took me in...well, most of it did, and in their company I was never treated as anything but a sister, a friend, a loved one. But outside...everyone knew I didn't fully belong. I've had no real place for most of my life. When people have looked at me, it was for the connection I might provide, rarely for myself. But you don't care about that."

"No. I don't care about any connection you might provide," he agreed. "You are more than enough all on your own."

Her eyes stung with tears and she blinked them away. "Thomas," she murmured. "You don't know how much I want...I want..."

He nodded. "I do know. Because I want it too. I want to touch your body like I touched your hand. I want to feel you shudder with pleasure. I want to learn your taste and the way your skin looks when it's flushed with sweat. I want you. Desperately."

The last word hung between them, filled with double meaning. She bent her head. *"Desperately."*

The curtain to the box pulled back and the mothers returned. They were both smiling, and Sasha forced one of her own. "I assume the ruse is being accepted?" she asked softly, ever mindful of those listening.

Queen Giabella took her hand and squeezed. "Indeed, it seems to be. That is one shining beacon after the last horrible day."

"You're doing wonderfully," Lady Bramwell encouraged. "A few people commented how lucky Thomas is in his choice of companion."

Sasha fought with all her might not to recoil from that statement. Of course that was the purpose of tonight. To keep the public unaware of Ilaria's absence, but also to continue the journey toward Thomas's marriage to the princess. Sasha was a stand-in. She would never truly have what her sister would eventually have.

The lights to the opera house lowered one by one and a chime rang, signaling the end to intermission as the orchestra settled in and began to play a low tone of music to welcome the revelers back. She took her place next to Thomas again, but she tugged her glove back on as she did so and then folded her hands in her lap.

He seemed to get the message, for he did the same. The lights went down, the opera continued with its star-crossed lovers destined for heartbreak. A tale that was a little too close to home in the end.

But a tale Sasha couldn't avoid. She had to stop pretending that she could.

The opera had not yet ended when Queen Giabella, Lady Bramwell, Sasha and Thomas exited out a private space normally reserved for the Regent or the King. Their carriages were waiting there.

"I'm sorry we could not see the end of the show," Queen Giabella said. "But we could not risk being seen too closely."

"Most operas end the same at any rate," Sasha said softly. "With separation and death and a lovely aria."

Thomas glanced her way. She had been very quiet since intermission, leaning away from him. A barrier they both needed, yes. But one that stung. Now he saw the sadness in her eyes, the brokenness that he so wanted to fix.

"What are your next steps?" his mother asked. "Is there any way we can help?"

"My first instinct is to limit any further public events for Sasha playing Ilaria. It is too big a risk to her." The true warmth in the queen's expression when she looked at Sasha was evident. Thomas was pleased that Sasha could return the expression, even weakly.

"But it is the risk I am taking of my own volition, Your Majesty," Sasha said, reaching out to take the queen's hand. "If it will help Ilaria, I will do...I'll do anything."

She looked his way before she dropped her gaze to the ground, cheeks bright.

Lady Bramwell shook her head in awe. "That you are so willing to put yourself in danger speaks of your enormous character, my dear. You were wonderful tonight. So brave and so certain of yourself."

"Thank you, my lady," Sasha said softly.

"I do like the response our coming out tonight created," the queen mused. "If you do not mind continuing the role, perhaps Lord Bramwell could call again in a day or two, assuming Ilaria has not returned in the interim. He and Sasha could go for a ride in the park."

Thomas caught his breath. Alone with Sasha in the park. Oh, there would be guards, of course, but they would have to trail behind since his curricle was only meant for two. They would truly get to be alone together.

"A fine idea," he choked out. "I'll send word to make the arrangements tomorrow morning."

Sasha looked at him fully then, her dark eyes soft with worry, but also desire. That cocktail was the same one in his own chest. But damn everything and everyone else, he was going to take the time he was offered. Steal it.

They parted ways at last. Sasha only nodded slightly as they did so. He frowned as he helped his mother into their carriage and followed her in. As they began to drive, he prepared himself for her to launch into a recap of the nights events. But instead she settled back with a satisfied smile and was quiet for the short ride to her home. After she had gone, Thomas was swept back to his estate.

He entered the foyer and found his estate manager, Gillingham, waiting for him. The man had served as his man of affairs for years and was the adoptive father of Aurora's husband, Nicholas. He was also the best of men, the only reason why Thomas had *any* chance of recovering his financial standing. So yet another person thrilled at the idea of this future union. Yet another person depending upon it.

They talked briefly, though Thomas was entirely separate from the words. He did not recall the topic of conversation the moment he left Gillingham and headed up to his chamber.

He pushed into the room, and only when he had shut the door behind him did he drag in the first full breath of the last few hours. He shrugged from his jacket and threw it on the ground behind him with little thought. The placard of his trousers was next, and he shoved aside the errant tails of his shirt to find his cock half hard already. A state he had been in since touching Sasha hours ago.

He let himself think of her, think of the way her breath caught when he touched her. Think of how she tasted when he kissed her. He spit on one hand and stroked himself, leaning against the bed with the other. Pleasure he had been denied all night arced up the length of his cock, settled into his balls, spread throughout his entire system. He drowned in it and in thoughts of her. Always her, forever her.

When he came, it was hard and fast. He grunted out her name as he sagged on the edge of the bed, a mess physically. A bigger mess in the places where no one could see.

He sank down on his knees next to the bed and sighed. Control had always been the hallmark of his life. He had to find a way to get back to that, or else he would find himself surrendering to imprudent desires that would only make it worse for them both.

CHAPTER 16

It was the second afternoon since the night at the opera, but Sasha was still unable to remove the memories from her mind. Alone in her chamber at night, she tossed and turned, her palm tingling as she recalled Thomas stroking his fingers along its center. And his words rang in her ears. Words of acceptance, of desire, of a future she had to keep pushing away so it wouldn't mob her with regret.

Alone in her bed, she had touched herself, finding pleasure and knowing deep within her soul that it was nothing like what she would find with him. Only she couldn't.

And now she would have to spend a nearly unchaperoned afternoon with him, for he would arrive soon for their ride around Hyde Park. She had been dressed and primped and curled to anyone's version of perfection, as close to Ilaria as was humanly possible. She stood alone in the middle of the chamber and stared at herself in the full-length mirror. When she turned her head just so it was if she vanished. There was only the illusion she was trying to create.

It should have made her happy, but it didn't.

There was a light knock on her door and she turned toward it to find Greenly there. "Lord Bramwell has arrived," he said softly. "He and the queen await you in the Blue Room."

She nodded and drew in a long breath as the butler stepped away. Then she made her way to the next stop alone this terrible road. One she feared and longed for in equal measure.

At the door to the Blue Room downstairs, she hesitated. It was partly open and she could hear Giabella and Thomas talking softly.

"...never anything but my own daughter," Giabella was saying softly.

Sasha bent her head. She loved that the queen was so vocal in her support, so absolute in her connection. It had always meant the world to her.

"I understand," Thomas said back. "I will protect her with my life."

Sasha's breath caught and she forced a smile to her face as she entered the room. "I'm so sorry to make you both wait," she said, hoping she sounded light and airy rather than nervous and uncertain.

They both turned toward her and her breath caught. Their expressions were so similar, twin versions of deep regard and concern, protectiveness. She expected it from Giabella, of course, but to see that same connection from Thomas was...*wonderful* and terrible and everything in the world to her.

"We have waited but a moment," the queen said. "Oh, you do look lovely in that dress, dearest."

"You do," Thomas agreed, his voice a little rough, the tone of it dancing up her spine in a way that made her entire body get warmer.

She cleared her throat and did a little turn at the door. "Do you think I look enough like Ilaria to pass in the park?"

Giabella approached, seemingly unaware of the tension between Thomas and Sasha. She caught Sasha's hands and squeezed both gently. "You do." She turned back toward Thomas. "Now you will have a carriage with guards leading you into the park and another following you, along with a few guards sprinkled throughout."

Sasha forced a laugh. "Will there be anyone in attendance who isn't working for Grantham?"

Giabella tilted her head. "You know your brother—once he has an idea in mind, he takes it to its highest level. You should be protected." Her breath caught. "I-I hope you will be protected."

Sasha leaned forward to press a kiss to the queen's cheek. It had been a long time since she'd done something so familiar, and Giabella blushed with pleasure. "Mama," she said softly, eliciting another smile. "I will be protected, by everything you have listed and by Th—by the earl. We will be careful, I swear it to you."

Giabella swiped at a tear and turned away. "Off you go then," she said. "I'll await your return."

Sasha took a step toward her, but Thomas reached out, touching her arm gently. She turned to face him and he shook his head gently before he offered his arm. She took it, electric awareness ripping through her once more when she did so. Together they left the room and moved through the foyer to the open door out to the drive. A fine curricle was parked there, drawn by two white horses. A footman stepped up to help, but Thomas waved him off and took her hand himself, helping her up to the high seat. Once he had joined her, he nickered at the horses and off they went, out of the gate and onto the street. They only had to turn a corner and enter the park, of course, but she took a deep breath as if they had just started an enormous journey.

She glanced toward him. "I feel as though I hardly greeted you," she said. "Good afternoon, Thomas."

"I was just as guilty of impolite behavior. I fear the way I wished to greet you was not the way I should." He glanced toward her briefly. "Good God, but you are beautiful."

She bent her head and felt her cheeks heat. "Thank you," she whispered.

For a short time, they rode in silence, entering the park. It was a fine day, with birds chirping, and visitors on picnic blankets and walking in pairs or groups dotted the park's large grassy area. All eyes turned toward their vehicle as they rode by and Sasha forced herself to wave as people called out to her as "Your Highness" or "Princess Ilaria".

She sighed. "The ruse is working, at least. I hope that will make it worth it."

"Did you only agree to come out today in order to further the ruse?" he asked.

She glanced toward him. The reins were loose in his hands and his body language seemed relaxed enough, but there was a tension to his jaw. Her answer meant something.

"I could tell you that," she said, sliding her hand across the miniscule distance that separated them, letting her fingertips slide briefly against his knee. He stiffened as she did so, his breath coming short just as it had in the opera house. "I could lie and tell you that everything is for Ilaria, as my family believes. But you know better, Thomas. I wanted to see you today. I needed to see you."

He said nothing, but turned the horses down a narrow side lane that led from the main path. The carriage that drove ahead of them didn't notice their exit from the route and kept on, but the following carriage pulled in behind them, parking at the top of the side road and stopping there to keep any other traffic from joining them.

Thomas pulled the carriage to a stop at the bottom of the side trail, positioning them behind a small cluster of trees. Sasha could only barely see their handlers through the branches and assumed the guards were similarly blocked. It wasn't total privacy, of course, but a little of it. As much as they could hope to have.

He stripped his gloves off just as he had in the opera house, and she unfastened her own with haste. When his fingers caught hers, she let out a shuddering sigh. "This is so unfair," she murmured, more to him than to herself.

"It is," he grunted, twisting to face her more directly. "I should have refused, but here we are. Tormenting ourselves as we do."

"At some point we'll have to stop," she whispered, leaning a little closer. Almost too close, but not quite. Still, she could feel the faint stir of his breath on her cheek. She wanted to feel it everywhere else.

"But not today," he said, his voice rough again. Hard.

She swallowed. "Every day since we last met, I've thought about what you said to me in the opera box that night. About what you wanted...what you wanted to do to me."

He bent his head. "I shouldn't have said those things to a lady."

She wrinkled her brow. "I liked it."

"But you're an innocent and—"

She shook her head. "Fascination with women's virginity is a puritanical obsession my country does not share, Thomas. I have known about pleasure at my own hand for years and haven't shied away from the concept of it with a lover. You aren't burning my innocent mind with your wicked thoughts."

He stared at her. "So you've been with a man."

She nodded. "Yes. Though I'd hardly call him a man, honestly. He got close to me in order to make himself visible to the last king. A foolish notion considering I was not visible to him, myself. We did consummate the union before I realized he was only using me. So I dismissed him and haven't spoken to him since." Thomas was still staring and she swallowed. "Does that change your view of me?"

"Not at all. I understand you more, and that pleases me." He frowned. "Though I hate that some fool didn't worship you as you deserved to be worshipped."

"How would you worship me, Thomas?" she whispered, her hands shaking.

There was a long pause. So long that she thought he would refuse to answer. Perhaps it was best, after all, she was inviting torture by having him tell her wicked things. It wouldn't make this better.

"I would want to see you," he said at last. "I would want to take every stitch of clothing off your body so I could see you and memorize every line of your body. And then I would touch you. Find all the places that make you shiver, make you moan, make you wet for me, ready for me."

"With your hands?" she asked, barely able to make coherent words. "With your mouth?"

"Both," he groaned. "I would take my time, too. Make you beg. Make you shake. And just when you couldn't take anymore, I would make you come. With my mouth, with my fingers and finally, finally, with my...my..."

"Your cock," she said softly. "I told you that you don't need to protect me, not from what I want to hear."

"Yes," he said. "With my cock."

They stared at each other, both flushed with these wicked words, with the desperate images they created. She felt weak with her desire for him, desperate for what she wanted, what she couldn't have. Or couldn't she? After all, Ilaria was off with Captain Crawford and she doubted the princess was denying herself. Couldn't she, too, have just a taste of what this was...what it could be?

"The...the king and queen and Remi are going out tonight," she said softly. "Some state supper. I'll...I want to see you. Not styled like Ilaria, not pretending like we are now. Thomas, I need to see you."

His pupils dilated. He knew what she meant, what she was asking for. What she was offering. He cleared his throat. "You are temptation embodied, and I may not be strong enough to deny you."

"Then don't," she pleaded.

He drew his hand from hers with a shiver. "It would be wrong and imprudent to put you in that position, considering what our future...our shared future...holds. Considering that we would have to see each other every—"

She shook her head. "I'm not going to stay with Ilaria."

His brow wrinkled. "What?"

Her hands were shaking. It seemed she had made the decision

that had been plaguing her since her conversation with Dash days ago. The only decision she could make, truly.

"I've talked to Dash about it—Mr. Talbot, he's on the queen's staff, her private secretary," she said, wishing she didn't sound so breathless. "He's offered me the ability to return to Athawick after Ilaria...after Ilaria marries. I will join the queen's staff, with a thought that I could eventually become secretary for the next queen. Grantham's wife."

His lips parted in shock. "So you...you wouldn't be here with Ilaria."

"No," she said. "I wouldn't."

They held gazes for a long moment, and then he let out a long, shuddering breath. "If we want to be alone, it would be better to go somewhere that is not Bleaking House."

She nodded. "Yes. I could easily sneak in and out. No one is watching me, in truth, and I've been helping Ilaria do it since..." She trailed off and shook her head. "I'm sorry, I shouldn't have said that."

His expression softened. "Ilaria isn't my concern." He glanced toward the guards on the path and she did the same. They were beginning to look restless. Their time for this discussion was running out. "I could meet you in the alleyway behind the estate. We could...we could go to my home."

Everything began to feel unsteady as she stared up at him. His home. His home. *His* home. "Could we not be caught there?"

He cleared his throat. "I will give the staff the night off. Most will happily go to spend a night with friends or family. The rest will go to bed early. I'll eat at my club...if I can eat at all."

She nodded, perhaps too swiftly and desperately, but it didn't matter that she showed her vulnerability. She trusted this man with her heart...her soul. She knew what that meant, but refused to name it, even now as she planned to rendezvous with him.

"Yes," she whispered. "Ten?"

"Ten."

"Your Highness," came a voice from the path.

It jolted them from their conversation and Sasha scooted away from Thomas a fraction as he turned the rig and jogged the horses back to the main path. They didn't speak of their plans the rest of the ride. She was too fearful to do so, in case she might talk him out of his agreement. In case she would find her own reasons to be prudent and wise, rather than daring and bold. Instead, they spoke of the weather and books as she waved to those who stared at them. She was well aware that her bright smile and the closeness with which she sat with Thomas was only feeding the narrative that he and Ilaria would wed and be happy.

But in that moment she didn't care what fiction she was creating. She only cared that the reality tonight would be him and her. Together, alone, able to give each other what they both wanted, needed for a stolen moment in time.

He eventually steered the rig back to Bleaking House and pulled to a stop. They stared at each other a moment before the footmen appeared to help her down.

"Ten," he said, repeating the time they had chosen to meet.

She nodded. "I'll be there."

She moved to get down, and he caught her hand. "If you change your mind, I'll understand."

She shook her head. "Ten, Thomas. Don't be late," she whispered, then stepped from the rig and went into the house. Somehow she managed not to look back, but she felt his gaze on her with every step. Felt the heat of him just as she would in a handful of hours when she could finally have a brief taste of everything she would eventually lose.

There had never been a night in the history of nights that had ever been longer than the one Sasha endured after she left Thomas. Every conversation seemed to drone on, the supper she'd shared with Dash had been unending, even the time after had dragged as she pretended to read one of the books he had helped her pick at Mattigan's Bookshop. She could only continue to stare at the clock, willing the time to pass.

But finally there were the ten chimes to indicate it was time for their assigned meeting. Sasha bolted from her chamber, hands shaking. She made her way downstairs almost blindly, tripping over the edge of the carpet as she reached the hall.

"If someone sees you, you're just getting a book. If someone sees you, you're just getting a book," she repeated over and over to herself under her breath.

But no one was looking for her. Most of the servants were in their private quarters by now. The ones still up were making preparations for the return of the royal family after their state affair, or readying for the next day's schedule. Sasha was nothing to them and so she was able to move with invisibility through the house and out the back to the garden.

She began to run the farther she got from the house, her heart pounding so loudly she feared Thomas would hear it even from a distance. At last she reached the gate and unlatched it, slipping into the alleyway there.

Thomas was standing beside the same rig he had escorted her in earlier in the day, though he had pulled up the shade to give them more privacy. Certainly, she was no longer styled as Ilaria to draw attention. When she moved toward him, he did the same, and then she was in his arms, lifting to his mouth, their lips colliding like two people starved. And she was, in truth, starved for his touch, starved for his taste, starved for this wicked connection.

They broke apart, both panting in the moonlight. "Hurry," she whispered, grasping his hand.

"Yes," he agreed, and they moved to the curricle. He helped her up and then they were off.

For a while, he was quiet. Not pensive, she didn't think, but simply unspeaking. He cleared his throat at last. "If Ilaria was sneaking out through that gate, going off to meet with her...her friend, I'm surprised King Grantham hasn't put a lock and four guards on it."

She smiled. "He likely would, but I think he would be thwarted. After all, it isn't just the family who uses the gate, is it? There's a whole household of maids and footmen and who knows who else who go to meet their lovers."

He cleared his throat softly at that word, and she shifted as heat entered her cheeks. They had said so many more passionate things to each other over the last few nights, but now the reality was so near. Lovers. They could be lovers, at last.

"Some forces cannot be stopped," he said softly.

They rode in silence again, but only for a few moments before he turned the vehicle into a drive and parked it there. She gazed up at the house, which was a beautiful white-stuccoed building with black wrought-iron terraces along every front facing window. Though it wasn't quite as large as Bleaking House, it was a fine prospect.

"Is this it?" she whispered.

He nodded.

"But it isn't five minutes drive to Bleaking House," she mused.

He laughed. "No, it isn't. Why does that shock you?"

"I don't know. I just never knew you were so close."

His gaze grew darker at that statement and he offered her his arm. "Come, let's go inside."

She allowed him to lead her through the door and into the foyer. The house was quiet and no servants rushed to assist, just as he had promised. For that she was pleased. She liked the idea of a little world that was just their own.

He drew her down a long hallway and stopped, a look of almost confusion on his face.

"Why the expression?" she asked.

He shook his head. "I'm just not certain where a person...does what we're about to do."

She wrinkled her brow. "The...the bedroom is traditional, Thomas."

He chuckled briefly at her words but he didn't move her toward his chamber. "Indeed, it is. But...let's go into the parlor. Talk for a moment."

She fought the spike of frustration that moved through her at that moment. All they were ever allowed to do was talk, and right now she didn't want words. But then again, this was Thomas's home, a place that would reveal so much about him. So she let him guide her into the parlor without argument.

He moved to pour her a drink and she smiled as she walked around the room, looking at miniatures of his mother, his sister and her husband, Mr. Gillingham, that were lined up on the mantelpiece. This was a family room, rather than a strictly public one. A place where Thomas would mainly gather with those he knew and loved.

And he'd brought her here. She shivered at the thought.

"Sasha," he said softly. He had poured the drinks but they sat untouched on the sideboard.

"Yes?" Her voice trembled.

"We're going to need to some rules, I think."

She laughed even though her heart was racing. "I should have known you would want rules. Very well, what are they?"

"I can't...take you," he whispered.

She stared at him. She'd been allowing herself that fantasy all afternoon, but when he said those words, she knew they were true. "Because of her," she whispered.

He nodded. "The same reason we can't do this in my bedchamber. God knows that is what I want, but if I do..."

"It will make the rest too hard," she agreed. "I agree. But you'll still...you want to...?"

"Make you come?" he asked. "As I promised? Oh yes, if you'll allow it. Will you?"

She nodded immediately. "Only I want to do the same for you."

His eyes widened. "I can't ask—"

"You didn't ask," she interrupted. "I'm offering. I refuse to take no as an answer. If you are to give, I want to give equally in return. That is not up for negotiation."

"I see that you were raised by royalty now," he said with a chuckle. "Very well, I acquiesce to this great sacrifice you are suggesting. The one I've been fantasizing about since the first moment I met you."

"On the terrace?" she gasped out in surprise.

"Yes."

She moved toward him slowly, loving how he tracked every movement. He didn't pull away as she rested her hands against his chest, sliding them up, feeling muscle beneath the surface. She lifted up on her tiptoes and brushed her lips to his gently. "Any other rules, my lord?"

"All the blood is rushing from my brain, so I cannot think of a one," he said. "Do you have any?"

She worried her lip. "This is a moment we're stealing out of time, Thomas. So I think my only rule is that we...we can't talk about it again after it happens. We can't moon over each other and have regrets about the moment when our futures diverge. Can you do that?"

She could see in his eyes that he couldn't. Nor could she, if she were honest with herself. But she was going to try. And as he nodded, her relief was so powerful she felt weak from it. But he was her support, he was her strength.

"Then will you please kiss me? Please."

CHAPTER 17

I t seemed to break him, that one little word. *Please.* Thomas moved toward Sasha and cupped her cheeks as his mouth collided with hers. She lifted into him, whimpering his name into his mouth, gripping his jacket with both hands like she could somehow tug their bodies together and get even closer.

He backed her across the room, their mouths never parting, the passion of the kiss only increasing. The back of her legs hit the settee and he gently lowered her onto the cushions, dropping to his knees before her. His fingers came into her hair, loosening the pins that held her style in place. When he dragged the tips along her scalp, she broke their mouths, arching back with a shudder of pleasure.

But he wouldn't let her pull away. He claimed her mouth again, and when he kissed her this time there was purpose, there was drive, there was a heat she could tell he had been holding back all this time. Trying to protect them both from the animal desires that flowed between them. Now that last barrier was gone. His tongue drove deep, swirling around her own, making her tingle from the roots of her hair to the sensitive nerves between her legs to the curling toes in her slippers. She felt alive, electric, and she never wanted it to stop.

"I want to see you," he muttered as his lips left hers and slid across her jawline, over her throat. "God, I want to see you."

"The dress buttons in the front," she gasped as he sucked lightly where her pulse fluttered. "So see me."

He pulled back and looked down at her, then nodded and unfastened the top button of her gown. She watched him as he made quick work of them all, then helped him tug the dress down to her waist. She was wearing a chemise beneath, but the soft, silky fabric was so finely made that it was almost sheer, and he stared at her. She smiled up at him, then dropped first one strap away and then the other, baring herself from the waist up.

"Good God," he muttered, dragging his fingertips down her collarbone and finally allowing them to crest over her breasts. She arched against him, groaning as pleasure ricocheted through her, sending a solid pulse to settle between her legs.

He bent his head and swirled his tongue around one nipple, tightening the sensitive flesh even further. She dug her fingers into his hair, holding him there as he licked and stroked and finally sucked hard, harder, and she let out a keening cry of pleasure. He looked up at her, dark eyes focused on her response as he slowed his tongue, lessened the pleasure, drew it out until she was lifting her hips toward him in silent request, demand.

He switched his attention to the opposite breast, cupping the weight, massaging gently and, at last, licking her flesh, sucking her nipple. She found herself tugging at his hair, holding him hard against her for more, more, more.

He smiled as he glanced up at her, and she bit back a laugh at how utterly mussed he now was. "I've destroyed your hair," she whispered.

He shook his head. "Good. I very much look forward to seeing that in the mirror later and being able to track every one of your fingers in the paths. Being able to remember that you did that when

I was making you moan my name. And, I hope, when I make you forget your own."

She blinked down at him, for his words were utterly hypnotic. She never wished to be free from this spell. "Then make me forget, Thomas. Make me forget everything but you and us and this."

He nodded, pushing up closer to kiss her once more. Then he returned his mouth to her breasts, lavishing her with attention, with the rough stroke of his tongue, with the faint scrape of the shadow of his whiskers.

Somehow in the fog, she noticed that his hands were moving. Down her stomach, across her hip, down her thigh. He caught the hem of her skirt and began to shove, piling the silky fabric as he revealed more and more of her.

When the dress was bunched around her stomach, she rested back on her elbows, watching him through a hooded gaze. Her heart was pounding so fast, she feared he could hear it, or feel it as her pulse fluttered beneath her skin like butterfly wings.

He focused his attention to her lower body, caressing her hips through her drawers, licking his lips like she was a feast and he a starving man. There was something about that dark flick of his tongue that made her shiver.

"May I remove these?" he asked, his voice shaking like her body was shaking.

She nodded and he untied the flimsy drawstring. She lifted her hips to help him remove the cotton, and then she was naked from the waist down, totally stripped of all propriety.

Part of her wanted to cover herself. He was staring so intently that she felt completely exposed. But the other part, the very wicked part, wanted to show him more. Wicked won, because this was the only night it could. She slowly parted her legs wider to let him see how slick she was with need, how ready she was for whatever he would do to pleasure her.

He let out a sound that felt like it came from the pit of his very soul. Low and harsh and deep, it rumbled through the entire room and called to her blood, heating everything, shrinking the chamber down until it was just him, just her. Just this.

He placed a hand on each of her thighs, pushing them even wider, creating a space there that he eased into. His fingers were warm against her flesh, warmer still when he squeezed gently, branding her with a mark that would fade away, disappear before this night was over.

The mark he made on her heart was something else entirely. But no, she wouldn't think of that. She wouldn't ruin this with maudlin thoughts. Tonight was for pleasure, nothing more.

"Please," she whispered, unable to find her full voice even though no one would hear her in the empty house.

"I intend to please you," he promised.

Thomas had always appeared to be an entirely decent man. She looked at him across ballrooms and terraces and in the moonlight and she always saw something upright, someone responsible and thoughtful.

Tonight, though, that man was gone, hidden for a little while by a rogue who had a twinkle in his eye. A man who knew how to make her quake and intended to do it, slowly and torturously until she came entirely undone on his settee.

As if to accentuate that point, he lowered his head toward her exposed sex. She found herself lifting to him, reaching for what he would give. He chuckled, low and possessive as he cupped her backside with both hands and pressed a kiss to her exposed flesh.

For a moment, time froze, and she stared down at him, his head buried between her naked thighs. This was happening. This moment was hers and hers alone and no one could ever take it from her, no matter what happened next.

He lifted his gaze to her and she held there, lost in his passion and his goodness. And then he peeled her outer lips open and returned his mouth to her, this time for an open-mouthed kiss, and she did exactly as he had said she would.

She forgot her name. She forgot her duty. She forgot her heartbreak and her fear. She forgot everything except for the wicked, silky stroke of his tongue against her folds. He lapped up the evidence of her pleasure from his touch earlier and created even more as he licked her from top to bottom, lavishing her with pleasure.

She gripped the edge of the settee, trying to find purchase as pleasure skidded through her every nerve, her every limb. It washed over her in one big wave that drowned out everything but him.

Once again she dug the fingers of one hand into his hair, holding him closer, urging him on as he licked and licked like she was the sweetest treat and he could indulge in her forever. Never get tired of her flavor. She found herself grinding up against him, seeking more, demanding more.

He laughed again, the reverberations tickling through her body. "Looking to be in charge, are you?"

She gasped for air, trying to find words. "I-I can't help it. I just want…I want…I need…"

"I know what you need." He blew a warm breath against her clitoris, and she jolted. "And I'll give it to you when I'm ready. I want to savor this, Sasha, so don't take that from me."

She nodded and relaxed further, closing her eyes so she could only focus on sensation. On how gentle his tongue was as he circled her sensitive clitoris with it. On how cruel he was when he withdrew to stroke her entire length again. On the building pleasure as he held her wider open, making her entirely helpless to him and his touch.

She felt his finger trace her entrance and glanced down. He was watching her again, gauging her reaction so he could best torture… or relieve her. He tilted his head as he pressed the tip of his index finger to her entrance and took just a few millimeters of space. She gasped despite how small the claiming was, lifting to demand a bit more.

His eyes were glazed, pupils fully dilated, and he let out a low curse as he pressed his finger inside to his first knuckle, then to his second.

"Yes, yes, yes," she whimpered, flexing around him, feeling him move within her.

He dropped his mouth back to her, this time focusing entirely on her clitoris. He pumped his finger in and out, mimicking what she wanted him to do with his cock, wishing it could be so. But this pleasure took away any other emotion. She rocked into him, unable to control the flex of her hips now, even if she tried.

He was pushing her up a mountain now, drawing her to an inevitable cliff of pleasure. She saw it coming in the distance, felt it as the tingles of pleasure grew stronger, faster, harder. He sucked on her clitoris over and over, scraping her gently with his teeth, soothing her with the tip of his tongue as he fucked her mercilessly with his finger.

She came in a burst of rippling waves, bending her back, tearing at his hair and the settee edge, wailing out his name into the quiet like it was the only word she knew. In that moment, it was, because her entire world was boiled down to him and the pleasure he gave.

He milked her through the crisis, drawing her release out until she went weak on the cushions, her breath only pants, her legs shaking around his shoulders.

Only then did he lift his head, looking as smug as any man could have done. He leaned up, kissing her so she tasted herself on his mouth. She drew him against her, wrapping one bare leg around his boot, wishing she could stay like this forever.

Pretending she could because the alternative was far too painful.

Thomas was no libertine, but he had been with his share of women over the years. He had become a student in bringing pleasure. Moreover, he *liked* doing it. There was nothing so powerful an aphrodisiac than watching a lover come undone. He was always left hungry for more in those moments.

But in all his years, he had never experienced anything like the power of Sasha's release. In that brief moment it was like they had become truly one, bound by the unceasing waves of her pleasure and his desire to give her more and more and more of the same.

He balanced next to her on the settee, running his fingers up and down the bare leg she had slung over him as she curled against his chest with a satisfied sigh.

"*That* was wonderful," she murmured, her lips moving against his jaw gently.

"It was," he agreed as he kissed her mussed hair, breathing in the scent of her. "As wonderful as I dreamed it would be for weeks."

She sat up a little straighter and smiled at him. "And now it's my turn."

He blinked. "I'm very happy to do it again if that's what you mean."

She laughed, the sound like music in the air, and shook her head. "No, my lord, we had a bargain. Have you forgotten? My pleasure for your pleasure. And since I shouldn't do…what I would like to do to trade it, I would like to touch you instead."

He was still on fire for her, his cock uncomfortably hard. Earlier in the evening, she *had* offered to give him the same release he'd given her, but he hadn't intended to hold her to it. Now, though, she set a hand against his chest, her fingers pressing warmth into him even through his jacket and shirt beneath. It was a spell and she weaved it around and through him until he couldn't think of anything, see anything, want anything but her.

She leaned up, kissing him as she trailed her hand down his stomach, his abdomen, and then she cupped his cock through the placard of his trousers.

"Christ," he grunted, slouching a little as stars burst before his eyes. "Sasha, I don't expect you to—"

"Hush," she whispered, her fingers working to free the buttons there. "You promised me a quid pro quo and I won't be denied."

She folded the fabric of his trousers down and his cock popped free at full attention. She stared at it a moment, her eyes wide, and then she licked her lips.

"Very nice," she murmured with a wink for him.

He didn't respond, he couldn't as she took him in hand and stroked him from base to tip in one firm motion. He rocked his head back over his shoulders, his vision blurring as she repeated that motion over and over. Her hands were like silk over the steel of his flesh, and she seemed naturally able to find the right tension and rhythm to please him. He lifted into her hand as she continued to palm him.

"I want to taste you," she whispered, her voice wicked and heated and close to his ear.

He opened his eyes and watched as she lowered herself to kneel before him as he had just been doing for her. Her gown fell back around her legs, though her breasts were still exposed. It was a lewd delight to watch her like that: dress around her waist, nipples hard as they brushed the edge of the settee, his cock in her hand, dark eyes holding his like some temptress sent to take him to hell. Or heaven. Either way, he was going with her, no questions asked.

She darted out her tongue and slid it across his head, swiping away the droplet of liquid that had leaked from his excited cock. She smiled up at him, then repeated the action.

Her mouth was steamy hot, and when she closed her lips around him and sucked him inside, he let out a cry that he couldn't have held back for any offer presented to him. She took him deeper, deeper, until he bumped her throat. Only then did she retreat, gasping for breath around him.

He tangled his fingers into her hair, pushing it away from her face so he could watch her fuck him with her mouth. Slowly at first, then faster, harder, deeper. She stroked the root of him with one fist, lubricated by her own spit, and sucked him as far as she could

JESS MICHAELS

take him until he was lifting to her, tugging her closer, reveling in the way she gasped and groaned around him. She was writhing on the floor, wriggling like she wanted him inside of her, enjoying this as much as he was. Her pleasure drove him toward the edge as much as her tongue. He was ready to fall, his balls tightening, his body thrumming with undeniable, unending pleasure.

"I'm going to come, Sasha," he groaned, trying to pull away.

She resisted his withdrawal, lifting her gaze to him with a wicked smile as she took him further, coaxed more. He couldn't hold back, he couldn't protect her, and he cried out as he spent.

She took every drop of him, swirling her tongue around him as she toyed with him through the release. He twitched as she continued to suck his ultrasensitive cock. Finally she let him go and rejoined him on the settee.

"You didn't have to do that," he panted.

She arched a brow. "You think I didn't want to know your taste like you wanted to know mine?"

He blinked at the confidence of that statement. Goddamn, but this woman could kill him. Or save him. If she could be his, he would...

But he couldn't and he shoved those thoughts away with near violence because they hurt too much. He didn't want to hurt right now, just feel pleasure and warmth and satisfaction.

She settled into his shoulder, and for a little while they just held each other. He traced the lines of her bare arms with his fingertips, she nuzzled her nose against his jawline, his ear. It was perfect, or as close as he would ever come.

"How did you come to be the adopted daughter of the King and Queen of Athawick?" he asked at last.

She tensed a little at his side, her fingers flexing against his thigh. This topic was clearly not a happy one. "I *wasn't* the adopted daughter of the King of Athawick," she said softly, after a few ticks of the clock had passed since he asked the question.

"The last king, I mean. King Alastair."

She shook her head. "King Alastair was my sovereign, but he was *never* my father in any way that mattered."

"My apologies," he said, kissing her temple. "I was curious, but I can see I've pushed too hard. You don't owe me an explanation."

"No, but I want to give one. To tell you. It's just so hard to know how to begin." She drew in a long breath. "My parents were in the king's inner circle in Athawick. My father had been a friend to him when they were children, and he was awarded with a place in courtly affairs. He and my mother were on a diplomatic trip to England, actually. On their return home, there was a terrible storm and the ship sank. Hundreds were lost, including Magnus and Sasha Killick."

"You shared a name with your mother," Thomas said, watching how her expression grew taut with pain.

"I did," she said. "And I suppose I must have shared even more, but I was six when they were lost. I hardly remember them now. Giabella had a miniature of them made for me, a kindness amongst a thousand other kindnesses. Now I remember them as that two-dimensional image, not as living, breathing people. I suppose it is better than no memories at all."

"What happened then?" he pressed, wanting to know more.

She sighed. "Dashiell Talbot was in my father's employ at that point. He came to me, managing what would be done with a little girl who had no other family, no other place. It was protocol that the remaining family be brought to the king and queen so they could offer their condolences." Her gaze became far away. "I shall never forget the feel of his hand that day. He was so big. I felt so protected."

"I've seen him with the queen, though I don't think we've formally met," Thomas said softly.

She smiled. "You should. He's brilliant and kind and funny, though he tries to hide that for propriety." The smile wavered. "He comforted me, but I was still afraid of meeting the king and queen. When I did, King Alastair was immediately dismissive. I was a child, he had little use for his own children. Certainly he had no interest in an orphan child of someone else, friend or not."

Thomas shook his head. "I'm sorry."

"It was fine. He was who he was, the good and the bad. He left the room almost immediately. But Giabella..." She trailed off and her face lit up with love. "She was warm and wonderful, as you see she always is. She thought I looked like her daughter, she knew I had no other place in the world. And then she said she would take me."

"You must have been shocked," Thomas said.

Sasha nodded. "I'm sure I was, though I was so young I'm not sure I truly understood what was happening in that pivotal moment that changed my life forever. All I knew was that I wasn't going to be sent away, which was what I'd been told before. Of course, Giabella had to thwart Alastair's disdain, so she and Dash made a plan for me to join the royal family."

"They overcame the king together," Thomas said, impressed.

She laughed. "They were always overcoming the king together over the years. Though sometimes it was via negotiation. He didn't want me..." Her voice broke a little, and Thomas was surprised at the anger that entered her gaze. "He made sure I knew it."

"How?" he asked.

She met his gaze. "That is the one thing I should not tell you, of all people, Thomas. Not after what we just did."

His eyes went wide. "What does that mean? What did he do?"

She bent her head, and he saw her struggling. Perhaps he should have released her from his demand that she spill this obviously painful truth. "Ilaria was about to be taken out into Society the year I turned sixteen. Giabella felt that would be the perfect time to make my position in the family a more certain one. She wished to give me...give me a title. Princess Sasha of Athawick, though I would not be allowed to advance to the throne, of course. She also wanted to give me a similar settlement as would be linked to Ilaria's marriage."

Her breath caught and he stared. Sasha with a title and settlement. That would mean he could...they could...

"Please don't look at me that way," she whispered. "King Alastair was livid when she and Dash presented their desire to him. I was not supposed to listen in on that conversation, but I was in the hallway, ready to be brought in so I could accept the offer when he agreed. I heard what he screamed at her."

Sasha's pain was so strong that it felt like a fist closing around his heart. He cupped her cheeks, kissed her gently, wishing he could take it away, wishing he could go back in time and never let it happen in the first place. "Breathe," he whispered. "Breathe and tell me."

She drew a few shaky breaths. "He said that he would never gift a royal legacy to common blood. Especially not mine. And he followed through on that. He made a law within hours. He cut me off from title and from fortune through the royal line...*and* through Giabella. Her own fortune, the one she had separate from his, was still controlled by him. He made it so she could not gift me a settlement either." She sucked in a harsh breath. "After that, I was thrown into service with Ilaria. I was made her double. And his courtiers always reminded me of my true place."

Thomas shook his head. "You were not fully a family member."

"With those who mattered, I was. But yes, that is the life. Always on the outside looking in, always on the inside looking out." She was calming now, the pain fading now that she had explained how close they had gotten to his love for her being something he could pursue. Something that had been thwarted by a dead man Thomas hated more than anyone on this earth.

"I'm sorry," he said softly.

"Don't be. There were heartaches and disappointments, but Dash took care of me, Giabella and the children took care of me. At first, Giabella had arranged for Dash to work for the king, but ultimately he moved to her office. He became her personal secretary. So when you say that I am the adopted daughter of the king and queen, that is why I say no. I am the adopted daughter of Giabella of Athawick and Dashiell Talbot."

She lifted her chin with pride, and he would have smiled, only her story created a troubling question in his mind. "You and Ilaria are very close."

"We are only two years apart, and since she had only brothers, she was thrilled to have a sister," Sasha said with a laugh. "We played together all the time—she included me in everything she did. She always wanted us to dress alike, which is how our similarity in appearance became even more clear in later years. I suppose it saved me, as it presented me with a vocation to prove my worth to a volatile king who wanted to thwart me entirely."

"And yet you would walk away from her," Thomas said.

She flinched and sat up, separating their bodies as she tugged her chemise back over her shoulders and buttoned her gown. It was wrinkled but somewhat serviceable. Her hair was still down around her cheeks—she dropped her head and suddenly it was a barrier. "Thomas…"

He could hear in her voice that she wanted to put an end to this conversation, that it hurt her, but he couldn't push these questions aside. "You told me this afternoon that you had decided to go back to Athawick and enter into service of the queen instead. Would you truly throw away your connection to Ilaria?"

"No. That's not what I could ever do. I love her too much." Sasha got up and paced away, picking up hairpins absently, wrapping her hair into a bun and pushing them in as she paced. "I'll just put some distance between us. If we were natural sisters, that would happen with a marriage, wouldn't it? We'll write. I'll see her when she…" She faltered and her hands began to shake. "…when you both come to Athawick for royal events. I'll sail to London whenever she needs me. I just can't be here every day, watching your family grow. Watching you slowly fall in love with her."

He pushed to his feet and fastened his trousers before he moved toward her. He had never intended to say the words that were on his tongue, to make this harder, but perhaps he had to now. If they were laying cards on a table, this was the only one that mattered.

"I want to make something very clear, Sasha. I will *never* love her." He reached for her "Because I...I..."

She backed away, shaking her head, her eyes wide and filling with tears. "No, please don't. Please don't say it or I won't be able to do what I must. Please."

They stared at each other for a long moment, a lifetime. "I won't say it," he agreed. "But nothing in the world can make me not feel it. Trust me, I've tried."

She breathed in and it was shaky. "I need a moment, I think, before we return to Bleaking House," she whispered. She motioned to the terrace doors. "May I?"

He wanted to say no. To catch her hand and pull her close and kiss her and start this madness all over again. To make her his and keep her here until the world stopped turning, until he drew his last breath. Perhaps in another life, he would have been able to. Perhaps in a future life, he would, after all.

But not this one.

"Of course," he said softly.

She nodded, turning away and slipping out of the room. When the door clicked shut behind her, he sagged against the back of the settee where he had just thoroughly pleasured her and been so powerfully pleasured in return.

People wrote sonnets about love, they told wide-eyed tales of the joy of it. And he hated them all. Hated everyone in the universe who had what he could not, who would go to sleep beside their heart instead of eventually watch it board a ship and sail away.

Most of all, he hated himself for not being strong enough to abandon everything to be with the woman on his terrace.

CHAPTER 18

S asha had controlled the tears as she told the story of her childhood. She'd kept herself in check as she revealed how close she'd been to taking on the role and dowry that could have allowed her to be with Thomas. But when he nearly said he loved her...*that* had been what broke her. Because she had known it all along, because she felt the same emotion in return. She loved this man. Deeply and completely.

She had been so good her entire life, doing what was expected, being who she was needed to be and now...

"It's not fair," she whispered as the tears she had kept in check began to flow. Anger rose in her chest, and she slammed both hands down on the metal railing until it reverberated with a clang. "It's not fair!" she repeated, louder.

"You may be right, princess. It's not fair."

She pivoted at the voice that came from off to the side and watched in horror as a stranger jumped over the railing and onto the terrace, just an arm's length away from her.

She didn't recognize him. He wore dark clothing and a hooded cloak that cast a shadow over most of his face, but when he looked at her, his eyes burned into her. As intense as a predator stalking his prey.

Ilaria had described her own attacker in a similar fashion a few days before, his eyes the one thing that had stood out to her.

"You," Sasha whispered as fear washed away every other emotion that had clouded her mind.

"You're not the princess," the man growled, rage entering those eyes.

She glanced toward the terrace door and he followed her stare. When she jolted toward it, he swung on her, backhanding her across the cheek hard enough that she flew back and hit the terrace railing with a second clang. She pushed away from the stranger, but he was looming over her now, closed fist drawn back, vengeance and horror in his eyes.

As he punched down toward her again, she recognized she might not survive this. In the blink of a moment, she thought of her family and how her loss would hurt them, she thought of her future that she would not ever get to experience.

And she thought of Thomas, who she loved so deeply, and how he would blame himself. Then the world went very dark and painful and cold.

Thomas had stepped from the room to allow Sasha her moment without staring at her through the glass like she was a fish in a bowl. He had taken a few breaths in the hallway, gathered himself, and stepped back into the parlor.

To find himself in the midst of a horror show. Through the glass doors to the terrace, he could see a man standing over Sasha. She was on the ground, unmoving as the bastard rained fists down over her.

He ran, bursting through the doors and hit the man with all his weight, hurtling him off of Sasha. For a moment their eyes met, and then the attacker pivoted and jumped from Thomas's terrace and off into the night.

Thomas dropped to his knees. Sasha's face was bruised already, but she was breathing. He gathered her in his arms, hating how limp she was, how unresponsive.

"Help!" he called out into the house. "Someone help!" A few of the servants were still in residence for their night off, and he could only pray one of them would hear him.

He focused his attention back on Sasha as he lifted her and carried her back into the parlor. He laid her onto the settee where they had given each other such pleasure. Her lip was bleeding, and a droplet slid down her jaw and stained the fabric beneath her.

"Wake up," he whispered, examining her injuries carefully. "Come now, you must wake up."

She moaned and lifted her hands, as if to protect herself from her attacker. Her palms were bruised, as well. But to his utter relief, she opened her eyes and her gaze cleared as she found him.

"Thomas," she whispered.

"You're safe," he assured her. "You're safe."

Behind him the parlor door opened and a footman entered, his shirt untucked and hair wild. "I heard you call, my lord, what is..." His gaze shifted to Sasha. "Oh my!"

"I need you to fetch a doctor," Thomas said.

"No." Sasha grabbed for his arm as she struggled to speak. "Not...not a doctor. If I'm found here...problems. I must go back... to the family. Their doctor...discreet. Please."

He wanted to argue. After all, she was a mess of bruises and scrapes, and he didn't want to ignore that and whisk her away in secret like she'd done something wrong. But he could see from the wildness in her stare that she was incapable of rational argument.

"Fine," he ground out through clenched teeth before he turned back to the footman. "Will you have the carriage prepared? And is Vickery here?" he asked, referring to his driver.

"No, sir. He's out visiting his mum." The footman shifted. "I can prepare the rig, sir, and drive it. My father was a driver and I learned."

Thomas nodded. "Yes. Good. Hurry."

The footman rushed from the room.

"He can't tell anyone, Thomas." Sasha gripped at his lapels. He was pleased that her voice seemed stronger, as did her grasp. "He can't tell."

"Hush," Thomas said. "He won't. I will be sure of it. And you shouldn't be worrying about anyone but yourself. What happened?"

"It was...it was the man who attacked Ilaria at the club." Her dark eyes sparkled with tears. "I know it. He was angry that I wasn't her—he must have followed us here."

"He was watching the house," Thomas murmured. "He didn't know that Ilaria was secreted away for her safety."

She moved to nod and then groaned. "Yes. He was there and then he hit me and I...I don't remember anything until I opened my eyes and you were there."

Thomas cradled her a little closer. "It's my fault."

"No, it isn't," she whispered. "If you'd known something like that could happen—"

"But I did, because it happened to Ilaria," he insisted.

She began to cry softly and he pushed aside his guilt, holding her close as he did so. "Is anything broken?" he asked. "May I look?"

She let him, turning her face so he could examine the bruises. She'd have a black eye. Her lip was cut, and her cheek. Her hands were what worried him most, but she was able to bend all her fingers when pressed. She was lucky and he knew it. The man on the terrace had been hellbent on destruction to beat an unconscious woman.

Thomas had almost lost her.

The footman, Martin, stepped back into the parlor. "The vehicle is ready, sir," he said.

Thomas picked Sasha up, holding her close, and carried her to the carriage. Once he had her situated, he turned back. "Bleaking House," he said to Martin. "And I must be clear that you must never speak of this night to anyone."

Martin nodded. "Of course not, sir."

"No one. Not in my employ, not in your own family. No one."

"I understand. I'll go as fast as I can and be safe."

Thomas got into the carriage with Sasha. She turned into his side, her fingers clenching against his shirt as they headed off, back to her family. To the consequences for their actions tonight and the heartbreak they had nearly wrought.

As the carriage pulled up to Bleaking House, Sasha tried to calm herself. She was now past the shock of what had happened and her foggy mind was clearing. Of course that left memories of that horrible man rising up over her to flash into her mind over and over. The pain was not gone, though. It came in waves of heat and sharpness. She had to think, had to focus.

"You could leave me," she whispered. "So they won't know I was with you."

Thomas stared at her with wide eyes. "Is that the man you think I am?"

"No," she choked out. "But I would protect you if I could. Thomas—"

He leaned down and kissed her gently. "It is not up for debate," he said firmly.

"Well, let me walk on my own, at least," she said as the door opened.

She could see how much he wanted to argue, but he didn't, instead climbing down from the carriage first, then reaching back to assist her. The door opened and Greenly appeared, silhouetted in light from the foyer. "You cannot park that here, sir, this is the private residence of—"

Sasha stepped into the light and looked up at him.

"Your Highness!" he gasped.

She moved closer. "No, Greenly, it's Miss Killick."

"My God," he said, and she winced, for she knew from his horrified expression just how bad her battered face looked. "Help her in, I'll fetch the family at once!"

Thomas took her arm, and slowly they eased up the steps together. She motioned to the first parlor—she had no energy to go deeper into the house. He took her there.

"Lie down," he said, his arms tight around her, comforting and warm.

"No," she said. "I can't frighten them like that."

She had scarcely finished the sentence when the queen and Dash rushed in to the room together. Giabella was wearing a robe and her hair was down. He was still in his attire from earlier in the evening.

But it wasn't their state of dress that unnerved her. It was the looks of pure horror on their faces as they stared at her.

"Sasha," Dash murmured, and then he crossed to her. She fell into his arms and the tears began to fall in earnest. "What happened?" Dash said, his tone harsher than she'd ever heard as he stared at Thomas over her head. "What happened to her?"

"She was attacked," Thomas said, never taking his gaze from her. She felt it burning into her even as Dash brought her to the settee and sat with her, his hands shaking as they clutched hers.

"Here?" Giabella cried out.

Thomas shifted. "No, madam. At…at my residence."

Sasha closed her eyes as the room grew entirely silent. There. It was out. She'd had no illusions that it wouldn't be, of course. But she'd hoped, dreamed that she could keep her feelings, her desires, her weaknesses a secret from these people she loved so desperately.

"Gia," Dash said softly, referring to the queen in a way Sasha had never heard before. He was always entirely formal. "Come."

He motioned her to him and stood, giving her his seat. The

queen immediately clutched Sasha to her. "My baby," she whispered. "We need a doctor. Greenly, have the king's doctor fetched at once. And where is Grantham, where is Remi?"

Greenly stepped into the room. "Prince Remington has not yet returned from his...his evening," he said with a blush. "King Grantham is being retrieved at present. His courtier, Mr. Blairford, was insistent on fetching him, himself."

Dash had stepped toward Thomas during this exchange and he was staring at him, unblinking, unmoving. "Would you like to explain yourself, sir?"

Sasha shook her head. "Dash, don't."

He glanced her way. "I will, Sasha. I may not have been able to be your father in every way I would have liked, but I will by God protect you tonight." He glared at Thomas again. "Speak."

Thomas straightened. "I understand your anger and it is justified. Taking Sasha to my home was...imprudent. And considering what happened to her there, dangerous."

Grantham burst into the room, fully dressed and clearly angry. "What the hell is going on that requires my presence at two o'clock in the..." He stopped as he stared at Sasha. "What happened to you?" he whispered, and crossed, dropping to his knees before her to gently trace the bruises on her face.

"I'm sorry," she murmured.

"You offered her as sacrifice," Thomas said, his hands clenching at his sides and his voice trembling with so much emotion that it made Sasha's heart break. "And *this* is the result of it."

Grantham got up and pivoted toward him. "What are you doing here? What did you do?" he snapped, and took a long step as if he would physically fight Thomas.

Sasha began to stand, but Giabella caught her arm. It was Dash who inserted himself, pressing Grantham back with both hands. "This will not help, Grantham!" he all but shouted.

The room fell into shocked silence, but at last, Grantham

stepped back, straightening his jacket. He cleared his throat and pivoted back to Sasha. "Take her upstairs," he said softly to his mother. "There will be no way to hide from staff that Ilaria is not actually abed sick. They will find out the truth and there is naught to be done about it. The doctor should be here soon, I assume."

Sasha got up. "Please don't, Grantham. Don't punish Thomas for what I did."

Grantham held her gaze evenly a beat and then bent his head. "We are all punished for the sins of others, Sasha. You only need worry about yourself. I will come up shortly."

She glanced toward her mother, and Giabella nodded. "Dash will keep them from killing each other," she said softly with a glance for her secretary that lingered.

Sasha wanted to fight their orders. To insist that she remain. But everything hurt; the burst of energy she'd felt after the attack, when it felt like she could take on the world...or at least her family...was fading. She caught the queen's arm.

"I'm sorry, Thomas," she whispered.

He shook his head. "You never have a need to apologize to me, Sasha. Never."

Tears stung her eyes as Giabella led her from the room. And she couldn't help but wonder if she would ever be allowed to see Thomas again. Or was everything destroyed after all, even the future that could have saved him.

Perhaps Queen Giabella thought that Dashiell Talbot would be the one to maintain the calm in the room when she took Sasha away, but now Thomas faced off with not one angry male relative, but two. King Grantham had stalked to the sideboard and poured himself a tall glass of what appeared to be Scottish whisky, and Talbot just stared at him, arms crossed, his pale blue eyes narrowed.

"I've asked you to explain yourself, my lord. I want that explanation now," Talbot said.

Part of Thomas bristled. Thanks to his position in life and his years, he was not accustomed to being taken to task like a schoolboy. And after the heightened events of the evening, the idea of coming to blows with either this man or the one glaring at him from the sideboard didn't actually seem like the worst end to a night.

Only he would imagine it would hurt Sasha. She had already been hurt enough and with more coming in the future.

"I'm not going to sport with the intelligence of either of you and pretend you can't see the connection between us," Thomas said.

Grantham slugged back a drink. "Are you not supposed to be developing a *connection* with Ilaria?"

Thomas arched a brow. "Are you trying to protect your investment, Your Majesty, or your sisters?"

Grantham flinched but said nothing.

"Ilaria doesn't love me any more than I love her. I am well aware of her situation with Captain Crawford and how and where exactly she came to be attacked a few nights ago," Thomas continued. "That this duty we are expected to perform together will keep each of us from the person we...we care for is most unfortunate." He shook his head. "Tonight I was desperately imprudent."

"Desperate seems to be the operative word," Talbot said, though he had softened somewhat.

"Perhaps. Imagine what it would be like to...to love someone and know you could never have her. I think that would make any man desperate."

Talbot turned away, and Thomas was sure he heard him mutter, "I don't have to imagine."

But King Grantham stepped forward and Thomas had to refocus on him. "I want you to understand, sir, that I am not pleased. But I think catching the blackguard who is threatening to harm my family is the top priority. So tell me everything that happened. Now."

Thomas nodded. "I agree. Sasha and Ilaria's safety is the most important thing. Everything else can wait. May I have one of those?"

Grantham glanced down at the whisky in his hand and then he grunted, "I think we've all earned one. Talbot, shut the door. I'll pour the drinks."

CHAPTER 19

The doctor gave her laudanum, and though Sasha appreciated it for the pain, she didn't like how groggy it made her. She'd woken a few times during the night, bleary and confused, and found various family members at her side. Giabella, Dash, even Grantham once.

But this time when her eyes fluttered open, she found herself alone. She moved and winced, for her body ached from the damage. She pushed to a seated position just as June entered the chamber, tray in hand. The maid froze as she found Sasha awake and stared for long enough that Sasha flinched.

"That bad, eh?" she asked.

June's gaze darted away, which was answer enough to Sasha's question. "Of course not, miss. I was simply surprised to find you awake."

Sasha caught a whiff of the food on the tray and her stomach rumbled. At least there was that. "That smells divine."

"Mrs. Woodrow asked about all your favorites and made them."

"So, they are talking about me," Sasha whispered. "The servants, I mean."

June set the tray down on the table and prepared Sasha's tea, then brought the entire contraption over so she could eat. Sasha assumed she was using the actions as a way to drag out her answer to the question. Her mouth was drawn into a frown as she said, "Yes. They're talking about your injuries. And also speculating on where Princess Ilaria truly is."

Sasha bent her head. Her imprudent night with Thomas had created all kinds of situations, it seemed. The family had worked hard to make almost all of those in their employ and all the Bleaking House staff believe that the princess was abed with a summer cold, not to be disturbed.

All that hard work was gone. Her appetite fled and she picked at the food on her plate.

"Where *is* the princess?" June asked softly.

Sasha lifted her gaze. "You know I cannot say. That isn't because you aren't trusted, June, but it isn't my place." She pushed the plate away. "Will you bring me a mirror?"

June pulled away slightly. "Miss, you don't want to—"

"Please," she interrupted firmly.

The maid sighed and went to the dressing table, where she retrieved a hand mirror. She returned with it and held it out with a shaking hand. As Sasha took it, June stepped away. Sasha drew in a long breath and looked at herself.

The left side of her face was a mass of bruises, her lip cut and swollen. As she stared, she recalled when the man on the terrace had struck her. Memories flooded her mind and she dropped the mirror onto the bed as she covered her face.

"Oh, love."

Sasha looked up to find the queen and Dash entering the chamber. She wiped at her tears and tried to force a smile, but Giabella shook her head as Dash took the tray away and the queen sat down on the bed. She wrapped her arms around Sasha and held her close.

"You cry now if you need to, dearest," she whispered.

So Sasha did, briefly, her face buried in Giabella's shoulder as the queen rocked her gently. When she had gathered her composure,

Dash quietly handed over a clean handkerchief and then they sat on either side of her, each holding one of her hands. June curtseyed and left the room, closing the door firmly behind her.

"We almost lost you," Dash said softly.

"But you didn't," Sasha replied. She forced a smile and tried to ignore the pain the action caused. "And I'm well."

"Are you?" Giabella asked, tracing her injured cheek with just the tip of her finger. She shook her head. "I was so blind. So focused on Ilaria that I could not see you."

Sasha's mouth came open in surprise at that recrimination. "But Ilaria is your child—of course, you would be thinking of her first."

Giabella stared at her. "*You* are my child, Sasha."

"Our child," Dash interjected, and he patted her hand, though he didn't squeeze it because of the bruising on her palms.

As Sasha sighed, fresh tears returning to her eyes, Dash and the queen met each other's stares over her. In that moment, they felt like a family, different from any other time in her life, save for that first moment all those years ago.

"I know I did something that hurt that family," Sasha said.

"No," Giabella began.

Sasha shook her head. "I did. I was imprudent and...I suppose it was selfish to only think of myself and what I wanted. What I-I needed."

She thought of Thomas, his fingers threading through her hair as he kissed her, his fingers thick inside of her as he pleasured her. She couldn't regret what they'd done. Only the consequences.

Giabella sighed. "You've spent your life, especially the recent years, sacrificing what you wanted or needed for the service of your country and your king. I know how difficult that is. How unfair when you did not choose this life but were either born or brought into it. Perhaps I was the selfish one for taking you in, for loving you so much that I couldn't picture this moment, when you might have to lose it all because of who we are."

Sasha gasped out a cry. "Oh no, no! I have never regretted being in your family, in your life. Mama, never think that."

Giabella smiled. "You so rarely call me Mama anymore."

"But I *always* think of you that way," Sasha whispered.

"This young man," Dash said slowly. "Bramwell. Does he care for you as much as you care for him?"

"He shows that he does in every action he takes," she said softly. "But what can I do? I don't want to hurt Ilaria. I don't want to hurt him."

Giabella put an arm around her and gently squeezed. "You let us worry about that. Grantham, Dash and I. And Remi, I suppose, because he intends to stick his nose in." She smiled. "He is champing at the bit to see you. Once he managed to stagger his way home, he was devastated that he wasn't here in your hour of need. I'll send him in after our meeting with Grantham shortly."

"Speaking of which." Dash glanced at his pocket watch.

"Yes, I know," Giabella said with another smile for Sasha. "Rest now, love." She kissed Sasha and then got up, smoothing her hands along her skirts gently.

As she did so, Dash leaned in and kissed Sasha's temple. "I'll bring you a book later."

Sasha laughed. He did know her so well. Together they left and Sasha stared up at her ceiling, thoughts bombarding her from every side. As comforting as they were trying to be, she was still over-whelmed by the consequences of her actions. Worse, now her feelings were out.

And she had no idea what that would lead to. She only knew that she had to send word to Thomas. Both to assure him that she was well and to simply connect with him. Because as she sat here by herself, she recognized one fact: the only person she wanted to see was him.

~

Thomas paced the breakfast room, ignoring the food that was perfectly prepared on his plate at the table. After a night of no sleep, after the absolute highs of pleasure with Sasha and the horrible lows of her attack, after surveying his garden in the moonlight, trying to see how her attacker had gained entry, he should have been exhausted. And he was, but more so he was restless. He couldn't hold still as thoughts of Sasha kept washing over him. The good and the bad, the desperate and the beautiful.

There was a rap on the partially open the door, and he turned to find Gillingham there. His man of affairs eyed him closely, concern in his fatherly expression.

"I believe you have forgotten an appointment, my lord." When Thomas wrinkled his brow, he continued, "Your sister and my son are here."

"Oh God's teeth, I did forget," Thomas said, running a hand through his hair. "Send them in, of course."

Gillingham vanished for a moment and returned with Aurora and Nicholas in tow. His man of affairs was slightly less formal with the couple since Nicholas was his adopted son and he adored them both. He even cracked a smile as Aurora kissed his cheek and spoke softly to him.

Soon the welcomes and small talk were finished and Gillingham stepped away. "I ought to return to my ledger. But I hope you'll come say goodbye before you go. Oh, and my lord, this missive arrived for you as I was fetching your guests. I promised Merryweather that I would deliver it to you."

He handed over the message and Thomas stared at the hand. Sasha's, he just knew it. Shaky, yes. Pained even, and that made sense considering the injuries to her hands. He flinched at the memory of the bruises and how she had gotten them. Slowly, he broke the wax seal that bound the pages and read the short message.

Around him, the others continued to talk.

"We must arrange for our next Sunday supper," Aurora was saying. "And Thomas, you truly must come this time."

Thomas heard her words, but almost like he was underwater. Focus was impossible now.

"Thomas?" Nicholas pressed gently.

"Yes, Sunday supper," Thomas said as he paced away, running his fingers across the letter. "Excellent notion. Gillingham will give me the particulars once you all arrange it. Now, why don't you get your plates from the sideboard and sit?"

Aurora and Nicholas exchanged a worried glance with Gillingham, but then he departed and the couple did as Thomas had suggested. He watched them from the window. Aurora always seamlessly adjusted to Nicholas's disabilities, handing him items only on his good side, and her husband's ability to make her smile or blush was like watching magic. His sister had never been happier, that was clear, and she gave the same joy to her husband.

Thomas was jealous. He hated himself for it, but there it was. The ugly, unvarnished truth.

Nicholas helped Aurora into her seat and then took his own place, but neither began eating. They both just stared at him. Finally, Aurora cleared her throat. "Politeness might dictate it, but I cannot sit here and pretend that I don't notice your troubled countenance. Thomas, what is it?"

He shook his head. "It is not your concern, I do not wish to impact your joy with my silly troubles."

"That's ridiculous," Nicholas said, folding his arms. "Family is meant to help each other, to offer support in times of trouble."

"Like Aurora allowed me to do last year?" Thomas asked gently.

Aurora's lips parted. "It's true I didn't turn to you when I was in trouble. I was trying to protect you, as you are trying to protect me. But didn't it upset you? Didn't we promise then that we would never keep secrets from each other again?"

He frowned. "Yes, we did."

Aurora stood and came to him. "Then let me help, Thomas. What is it? Something about Father?"

He huffed out a humorless laugh. "In a way." He stared at the letter in his hand. Sasha had meant for it to be private correspondence and there was part of him that wanted to protect it as such. But another part felt the pressure growing inside of him, eventually he would pop and the damage would be irreparable. And if anyone could understand the desperation of love that couldn't be, it was Aurora and Nicholas.

He wanted their help, their counsel, their support. And since saying the words out loud was too much...

"I'm sure Mama has told you all about Princess Ilaria of Athawick and her grand plans for my union with her," he said softly.

Aurora nodded. "Yes. The world knows that is the plan, I think. Is this about her?"

He cleared his throat. "She has an adopted sister, Miss Sasha Killick."

"Oh yes, we met her at that gathering at Bleaking House a few weeks back," Nicholas said. "Lovely woman, sharp as a blade."

Thomas hesitated and then handed over the letter to his sister. She took it, her brow wrinkling before she read it. She gasped and glanced up at him when she was finished. "Thomas!"

"Read it out loud so that Nicholas might know, as well. And because I need to hear the words. Perhaps once I do, I'll know what to say, what to do, what to feel."

She sucked in a ragged breath and read, *"Dear Thomas, I do not know how to begin to say thank you to a man who saved my life."* Aurora lifted her gaze. "How did you save her life?"

He shook his head. "That is one piece of information I best not give. Please continue."

"More to the point, how can I thank a man who has brought me back to life from the first moment we met on that terrace. I've tried to pretend it away, tried to push it away, tried to let myself believe that I could find a way not to break both our hearts if I just didn't say what I felt. But last

night, when the fear of death gripped me, what I thought before all other things was how much I loved you and how sad I was that I would never be able to say it to you. So now I say it. I love you, Thomas."

Nicholas pushed to his feet and grabbed for his cane, slowly making his way to Aurora's side. He stood near her, watching her as she read. And once more Thomas felt nothing but jealousy. Especially when Sasha's words rang in the air around them.

"I know this declaration changes nothing. We are on different paths, we will be no matter what we wish to be true. So I will love you enough not to ruin you. I do not expect a response, but I wanted you to know, whether that is a kindness or a curse. With all my heart, Sasha."

"Sasha?" Nicholas repeated, his attention shifting to Thomas. "Miss Killick is the one who wrote this?"

"Do you love her in return?" Aurora asked softly.

Thomas nodded. "I do. More than I ever knew I could love a person."

"Then what is stopping you from being with her?" Aurora asked.

He stared at her. "You bloody well know what. Father. What he did."

Nicholas thumped his cane against the floor, the thud of it punctuating the anger that all but permeated off of him in waves. "That bastard. Years after his death he is *still* hurting the people I care for."

"Nicholas." His sister's voice shook.

"It's true, isn't it?" he asked her. "He kept you and I apart for a decade. I lost *ten years* of happiness with you. It is unforgiveable. And now his actions are causing your brother to be pushed into an untenable situation. I won't apologize for despising that man and hoping he is burning in hell."

"You needn't," Thomas said. "At least not on my behalf. But you and Aurora must know, better than most, that the situation is helpless, hopeless."

The room was quiet a moment as they all let that truth sink in. He expected Aurora to comfort him, for Nicholas to slap him on the back and commiserate. But instead his sister's eyes brightened with emotion and she reached out to push the letter back into his hands.

"That is poppycock!" she burst out. "Look at what this woman has written you—that is real. That is true. That is more valuable than whatever you think you will gain by turning away from her."

"You don't understand," he groaned.

"Don't I?" Aurora asked. She motioned toward Nicholas. "Because of his sacrifice in the war, Nicholas was almost granted a title. Only my...my situation would have made it impossible. He chose *me* over what might have been easier for him. And he doesn't regret it. I don't have to ask him if that is true, because I feel it every moment we are together. But you can ask him if he would have regretted losing what we have in trade for being marquess."

Thomas shifted his gaze and found Nicholas' jaw twitching. "I would have regretted it every moment of my life if I had lost your sister again. I did it once—I do not recommend it, Thomas. You will spend every night trapped in a prison of your loss. Knowing you had the keys to your salvation and you turned them away."

"You have a right to love, Thomas," Aurora insisted. "To a real future."

"But Mama—" he began.

"Is not your problem," Aurora said softly. "I adore her, just as you do. But she will always be taken care of. And if you are happy, she will also be happy in the end. Watching you burn alive in a fire of regret would devastate her, even if she cannot see it at present."

What his sister was suggesting was like a sparkling beacon of hope at the end of a dark, smoky tunnel. Thomas could see it, but could he reach for it? He wasn't yet sure.

"It is a great deal to think about," he murmured, running a hand through his hair. "A great deal to consider."

Aurora gestured to the letter he now clutched. "The lady is not expecting a response, she says. So take your time deciding what to do. But my God, Thomas, choose for your own happiness. Yours is the only life you must lead, the only skin you must inhabit. Everything else can be arranged."

He nodded slowly and then motioned to the table. "Come, our food is growing cold. Let us speak of other things."

His sister was kind enough to allow it and she and her husband retook their places, as did he. But he hardly tasted his food as he ate it, hardly heard their light conversation meant to comfort him.

Because all he could think about was this new powerful thought that he could have Sasha. That he could choose for his own heart. And if he did, what a life they could have.

CHAPTER 20

Sasha was lying on the bed, her back to the door, pretending to sleep. It wasn't that she hadn't been sleeping in the day and a half since her attack. The laudanum forced her to when she was pressed to take it. But she needed it less and less as the initial swelling from her injuries began to recede, leaving only ugly bruises.

No, she was lying in bed because she was suffering in a different way. Her heart hurt.

She'd written that letter to Thomas the previous morning, and yes, she had told him she did not expect a reply. She'd wished to unburden her heart and knew it was unfair to expect him to be able to do the same. But the fact that he had not responded, at least directly to her, was difficult. Grantham had said Thomas had checked on her via letter to him.

But nothing to her.

The door behind her opened, and Sasha held very still. She was in no mood to see anyone. No mood to talk and talk and talk about what had happened and how she was recovering and what and why and how. She just wanted to lie here in her sadness and wallow a while.

"Sasha?"

Sasha's mouth dropped open. That was Ilaria's voice. She lifted her head, rolling to face the door, and found that the princess did, indeed, stand there, the queen behind her. There were tears in their eyes.

"Sasha," Ilaria repeated on a sob, and raced to her. Sasha opened her arms and drew her in.

"Hush, I'm safe," Sasha whispered. "I'm fine."

Giabella moved closer and shook her head. "We are very lucky, my love."

Sasha smiled up at her. Since their talk the morning after the attack, she had felt such a closeness to Giabella. If this was the positive she received from this heartache, she would take that small bit of comfort.

"I'll leave my two girls alone," the queen said, "and see what Captain Crawford is talking about with the king, Remi and Dash."

"I'll be down shortly," Ilaria said.

When she was gone, Ilaria perched on the edge of the bed. "Tell me."

Sasha closed her eyes. "Very well."

She struggled for a moment. She had told the story of her attack so many times that it felt like it should have been easy to recite it again. But when she began, it always brought back those horrible memories. That terrible moment when she had realized she would not make it. When she'd flashed to all she'd lose.

"Unless you don't want to," Ilaria whispered.

When Sasha opened her eyes, she watched as Ilaria toed off her slippers and raced to the other side of the bed. She climbed up, and for a moment Sasha saw her as a little girl, shoving into Sasha's bed for a snuggle when Ilaria had had a bad dream, or when they'd just wanted to tell each other stories. Now she put her arm around Sasha and gently guided her to rest her head on her shoulder.

"I need to," Sasha said. "The danger is to you, after all. Not me."

"I knew it was my fault," Ilaria breathed. "I'm so sorry, Sasha."

"It's not your fault." Sasha shook her head. "I was...I was out." She thought of Thomas. Of the pleasures they'd shared. She'd worked very hard not to conflate them with the pain after. She refused to let that be ruined by some heartless, violent blackguard. "Don't ask me more about it. I was out and I stepped onto a terrace, and suddenly there was a man there, coming toward me, his arms raised and his gaze wild. He stopped short when he got close enough to see I wasn't you."

"Did he have a piercing stare?" Ilaria whispered.

Sasha heard the moan escape her lips as an image of his bright eyes filled her mind. "Like he could see down to my every fear. I tried to back away, but he was too fast. He was enraged that he'd been tricked. That he thought I was you and I wasn't. He hit me so hard I fell and...and then everything gets dark and quiet and painful. I don't know what happened next until I woke up in Thomas's arms. He saved me."

"Thomas?" Ilaria repeated in confusion.

Sasha blinked. Did Ilaria not know Thomas's first name? The man she would marry when this was finished? The man who was sacrificing everything for her? "The Earl of Bramwell."

"Oh!" Ilaria gasped, and now when she looked at her, Sasha sensed understanding dawning. Far too much of it.

Sasha glanced away. "He and I were much thrown together, you see."

"I'm glad he was there," Ilaria said at last, Sasha thought carefully. "We owe him everything for saving you."

Sasha dropped her gaze. While she had been embroiled in her own situation, Ilaria had also been off with someone she loved and would lose. How Sasha felt for her. "How were things with Captain Crawford?"

She shifted. "Wonderful. Brief. Over."

Sasha knew that tone. It was the same as her own any time she spoke of Thomas. A lilt of longing and sorrow and broken heartedness. How she hated that everyone in this situation must endure it. "I'm sorry, love."

"I'm so sorry you were hurt because of me. But I'm glad Grantham sent word to bring me back. I need to be with you now, be with everyone. I need to stop this."

"Grantham sent for you?" Sasha asked. "I didn't realize he was doing that, though they certainly haven't spoken to me about everything in the last two days since the attack. And what do you mean that you need to stop this?"

She didn't like Ilaria's expression. She knew it well. It was the same one the princess always got when she was about to slip her guards and go make trouble.

Ilaria stood up. "Don't you worry about it. I'll come back up later. Would you like me to sleep with you tonight? Like we used to do when we were little."

Sasha laughed, for she had just been thinking of those same nights. She did love how connected they were. "You snore," she teased.

Ilaria laughed. "I do not! I've never snored in my life—it isn't what princesses do."

"I would like your company," Sasha admitted.

"Then I'll see you later," Ilaria said before she slipped from the room.

Sasha shook her head after she was gone. Having Ilaria back was wonderful, no matter what trouble she would ultimately cause. But there was no denying that having her back here also signaled one more step toward the end for them all.

When Ilaria returned hours later, it was with a look of stubborn certainty in her eyes that frightened Sasha. She was sitting up, propped against the pillows, and she tilted her head.

"What did you do?" she asked.

Ilaria laughed. "Do you know me so well?"

"Better than anyone. What did you do?"

Ilaria's expression fell, and for the first time, Sasha felt her fear. With a heavy sigh, Ilaria climbed into the bed with her and they held hands as she said, "I'm going to offer myself as bait to the man who attacked us."

"Bait?" Sasha repeated. "Ilaria, no."

"Don't you start, I already had to argue with Jonah, Grantham, Remi and Mama about this for hours. I'm not about to do it again."

"Well, you may have to. I saw that man, Ilaria. He is a monster, hellbent on your destruction and willing to harm anyone else who gets in his way."

"I don't care about anyone else but you," Ilaria said softly. "He harmed *you*."

Sasha rested her head on Ilaria's shoulder. "I don't like it."

"Jonah will be there, as will a great many guards and others, all to protect me. When it's done, we'll know if this is one man or a group after Grantham and his throne."

She was too exhausted to argue. If somehow Ilaria had convinced the rest of the family to go along with this madness, then they must have a plan to protect her. And the princess had always done as she pleased. Sasha certainly couldn't talk her out of it.

"Does Thomas know?" she asked.

Ilaria glanced at her. "Bramwell? No. Why would I tell him?"

Sasha stared at her. "Because he is your future husband, isn't he?"

Ilaria's expression crumpled slightly, and then she nodded. "I suppose he is that."

"He has a right to know of your plans. You must tell him."

Ilaria turned to face her fully, tucking her legs beneath her on the bed. "Are you certain *you* don't want to tell him?"

Sasha caught her breath. She did want so desperately to see him again. To touch him. To be able to feel his comfort. But she slowly shook her head. "I...I wrote him a letter. He didn't respond."

"Bastard!" Ilaria burst out.

"No," Sasha interrupted, holding up a hand to stay Ilaria from her censure. "I told him he didn't have to write back to me. I just wanted him to know...to tell him..."

"That you love him," Ilaria whispered.

She nodded. "You must despise me."

"I could never despise you," Ilaria insisted. "But my God, the idea that you would have to give up your heart because of me and the future of Grantham's throne. It is monstrous."

"And it is the way of royal life. We don't get to choose." Sasha sighed. "I can't talk about it anymore, Ilaria. I can't with you, you understand that. And I can't...I can't stay with you after. Not when you marry him. It would be unfair to us all."

Ilaria drew back and tears filled her eyes. "To lose you... God's teeth."

"I'm sorry."

"No. You needn't be. And I *will* tell Bramwell of my plans. We have a few days to arrange logistics and the like. I'll go tomorrow and tell him."

Relief flooded Sasha. "Good."

"Now, I'm tired, you look exhausted. I think we could both do with a nap. Are you still reading that wonderful gothic?"

She nodded. "Yes. It's in the bedside table."

Ilaria leaned over and rummaged through the drawer, coming back with the leather-bound book. "I'll read it out until one of us falls asleep."

Sasha settled back and closed her eyes as Ilaria began to read. But she didn't picture the romantic saga from the page. She just let herself fantasize about Thomas instead, and it was with images of him in her mind that she fell asleep at last.

JESS MICHAELS

T homas was at his desk, staring at the letter he'd started and stopped so many times over the last day. As far as he'd gotten on its current iteration was *Dear Sasha* and nothing more. How in the world could he respond to her? He had no answer. How could he tell her that if he broke the suggested union to Ilaria he would come to her as a man of no means and even worse reputation? Word of it would spread like wildfire, he had no doubt, burning him even further. How could he ask her to throw away a life in a palace for that? Love or no love.

He looked up to find Gillingham at his study door, a strange expression on his face. "Er, you have guests, my lord. Royal guests."

Thomas set his quill down and stood, smoothing his jacket reflexively. "Send them in."

He expected to be joined by King Grantham and the queen, perhaps with news of Sasha, though he'd heard earlier via short message from Dashiell Talbot that she continued to recover. But when Gillingham returned it was with Prince Remington and Princess Ilaria at his heels.

Thomas shook his head. "You are back."

Ilaria nodded. "I am. I returned yesterday after the news that Sasha had been attacked. You remember Remi, don't you?"

"Your Highness," Thomas said, inclining his head first to the prince and then the princess. Gillingham excused himself, and Thomas motioned for the settee before his fire. "Please sit. Would either of you like tea?"

The offer was refused and so Thomas sat across from them, staring. "Has something happened to Sasha?" he asked. Prince Remington exchanged a look with Ilaria, who was actually smirking. "Is there something funny about that question?"

She nudged her brother. "No, not at all. I wagered a pound with Remi that you would first ask after Sasha, and I won."

"*And I won*," Remi repeated under his breath in a mocking tone that made Ilaria smile. "Sasha is fine, my lord. Getting stronger

200

every day, thank God. That is not the reason my sister strong-armed me to escort her here today."

"I don't understand," Thomas said.

"Since my return, I've been watched far too closely, but I didn't wish to come here and speak to you with an entire army of interested parties pushing us close together and trying to make a match like they have been since our arrival in London." Ilaria sighed. "So Remi and I devised this solution, where he would escort me for a walk in the park, only instead we strolled over here."

"In broad daylight? With a killer tracking you?" Thomas asked blankly.

"God, you sound just like Jonah and Grantham," Ilaria murmured. "I was wearing a hood, my lord. No one could see my face and we exited through a side door. I promise you, I was not in danger."

Thomas wasn't entirely sure of that, but it was obvious that Ilaria could not exactly be controlled. At any rate, he was more curious about why she'd come to him after all these theatrics rather than, say, Crawford, who he was fairly certain was her lover. The other was not his problem.

Yet.

"So why did you come to me?" he asked.

"Because Sasha insisted that you must know what is about to happen." Ilaria swallowed. "We are planning a ruse tomorrow night where I will be offered as bait for the man who attacked me and later Sasha."

Thomas drew back. "What the hell are you talking about? Your Highness, this is foolhardy. Does your family know you plan something so reckless?"

"They do. And while they argued against it just as strenuously, they have come around to the idea. I will be guarded as closely as I can be. There are a great many parts in motion, I assure you."

"So you came here to inform me," Thomas said softly.

She nodded and then glanced at Remi. The prince gave a heavy sigh and got up, moving away so they would at least have the illusion of privacy. She drew a long breath. "I also had another question for you. What do you intend to do about Sasha?"

Thomas flinched. It didn't surprise him that she knew about the connection between them, though he wasn't certain Sasha would ever tell her about the details of their few encounters. He shook his head. "I don't know. What do *you* intend to do about Captain Crawford?"

The flutter of pain that worked across her face was as real as his own. For a moment it connected them more than any forced moment on a ballroom floor ever had.

"You know about him, do you?" she asked.

He shrugged. "Yes."

"I don't know what is going to happen after this nightmare is over," she said after a small hesitation where she appeared to be gathering her thoughts. "My family is important to me. The threats against me, against Grantham's throne, make it abundantly clear that I may have to choose duty over love. I can't say that I'll refuse that order if it is given again. But I also cannot say that I will walk a path that will only lead to pain and ruin for so many. I would not do that to you, but most especially to Sasha and Jonah...and to myself."

He leveled a stare at her. "And you are telling me this...why? To prepare me for the destruction of the plan?"

"Don't you want it destroyed? Don't you want to be able to give Sasha your heart without anything else in the way?"

He snorted out a laugh. "It won't be that easy, Your Highness. Even if the desired engagement doesn't take place, there will be a great deal in the way of my offering for Sasha, no matter what my heart wants."

"I hope that isn't true," she said softly. "Because if you were to turn her aside, even though there were no barriers in the way, she would be heartbroken. You want to protect her, I can see that in every part of you. But you won't protect her by denying her your love."

Prince Remington cleared his throat from the window. As much as he was trying to pretend like he was giving them privacy, there was no way he hadn't heard every word between them. "Ilaria, we should return before Grantham sends out a guard to collect you and murder me."

She nodded and got up, and Thomas did the same. As she moved toward Prince Remington, he leaned down and said something to her. She frowned, but then returned her gaze to Thomas. "It seems this is farewell. Please think about what I said, Lord Bramwell."

"Thinking of Sasha is all I do, I assure you. And I will take your words to heart."

She left the room, but Prince Remington stayed, his arms folded across his broad chest. Thomas sighed. "Still feel you need to protect Sasha, then?"

"She's still the one who needs protecting, it seems," the prince said. "I don't really believe in love, you know."

"You...don't believe in it?"

"No. I've seen people who thought they loved each other tear the other to shreds. I've seen it fade. I believe in attraction and infatuation." He paced away. "But that is not the end that either of my sisters desire. *They* believe in love. And both of them feel it for the wrong man."

Thomas sighed. "I want to do what's best for everyone."

"But you might not be able to do what's best for *everyone*." Remington stared off for a long moment, and when he spoke it was with hesitancy. "I...was with my father...at the end. Did you know that?"

Thomas shook his head. "I didn't."

Remington's expression grew faraway. "We never got along. He was not a kind man and he always made his disdain for me utterly clear. But as he lay there dying, he grabbed my hand, and do you know what he said to me?"

"What?" Thomas asked.

"'I wish I'd been more like you.'" The pain that flickered across

Remington's face was the most real emotion Thomas had ever observed in him.

"What did he mean by it?" Thomas asked.

"I could make some flippant comment," the prince said. "But the thing he always railed at me for, focused on, was that I did what was best for me. When I wanted something, I took it. When I needed pleasure, I found it. So I must believe he meant that." He moved closer. "You will make a handful of people pleased for a brief moment if you do what you are convinced is the only 'right' thing. But you will harm a great deal more in the long run."

Thomas shut his eyes. Those words rang so true. "I have been trying to write a letter for the last day. I've been trying to find the words to tell her how deeply I love her. To ask her if she would be willing to sacrifice so much to be with me. I don't know how to say those things when everything is so upended."

Remi nodded slowly. "It is that. You should see them all run around Bleaking House like chickens with their heads cut off." He stared at Thomas a moment. "Wait another day."

"Won't that torture her?" Thomas asked. "She has been waiting for my response, I know that."

"I'm sure she is," Remington agreed. "But right now not one person in my ridiculous family is ready to make a rational decision. It will be better after Ilaria has performed her utterly foolhardy attempt at catching an attempted murderer tomorrow night. When she has, when this situation is resolved, *that* will be the best time to address the future. Will you do that?"

Thomas nodded. "Yes. I'm sure you're right that the family is too distracted by the danger to fully deal with what will happen next." He thought of Sasha's crumpled figure on his terrace and flinched. "Tell me that they have at least doubled your guard at the house. That Sasha is being protected as strenuously as Ilaria shall be."

Remi cocked his head. "She will never be as protected as you would like, I think. Not unless you can see her."

"Then I should come," Thomas said. "Tomorrow I should come

and sit outside, watch the house. Be a pair of eyes that only cares for Sasha and her well-being, not the future of a monarchy."

"You do love her, or as close to it as one can," Remington said softly. He nodded. "I like that idea. The advantage of it is that you will be aware the moment Ilaria has returned from this fool's errand. And that will be your moment to declare your heart."

There was a certainty that filled Thomas in that moment. A peace he had only felt recently when he was with Sasha.

"Remi!" Ilaria's voice came from the hallway, and none too patiently.

The prince laughed. "You see what I have to deal with."

Thomas managed a chuckle. "Better go to her then. But thank you, Your Highness. I appreciate your counsel more than I could ever say."

Remington pulled a face. "Ugh, don't say counsel, it makes me sound wise and I cannot be believed to be that." He extended a hand and Thomas shook it. The prince smirked slightly. "I look forward to welcoming you to the family, my lord. I just hope it is the right way."

He turned away then, leaving Thomas to ponder things alone. He poured himself a drink and then sat staring at the fire to do just that before he returned to his desk and the letter waiting there. He sat down and finished it, even though he wouldn't send it, even though he needed to have a little patience.

Dear Sasha, I am coming for you. One way or another, I will come for you.

He stared at those words, praying that they could be true. That they would be true. And that he could overcome all the pain this decision would cause, because he couldn't bear the pain if he didn't choose his heart.

CHAPTER 21

S asha paced the parlor with the remaining family, waiting for Ilaria's return from her desperate mission. Every moment stretched so long, she found herself walking to the clock on the mantel to check it had not broken. And she was not the only one anxiously seeking something to do. Grantham had gone after Ilaria and Crawford, though he had been made to promise that as king, he would not involve himself in the danger.

That left Remington, who was standing at the fire, jabbing it restlessly with the poker. His usually playful expression was now dark and dire, troubled as she knew her own was. She squeezed his arm as she turned to look at Queen Giabella and Dash. They stood together at the window. She worried her hands together, nearly rending the handkerchief she held in two. Dash didn't touch her, of course. Propriety dictated that he not. But he stood as close as one could without touching, murmuring soft words of comfort that no one could hear but the two of them.

"Ilaria's fine," Sasha said out loud, at last. "Certainly she is fine. She would never be otherwise."

Remi turned toward her and nodded, though the certainty didn't reach his eyes. "She's fine," he repeated.

"How could I have allowed this?" Giabella groaned, moving away from Dash's side and pacing the length of the room. "How could I have let her go?"

Before anyone could answer, the door to the parlor opened and Grantham and Ilaria entered with Captain Crawford. Ilaria clung to Crawford's arm, pressing her hand into what was once a white shirt but was now stained red.

"Great God!" Giabella cried, rushing forward and ushering them to the settee. "What happened?"

"A flesh wound, madam," Crawford said. "Nothing more."

"Hush," Ilaria said. "The doctor is already on his way."

"Are you injured?" Sasha asked her sister.

Ilaria lifted her gaze, and Sasha saw what a harrowing night she had certainly had. She shook her head. "No. Our plan worked, at least in part. I was approached, but the man attempted to take me and Jonah fought him off. That was how he was injured."

"Did the attacker escape?" Giabella asked.

"No." Ilaria met Sasha's eyes again. "He's dead. He took some hidden poison. He cannot hurt us now."

Sasha's knees buckled slightly and she gripped the back of the closest chair to shore herself up until Dash came and held her elbow, squeezing gently. She leaned into him. "So…is it over?"

"For now," Grantham said softly. "I don't know if this man was truly part of some larger conspiracy tied to the unrest after my ascension to the throne, or if he was just an unhappy subject trying to make some point. We will look into it further. But for now, this nightmare seems to be over."

"I'm telling you, I will not wait to be announced," came a voice from the hall. Sasha stumbled toward it, for she knew that voice as well as she knew her own.

Thomas, she mouthed in shock as the door flew open and Thomas, indeed, did enter with a frazzled Greenly on his heels.

He scanned the faces and found hers, holding her stare evenly. Relief flowed over his features. Good God, but he was handsome.

She always forgot, and then he was there and it was so obvious that it filled her every sense until there was only him.

"You are well," he said, speaking to her, although she had been safe the entire time.

"What are you doing here?" Sasha asked, and Grantham turned away from Crawford to spear him with a confused look.

"I might ask the same question. We didn't expect you tonight, my lord."

Thomas's lips pinched. "I took a place of watch from across the street, Your Majesty. I thought an extra pair or eyes in this circumstance would not be unwelcome."

Grantham opened his mouth to speak, but Sasha interrupted him. "You were watching over us?"

Thomas held her stare and said nothing, but his gaze spoke volumes. Not watching over all of them. Over her. He had come to watch over her, a guardian with only her safety and well-being at heart.

The doctor arrived then, cutting off any hopes Sasha had of further conversation. She focused on Ilaria as they were all ushered from the parlor so he could examine Captain Crawford. She took her sister's arm as they made their way to another chamber to wait.

"You are pale," Sasha whispered.

"It was terrifying," Ilaria said. "When he attacked me before, I lost consciousness from the fall. I didn't have time for anything beyond the initial flare of fear. But this time I felt it all. And when he slashed Jonah…" She covered her mouth. "I can't lose him."

Sasha pursed her lips, letting Ilaria pace away to speak to her mother. Thomas was standing at the window, talking to Remi but watching her. Always watching her. She moved toward him, drawn to him as she had been from the very first moment.

"Ilaria told you about the danger," she said.

Thomas inclined his head. "She and the prince visited me yesterday afternoon to inform me."

Her lips parted and she stared at Remi. "You did? I had no idea. Why didn't you tell me?"

Remi glanced at her, then at Grantham and Ilaria and the queen, who were all gathered together across the room. He did not answer low, just for her ears, but loud enough that the room could hear. "I am not the one who normally resolves problems in this family," he said. "But this one I could not ignore. There are things that must be dealt with, don't you agree, King Grantham?"

Grantham froze at the formal address and stared at Remi a moment. Then he looked at Sasha, then Ilaria and back to Thomas. He let out a long sigh and nodded. Sasha nearly buckled. He knew. Grantham had remained quiet, ignoring the tangled web that had been weaved and would threaten all his plans. But he knew the truth, he knew her heart, he knew Ilaria's.

"I suppose it must, yes," Grantham said softly. "Excuse me a moment, I will go to Captain Crawford."

"I'm coming with you," Ilaria burst out, but Grantham held up a hand to stay her.

"Ilaria, I must speak to the man alone," he insisted.

She shook her head. "Then I will wait in the hallway until you are finished with whatever kingly attitude you must lord over him. But I *am* going."

Grantham looked annoyed, but he said nothing as he allowed her to follow him out the door and into the hallway. Sasha continued to stare at Thomas. She wanted to talk to him, but all the things she had to say were better spoken privately.

Giabella approached, making that conversation even more impossible. "My lord, won't you sit? I'm so sorry we are distracted."

"Yes," Thomas said, and moved to the settee.

Sasha would have gone to him, but Giabella took the place beside him instead, and for the next few minutes there was nothing but awkward small talk. They spoke of the roads, for heaven's sake! As if this were all normal and not the culmination of weeks of longing and regret and hope, just a tiny flare of hope.

Grantham returned to the parlor and motioned to Giabella. The queen nodded to Dash, and the three stepped into the hallway together. Grantham shut the door behind them. Remi rolled his eyes and motioned at Thomas and Sasha.

"Go on then, you've been waiting this long." Remi moved to the door. "I'll listen for the return of the gatekeepers."

Thomas moved to her and she to him, wrapping her arms around his neck and just holding him close to her. "I have missed you," she whispered into his neck.

"I've missed you too," he said, his fingers clenching against her back like he could somehow bring her even closer.

"Someone is coming," Remi said, and they parted, stepping away as Giabella returned, but without Dash and Grantham. She was smiling and that expression moved toward Sasha briefly.

"Lord Bramwell, I'm afraid that we have an announcement. One I believe you may not be so upset about as might be believed."

Thomas moved toward her. "Ilaria will marry Crawford?" he said softly.

Sasha's knees buckled and she reached out, catching Thomas's forearm to steady herself. Giabella looked toward her. "Yes. Dash has gone to make some arrangements. But they are engaged. Or they will be as soon as Grantham gives the permission and hopefully allows poor Captain Crawford to make his own overtures."

Thomas bent his head for a moment, and then he nodded. "Your Majesty, as you have said, I might be more pleased with this announcement than some would believe. I wish the princess nothing but joy. She seems to truly love Crawford, and I would never separate anyone from someone they cared for."

He looked back over his shoulder at Sasha when he said that, and she melted a little. Still, he had made no move to propose to her. It still might not be possible. But other things were now. Other futures. And she saw his desire for them sparkling in his eyes.

"Thank you for your kindness," Giabella said. "And I do know that there may be other things to discuss." She glanced again toward Sasha. "But perhaps you would forgive us if we do not deal with them tonight. It has been an exhausting evening for everyone, and I would like to focus entirely on...on those other situations when the time is right."

Sasha's heart sank. She might have expected this. The engagement of a princess, especially after everything else that had happened, would take precedence. And even if her family would allow a union between her and Thomas, even if he wanted that, it would likely involve a great deal of negotiation and settlement.

So her joy would have to wait. And she ached for it.

Thomas looked just as chagrined as she did over that fact, but he nodded. "Then I think I should leave your happy celebrations to your family now," he said. "But do tell Princess Ilaria and Captain Crawford that I fully support the union and will do everything in my power to make that publicly known."

He stepped away from Sasha to kiss the queen's hand and then shake Remi's. When he at last reached for hers, he whispered, "We need to speak alone. *Now.*"

Her eyes went wide at the edict but she smiled at him as she whispered back, "My chamber in five minutes. Four doors to the right after the stairs."

He bid her a far louder farewell before he left and she worried her hands as Giabella approached her. "I'm sorry, my dear. I know you might have hoped for a clearer resolution to all this, but I do want to give your future as full an attention as I do any of my other children. And Dash will want to be part of that, as well. You understand?"

"Of course," Sasha assured her. "But I am a little tired after all this excitement. May I retire?"

Giabella's expression turned to one of concern. "You are in pain?"

"No, no," Sasha said, squeezing her hand. "But weary. Tell Ilaria I am very happy for her and I cannot wait to hear every moment of her proposal and celebrate properly as we tell the world of her joy."

Giabella nodded and kissed her cheek before Sasha slipped into the hall. Grantham was coming out of the parlor where Captain Crawford's wound had been stitched, and she ducked away before he could see her. She didn't want to get caught in yet another conversation about the reasons she would have to wait for her happiness when it waited for her in her room right now.

She almost staggered in her excitement to mount the stairs and found herself nearly running to her door, her heart throbbing. When she threw it open and burst into her chamber, it all but stopped.

Thomas was there, standing in the middle of her room. He turned to her as she stepped inside, as she shut the door. And then he was moving toward her, catching her in his arms and dragging her in for a deep, powerful kiss that seemed to melt her from the inside.

"We need to talk about this," he murmured against her mouth before he pulled away. "You have waited far too long for a response to your beautiful letter of two days ago."

She stared up at him. She saw his love for her, she recognized it completely, just as she recognized her own. But beyond that love were doubts, uncertainties. Questions that had to be answered, problems that might very well be insurmountable thanks to two reckless and cruel fathers who had never thought of anyone but themselves.

And in this moment, this beautiful moment when Thomas was truly free of the connection to Ilaria that had kept them apart physically, she didn't want to talk about all the other problems that might cloud the future.

She lifted her hands to his cravat and began to untie it. "Please don't talk, Thomas. Not yet."

"Sasha," he began, pulling back a fraction. She cupped his face in her hands to keep him close enough that she could feel his breath tickle her lips.

"I know we have so much to say. But I'm not fool enough to believe we have more than this moment in time. So I want you to make love to me. Do you understand? There are not barriers to it anymore, there are no reasons not to do it. And I want you, I want *this*. Later we can debate."

He held her gaze for a moment, and she saw him break. Saw that he would give her anything, everything in the world that she wanted if he could. Tonight he could, at least when it came to this.

He bent his head and kissed her. Deeper this time, slower, with more purpose, with more passion. And she knew that she would get what she wanted. Finally.

~

Sasha was too much to resist, that was all there was to it. Especially when she was offering herself, demanding he take her. No man would be strong enough to say no, but especially not him. But he did want to savor this, because she wasn't wrong that it might be their only chance. He wanted to celebrate it because it was rare and beautiful and something he had dreamed about for weeks.

He broke the kiss and caught her shoulders to turn her around so her back was to him. He leaned in and kissed the side of her neck gently, then sucked not so gently. Her backside tipped against him and she ground there with a gasp.

He had to focus. Somehow. He tried as best he could and carefully unfastened the top button of her gown. Bare flesh was revealed, and he leaned in to kiss there.

"Please," she breathed, reaching back to press her palm against the side of his thigh. "Please."

He unfastened the second button, the third, and kissed along the trail he had uncovered until he reached the edge of her chemise. He brushed his fingers beneath the lacy detail work, loving how Sasha shivered with even the barest touch. He already knew the flush of her skin when she came. He wanted to feel that same thing around his cock now, milking him, making him lose control.

He unfastened the last few buttons and drew the dress down, dragging his tongue along the path he created. She pushed the silk away from her arms and then her hips gave a little shake to get the garment off. It pooled at her feet and she kicked it away before she turned toward him slowly.

He caught his breath. She was exquisite in the short, thin chemise that just barely skimmed her thighs. All soft curves and kissable lines. He wanted to worship her like the queen she was. No, more than a mere queen. A goddess. His goddess. He cupped the back of her neck and tugged her closer, molding her against him as she gazed up at him in desire and adoration.

He never wanted this moment to end. He kissed her and he wanted to kiss her forever, sustained only by her flavor, by her sighs. Never leave this room, just live to be her pleasure.

That felt like it could be a satisfying life, indeed.

She pushed back slightly. "I want to see you," she whispered, voice trembling.

He nodded and backed up, taking a seat on the chair before her fire to remove his boots. She had already untied his cravat, but now he unwound it at lightning speed and tossed it away, then shrugged from his jacket and made quick work of unbuttoning his shirt. When he tugged it over his head, she covered her mouth with one hand.

"Oh, is she horrified?" he teased.

"Captivated," she corrected, moving toward him, hand outstretched to touch the muscles of his chest, to slide her fingers down the line of his flat stomach and catch them on his waistband. "Bewitched."

"Take off the rest," he said.

She didn't argue, but slipped her chemise straps down and shrugged out of what was left of her clothing. She was naked and he was overcome. How could he be so lucky as to love this woman? And to get to touch her? What had he ever done in this life or another to have earned that privilege and that pleasure?

He couldn't squander the opportunity. He tugged her against him, loving the feel of her breasts as they flattened against his chest, the soft brush of hard nipples against his skin. He kissed her, backing her toward the bed. He lifted her to the edge and she opened her legs, wrapping them around his waist to tug him into that snug spot.

He cupped her naked backside, grinding against her, reveling in the way her head lolled back and she gasped. Pleasure. He wanted to give her so much pleasure. That was all that mattered now. That was all he cared about.

Thomas pressed a hand against her shoulder and nudged until she was flat on the bed. He bent over her, his dark gaze glittering with possessive, smug male power. She was his. His expression said it all. This was a claiming at last and she ached for it.

He pressed his lips to her throat and sucked. Tingles of pleasure ricocheted from that spot, settling in her nipples, tugging heat between her legs where she needed him so much. But he was going to deny her a little longer, it seemed. In trade for other pleasures.

His mouth dragged lower, hot and wet on her skin as he crested over her right breast. He tugged her nipple between his lips, sucking and swirling his tongue around and around until she gasped and arched beneath him. He smiled against her skin and moved his attention to the opposite breast, teasing her all over again.

And then he was gone, mouth moving lower. She sat up and leaned on her elbows, watching as he ducked his dark head between her legs, as he'd done a few nights before. He licked her gently at first, tasting the entire length of her sex. She pressed her hands there, opening herself to him, granting him access she never wanted to deny again. He glanced up at her with a low chuckle that burned into her very blood. When his mouth returned to her flesh, it was with drive and purpose.

He didn't tease. He didn't torment. He didn't play. He gripped her thighs, pushing her legs wider, and he worked her hard and fast toward orgasm. His tongue tapped over and over again against her clitoris, his fingers massaged her inner thighs. She lifted into him, shamelessly riding his tongue until at last the building wave of pleasure broke. Her hips jolted out of control and she cried out, loud enough that he lifted a hand to cover her lips gently. She sucked his fingers instead, using them to silence herself.

He groaned with pleasure and looked up at her, his chin slick with her juices, his eyes dark with purpose. He pulled his fingers from her mouth, stepped away, and unfastened his trousers. The fall front fell away and his cock came free. He pushed the trousers away and stood before her, fully naked.

She licked her lips at the sight of this beautiful man, unbelievably here just for her pleasure. She wanted to take it all, everything else be damned. She reached for him and he retook that spot between her spread legs. Only this time there was nothing between them.

She caught his cock, stroking once, twice and then aligned him to her entrance, still dripping wet from his tongue, from her release. "God, Sasha," he murmured as she stroked him back and forth through the evidence of her desire. "You'll unman me."

She smiled. "That's the idea, my lord."

He caught her hips with both hands, his fingers pressing into her flesh, marking her with his passion. Then he thrust. She took him, inch by inch, stretching for him, welcoming him until he was fully seated inside her still-fluttering body.

She lifted up further, drawing his mouth to hers and kissing him. First slowly, then deeper and faster. He began to move as she did so, licking her flavor from his lips. He ground her against the edge of the mattress, stroking her clitoris with his pelvis on each powerful thrust.

She met him stroke for stroke, racing for more pleasure, for this final connection that meant everything in this heated moment. When she came again, he caught her cries with his mouth and thrust hard through the crisis, drawing her to the edge of control and beyond. It was only when she went limp with pleasure in his arms that he let himself go. She watched in awe, flexing around him as his thrusts grew wild, sweat broke on his brow, his eyes grew unfocused. He was no longer a proper earl, a man with duties. He was her lover. He was her everything, and nothing else would ever matter but this.

He came with a groan of her name against her neck and filled her with the heated flood of his release. They collapsed back on the bed together, shifting to lie properly against the pillows, their arms and legs a sweaty tangle.

Sasha didn't know what would happen next. In some ways it didn't matter. Right now was what mattered and right now was enough for a while.

Thomas smoothed his hands over Sasha's hair, over her shoulders, over her bare back. There had never been anyone else in the world like her, and he was so lucky as to hold her in his arms. There was no denying he would do anything for her, anything to have her. And it would be difficult, but oh, so worth it.

"I love you," he admitted, catching her chin and tilting her face toward his so she would be sure to understand what he was saying. "I have longed to say it to you for a while, but kept it to myself as to not make things worse. But I love you, Sasha, with all that I am and all I will ever be. I love you."

Her eyes filled with tears at the confession, but her smile told him they were nothing but joyful. She leaned up and kissed him again, but it was like it was the first time all over again.

JESS MICHAELS

"I love you too," she whispered. Then she cuddled closer. "But we both know there will be challenges. So what do we do now?"

He didn't get a chance to answer, to paint her the most beautiful picture he could imagine from the future they could have. Before he could, the door to the chamber opened and Ilaria appeared, staring at them as they lay naked and tangled on Sasha's bed.

CHAPTER 22

"Ilaria!" Sasha gasped, tugging for the blanket to cover herself and Thomas.

Ilaria threw herself into the room, shut the door behind her and held up a hand as if to block what she was seeing. "I thought you might be together, but I didn't picture *this*."

"I'm not going to apologize," Sasha gasped as she finally managed to cover them both up with the blanket.

Ilaria peeked through her fingers and sighed as she realized there was nothing left to see. "No one is asking you to apologize, I assure you." She stepped closer. "So...it's done."

"Christ, Ilaria," Thomas grunted.

She smiled in response. "I'm happy for you. We should all be happy—we all deserve it. But Mama wants negotiation and Grantham will insert himself into this just as he is bound to do with Jonah and me."

Thomas glanced down at Sasha. "And then there is my mother," he said, his tone laced with concern.

"We know the barriers," Sasha said. "We know the questions. We are strong enough to fight them, aren't we?"

Before Thomas could reply, Ilaria stepped closer. "Run away."

Sasha stared at her. "I can't run away! Think of what it would do to Dash and Giabella! What an outrage it would cause for everyone. There will be enough of that when the public realizes you aren't marrying Thomas, as was the obvious original plan."

Ilaria rolled her eyes. "Not permanently, and it is exactly because of the potential scandal that I'm suggesting it."

"May I get dressed?" Thomas asked. "This is an outrageous conversation to be having while I'm half covered in a blanket."

"Well, you should have locked the door," Ilaria said with a glare for him. "How much is your...what do they call it here? A special license."

Sasha's mouth dropped open. She and Thomas had declared their love, but he hadn't proposed. Ilaria's assumptions were awkward at best.

But Thomas didn't hesitate. "Five pounds sterling is, I believe, the going rate."

"I have sovereigns," Ilaria said, rushing to the adjoining room. When she was gone, Thomas moved to throw back the covers.

"She'll be right back," Sasha said softly. "We'll start all over again."

"This is not the way I pictured the rest of this night going," he huffed. "I was supposed to make love to you at least once more and then have an incredibly detailed conversation."

Sasha blushed at his teasing. "I would have enjoyed that."

Ilaria burst back into the room, holding out a small drawstring bag. "There's at least ten sovereigns in there. More than enough, yes?"

"I'm not asking you to give me—" Thomas began.

"Not a word," Ilaria interrupted. "This is my gift to you." She returned her attention to Sasha. "If you two run away and get married, there will be no arguments, no hesitations, no question of how it will be done or if it is possible."

"That will not make people talk less and Grantham will be furious," Sasha said. "Not to mention Lady Bramwell. She doesn't even know that the engagement is broken."

"She is still counting on this engagement to raise our fortunes," Thomas admitted with a frown.

Sasha could feel his anguish at the truth of his mother's pain. "It isn't simple, Ilaria."

"But it *could* be," Ilaria said. "The campaign that is about to be waged by this family will be so powerful I almost cannot describe it to you. They are going to turn the tale of my future with Jonah into a fairytale worthy of any French literary wit. By the time we're finished, the entire British Empire will be cooing over us, *begging* for invitations to the royal wedding on Athawick. And I can make sure it is known that a secondary, just as happy and secretly planned marriage has already taken place."

"You think you can convince them that you and I were not intended for each other?" Thomas asked incredulously. "That this isn't a scandal?"

"I will do that and more. I will fix this," Ilaria insisted. "And all you two have to do is run away and get married. As soon as possible. Spend a few days hiding away and doing..." She waved her hand at their position on the bed. "...*that* and come back refreshed and ready to declare the truth: that you love each other. And that love conquers all in the end."

Sasha glanced up at Thomas and he back to her. Ilaria sighed at their silence. "I'll just step outside, go back down and tell Mama and the rest that you are resting more than comfortably and to not disturb you the rest of the night. If I wake in the morning and you are still here, we will have a talk. But if not, then know I will launch an offensive that will put any fought by our navy to shame."

She smiled at them and then slipped away. When she was gone, Sasha shook her head. "I—"

He covered her lips with his fingers. "How quickly can you gather some things?"

Her eyes filled with tears and she flung herself from the bed, racing to the adjoining bedroom, where she collected a small port-manteau. She threw gowns and chemises inside, a few pairs of slippers, some stockings and the rest of the accouterment that would be needed for even a short escape from reality. When she returned, he had fully dressed and somehow appeared entirely unmussed. As if the glorious moments they'd shared were a dream.

She faltered a little, but he held out her dress. "I'll help you."

Soon she was as ready as he was, and he took the small bag and her hand, and peeked out into the hallway. It was silent. Together, they snuck down the back stair, out into the garden and toward the stable, where his carriage had been brought earlier. His driver was swiftly found and then they were off. A whirlwind of activity that left Sasha's head spinning.

It was only when they had driven down the road out of London for a quarter of an hour that she drew a deep breath. "Ilaria is convincing, I know. And it is easy to fall under the spell that you owe me a union after we made love. But Thomas, I know this isn't easy. You have more to think about than just yourself."

His brow wrinkled. "Do you know that I tried to write you a letter to answer yours after our last night together that ended with the terrible attack?"

She blinked. "You did?"

"Yes. I could not find the words to properly express myself. Perhaps I shall do as poor a job at it now. But you inspire me, so I will hope for the best."

He leaned forward and took her hands in his. "I have already said that I love you, Sasha. And while I appreciate that you are trying to offer me a way out, there is no escape I wish to make. I want to marry you. I knew that before Ilaria announced she would marry Crawford. That made it easier, but the outcome would have been no different. You are my heart. My soul. My everything. And you always will be."

"But what about—"

He shook his head. "There will always be the *what abouts* that we will have to face. But by God, I'd rather face troubles at your side than have smooth sailing with anyone else." He squeezed her fingers lightly. "If you aren't prepared for that, I understand. And then we will have a very different conversation. But as for my part, this is the only place I wish to be."

She could hardly think, hardly find words to express the powerful, swelling adoration she felt for this man. The joy and the pleasure and the sweetness were so large, they overwhelmed her, they overtook her.

And yet she fought the tide and met his stare. "You are worth anything, Thomas. Any battle, any war, any trouble. I can't wait to be there by your side for it all, and for all the joy and wonder and light that will come, as well."

"Then since I realize I have not yet actually asked you this question." He dropped to his knees before her, cupping her cheeks gently. "Will you marry me?"

"Yes," she murmured as she leaned in to kiss him. "Oh yes, I will."

He pulled her to him, back against the opposite seat, his kiss turning from joyful to one of desire, one of certainty that this was forever. And nothing would ever change it.

EPILOGUE

One week later

In the end, the Earl and the new Countess of Bramwell fled only a few towns outside of London, where they found an agreeable friar who took their sovereigns and they were wed. The next few days were spent in wondrous, total bliss. But now, as their carriage pulled back up to Bleaking House, Sasha sighed and cuddled a little closer to her husband.

Husband! That one was still taking some getting used to.

"I do not know what we will face there," she said softly.

"A great deal of family faces," he said with a broad smile that had not left his expression the entire time since their wedding. "I sent word to my mother to meet us here too. I assumed it would be better to meet the entire firing squad at once."

"Oh, don't joke about that. Grantham is a king—he is only three generations away from a man who *did* order the execution of a man who secretly wed his daughter!"

Thomas pulled a face. "Did it happen?"

"Well...no. She convinced him of the young man's worth," Sasha admitted.

"Then you have a great deal of pressure on your shoulders," Thomas teased as the carriage door opened. "Best of luck to you, Lady Bramwell."

She stuck her tongue out at him before she allowed the footman to help her down. But if she expected a dour welcome, she found anything but. The staff was all smiles and the house was filled with laughter as they were led into the foyer and down the hall to the largest sitting room.

When the doors opened, Sasha's grip on Thomas's arm tightened. The entire family was there. Grantham, Giabella, Ilaria and Captain Crawford, Remi, Lady Bramwell, the Gillinghams and, of course, Dash. For a moment everyone stopped what they were doing and stared.

And then the room became a burst of congratulations. Sasha was pulled from Thomas for many hugs, including one from the dowager countess, who clung to her tightly as she whispered, "Welcome home, my dear."

As both of them extracted themselves from the welcome, Sasha shook her head. "Not that I am complaining, but I did not expect such a joyous reception after we snuck away to wed like thieves in the night."

Grantham arched a brow and tried to look stern. "As a member of the royal family, I do lodge a formal complaint that you did not ask your sovereign's permission. But I also grant you forgiveness for the transgression."

Giabella smiled. "It was the direction we were headed, I think we could all see that. And Ilaria insisted that your happiness could be folded into the story of her own. If you have not taken time to look at the London papers during your time away, they are filled with romantic retellings of how our family always intended our beloved adopted daughter to be married to the dashing Earl of Bramwell."

"I think some people even believe it," Ilaria said with a laugh as she wrapped her arm around Captain Crawford. Her glow said everything Sasha needed to know about her happiness. "And anyone who acts as if they don't is reminded that the invitation to the royal wedding we will be holding in the fall is going to be a most coveted one. And that shuts them all up."

Crawford laughed. "My future wife, more cunning than any admiral I served under in the navy."

Tea was brought and Sasha and Thomas were pulled from family member to family member for congratulations and whispers and smiles. She watched him as he moved amongst her adopted family, especially interested in the exchange with Dash. There was no hesitation between the men now, these two who had only ever cared about her happiness.

And that gave her more of it than she ever could have hoped. With a sigh, she separated herself and stepped out onto the terrace. She breathed in a long gulp of air and smiled as the terrace doors closed behind her. She turned, expecting to find Thomas there, but instead it was Queen Giabella, her hands clasped before her.

"Your Majesty," Sasha breathed, and then smiled. "Mama."

Giabella stepped forward and caught her hands. "It is a whirl-wind in there. But I wished to speak to you alone. Dearest, why didn't you tell me? Why couldn't you talk to me?"

Sasha bent her head. "It was so hopeless for so long. How could I drag my own pain into your realm? I knew that there was no way I could break the engagement you had planned for Ilaria, not without causing everyone pain. And then there was Thomas's situation."

She stepped away and worried her hands. "We've talked about it at length. I bring nothing to the marriage thanks to—"

Giabella's expression grew dark. "Yes, thanks to Alistair and his horrible machinations. Hateful man. What he did to all my children, but most especially to you, is unforgiveable."

"But it *is* what happened. Laws were changed, edicts signed. I know there is no undoing it. Thomas has worked hard to recover his family from the ruin his own dreadful father put them in. And I will do all in my power to help him. It will not be so regal a life as I've been privileged to live all these years with you, but I want you to know that I look forward to every day with him. For richer and for poorer. I will not suffer. I refuse to do so when there is such love to be shared with him."

Giabella smiled gently. "Are you quite finished, my love?"

Sasha cleared her throat. She had been rambling passionately, about her now-favorite subject: her future with Thomas. "I am, Your Majesty."

"The reason I asked you and Thomas to wait before you had your conversations and made your plans was that I wished to speak to Grantham. He...he didn't know what his father had done to harm you, to snatch acceptance from you."

"No, what would have been the point in telling him or Remi or Ilaria? Their feelings about the late king were already so fraught."

"But he needed to know. They all did." Giabella shook her head. "I should have done it as soon as Alistair died, but there were so many things that hurt you children, I feared creating one more scenario. Once it was realized that you two had bolted in the night to marry in secret, I did confess Alistair's terrible actions to your brothers and sister."

Sasha lifted a hand to her mouth. "They were angry?"

"Livid on your behalf. Remi threw a glass against the mantelpiece, Ilaria used language that made her former sailor husband blush and Grantham just...stared, silent for a full five minutes. It was all very dramatic, as we apparently are wont to be, judging from the last few weeks." Giabella shook her head sadly. She reached for Sasha's hands again. "Yes, Alistair made a cruel law to lock you out. But your brother is twice the man his father was."

"Ten times," Sasha whispered.

"Indeed. He declared then and there that his first order of business upon our return to Athawick would be to nullify that law."

Sasha's mouth dropped open. "Can he do that?"

"He is king. He can do whatever he wishes...within reason," Giabella said dryly.

"What did the courtiers think of that?" Sasha asked, picturing Blairford and his cruel treatment in the past few years.

"There were loud arguments, but in the end they serve at the king's pleasure. If they wish to do continue to do so, they will head his commands."

The door to the terrace opened again and both women glanced back to watch Grantham, Dash and Thomas step out together. Dash was smiling, as was Grantham, which was a rare enough thing since he took the throne.

"Did you tell her? Did I give you two enough time?" he asked.

Giabella nodded. "I did. And now I shall allow her sovereign to do his duty."

She inclined her head and stepped away as Grantham motioned Thomas to stand beside Sasha. He did and took her hand.

"He is being very mysterious," Thomas whispered. "I fear a beheading is eminent."

Grantham arched a brow. "I'm considering it. Now hush. I believe what our mother has been telling Sasha is that I intend to reverse the cruel law my father enacted to deprive her of an inheritance or title. Once that is done, I would like to gift her with a dowry that will equal the amount we have granted Ilaria."

Thomas's mouth dropped open and he stared, mute. Sasha couldn't help but smile. He had never mentioned any hardship his choice of her might create, but now she saw the recognition of the freedom such a boon would grant.

"Additionally, I will be granting her title of Princess Sasha of Athawick," Grantham continued. "An equal partner to her very proud and loving siblings, should she wish it."

Sasha gasped, unable to speak for all the love and shock that lifted up in her. "I…I cannot believe it," she said, looking at Dash for guidance.

His eyes were misty with tears. "No longer on the outside, my love."

She nodded slowly. "I cannot believe you would do this," she said to Grantham. "That you would offer me so much."

He leaned forward and kissed her cheek. "I would offer you so much more if I could, but *that* is no longer my job." He shook Thomas's hand. "Now you see, this is why when a king or queen asks you to wait, you *wait* instead of running away."

They all laughed. She hugged each of them in turn and Thomas shook their hands, his expression still shocked.

When the rest left so they could have a moment, Sasha drew him close. She lifted her arms around his neck and stared up into his handsome face. "You are astonished."

"I am," he admitted. "I have married a princess after all. My mother will be over the moon, though she already was."

Sasha smiled. She felt she would never stop smiling after today. "And now you will not suffer for your choice. You will have all the benefits."

He leaned in to kiss her. "Let me make one thing very clear: I would *never* have suffered for my choice. And the only benefit I need, my love, is you."

She leaned up for another kiss, but he laughed and she pulled away in confusion.

"When I first met you, I called you Your Highness," he said. "I suppose that is now true."

"Call me wife," she said. "That is the best title I shall ever have."

"Then kiss me, wife," he murmured.

And she did.

ENJOY THIS SNEAK PEEK OF PRINCES
ARE WILD

BOOK 3 OF THE REGENCY ROYALS SERIES

Remi wrinkled his brow and looked at all the things she had pointed out. He was so accustomed to his home, he sometimes forgot how bright and beautiful it might be to a stranger. He smiled as he saw it through her eyes.

"We like it," he said.

She lifted those same eyes to him and he was surprised when his breath hitched. Good Lord, but that stare was something. She hadn't fully turned it on him since they met but now he couldn't turn away.

Her eyes were such a stunning green. When he didn't look away from her, her cheeks brightened with the hint of a blush.

He cleared his throat. "Would you like to dance with me, Miss Linfield?"

Her lips parted as if she were startled by the request. Truth be told, he was a little startled himself. He normally had to be dragged into dancing with the eligible ladies and limited himself to those he could seduce without consequence.

"Er, are you asking me to dance, or only if I'd *like* to do so," she asked.

He wrinkled his brow. "Why would I ask if you'd like to and then not mean to follow through."

She blushed again, but this time it wasn't a pretty flush of nervous attraction. It was something far sadder, more embarrassed. "It has been known to happen. As a jest or a tease."

He arched a brow. "I think you'll come to find out, Miss Linfield, that I am a rogue, *not* a cad. Let me rephrase. Will you do me the great honor of dancing the next with me?"

Her mouth opened and shut, but finally she nodded. "Y-Yes. I would like that, thank you."

The timing of her response was perfect, for the first dance had just ended and the floor was emptying of one set of revelers and filling with the next. He extended a hand and she glanced up at him once more before she took it. He guided her to the center of the floor and they waited together there.

"Everyone is watching," she said softly.

He glanced around. Indeed, she was correct. While his sisters had danced the first with their husbands, he was the first royal family member to choose a partner outside their realm. He should have realized what a stir that would cause.

"Are you a good dancer?" he asked.

"Fair," she admitted, her breath a little shorter.

He extended a hand again as the music rose and drew her closer. "Then you'll just have to trust me to lead you."

They spun out into the steps together. For the first few turns, she was a little stiff, but she relaxed as they turned. Once she did, he realized how she had undersold her talent on the floor. She was actually a very good dancer, with natural grace and a smooth fluidity to her movements. She could adjust easily when he maneuvered her and never lost her rhythm even when they had to dodge less talented dancers around them.

"Are you related to the Duke and Duchess of Gilmore then, that they would bring you with them to such an event?" he asked.

She shook her head. "No. I would think you'd know that from looking at me and Ophelia, we are nothing alike."

"Plenty of people are nothing alike to their blood siblings," he said, glancing toward Grantham briefly. "But yes, you two do look night and day."

The light in her gaze flickered a little and for the first time, she stumbled in her steps. He firmed his arms around her, keeping her from tripping. Now why had that bothered her so much?

"Well, that may be true. But Ophelia is my oldest and dearest friend. And like a sister, no matter how...how much lovelier is than me."

He wrinkled his brow. Ah, so she'd believed he compared them and found her lacking. Or else she was fishing for a compliment. But no, that didn't seem correct. She wouldn't look at him and her cheeks were filled with high color.

"I never said she was lovelier," he said simply. "I never thought it, either."

Her lips parted, but she still refused to lift her gaze to him. She just continued to turn in his arms and her fingers, which had been resting lightly on his shoulder, tensed slightly.

"You-You must be happy for your sister," she stammered.

He smiled and allowed the subject change. "I am. For both of them. Ilaria is my blood and I am happy for her joy. Sasha was adopted, but she is just as much my sister, as has been proven by the fact that she will be coronated a true princess once the royal wedding has taken place. I could not be more pleased for both of them, nor love them more."

She stared into his eyes and shook her head slightly. "Those are lovely things to say, to feel. They are not quite you reputation."

He choked on a laugh at her unexpected cheek. "Oh really, Miss Linfield?"

She caught her breath and staggered again in the steps. "I'm so sorry, I should never have been so forward with you, Your Highness."

He arched a brow. "If you are so aware of my character, you should know I like forward. I like unforeseen depths like the ones you just showed." He leaned a little closer and caught a faint whiff of her scent: vanilla. Simple but warm and surprisingly intoxicating. "Now tell me, Miss Linfield, what exactly have you heard my reputation to be?"

"Oh…I…I couldn't…" she stammered.

"Nonsense. I demand you tell me," he teased. "By royal edict."

The music was beginning to slow and she swallowed hard. "Wild," she said, so softly that the one word almost didn't carry. "You are wild. Untethered. That you care for nothing but fun."

While he might agree with the first two adjectives, her last descriptor stung a little. She might not be the only one to believe it, but he hated to hear it.

"I do care about my family, Lady Priscilla," he said.

She nodded. "I can see that. I'm sorry I assumed incorrectly."

He chuckled. "Oh no, the rest is absolutely correct. I am entire wild, completely untethered. I hear that is the attraction." He was holding her too closely now. He knew it. He couldn't seem to stop it. "Sometimes a little wild is what is needed, wouldn't you agree?"

ALSO BY JESS MICHAELS

Regency Royals
To Protect a Princess
Earl's Choice
Princes are Wild (Coming Soon)
To Kiss a King (Coming Soon)
The Queen's Man (Coming Soon)

The Three Mrs
The Unexpected Wife
The Defiant Wife
The Duke's Wife

The Duke's By-Blows
The Love of a Libertine
The Heart of a Hellion
The Matter of a Marquess
The Redemption of a Rogue

The 1797 Club
The Daring Duke
Her Favorite Duke
The Broken Duke
The Silent Duke
The Duke of Nothing
The Undercover Duke

The Duke of Hearts

The Duke Who Lied

The Duke of Desire

The Last Duke

The Scandal Sheet

The Return of Lady Jane

Stealing the Duke

Lady No Says Yes

My Fair Viscount

Guarding the Countess

The House of Pleasure

Seasons

An Affair in Winter

A Spring Deception

One Summer of Surrender

Adored in Autumn

The Wicked Woodleys

Forbidden

Deceived

Tempted

Ruined

Seduced

Fascinated

To see a complete listing of Jess Michaels' titles, please visit:

http://www.authorjessmichaels.com/books

ABOUT THE AUTHOR

USA Today Bestselling author Jess Michaels likes geeky stuff, Vanilla Coke Zero, anything coconut, cheese and her dog, Elton. She is lucky enough to be married to her favorite person in the world and lives in the heart of Dallas, TX where she's trying to eat all the amazing food in the city.

When she's not obsessively checking her steps on Fitbit or trying out new flavors of Greek yogurt, she writes historical romances with smoking hot characters and emotional stories. She has written for numerous publishers and is now fully indie and loving every moment of it (well, almost every moment).

Jess loves to hear from fans! So please feel free to contact her at Jess@AuthorJessMichaels.com.

Jess Michaels offers a free book to members of her newsletter, so sign up on her website:
http://www.AuthorJessMichaels.com/

[f] facebook.com/JessMichaelsBks
[y] twitter.com/JessMichaelsBks
[o] instagram.com/JessMichaelsBks
[BB] bookbub.com/authors/jess-michaels

CPSIA information can be obtained
at www.ICGtesting.com
Printed in the USA
BVHW030847160921
616792BV00024B/121

9 781947 770638